While they chatted about fabrics and fashion, both of them realized that this was not the sole purpose of her visit and that what they said to each other about the texture and pattern and softness had secondary meanings to do with hair and skin, beauty and availability, desire and attraction.

For Etta this was a new way to conduct a flirtation, and as she watched his strong, elegant hands fondle the materials, she could almost feel the effect upon herself, warm and sensuous, silky smooth.

"I should return home," she said, lifting a handful of sheer silk to her face. She could almost taste its beauty.

He was close, perhaps too close for a new acquaintance. Turning, she found that he, too, was holding the same silk behind her head, easing her toward his lips while swathing her in its warm luxury.

"This is what you should wear," he whispered, bending his head to hers.

"But it's transparent."

"Yes. As I said, it's what you should wear. But only for me."

It was dangerous talk.

Author Note

Eighteen years further on from *Betrayed, Betrothed and Bedded*, Sir Jon and Lady Raemon are now the middle-aged parents of Henrietta, the lovely stepdaughter whose natural father was King Henry VIII.

His mistresses are well documented, so I have used some artistic license to invent Henrietta's mother, though in fact several of his offspring resembled his daughter Elizabeth quite closely. Lady Catherine Grey was one of these, a young woman who unfortunately did not share the characteristics of her brilliant older sister, Lady Jane Grey. By including some factual characters in *Taming the Tempestuous Tudor*, I hope to create enough reality to make the fiction sound plausible—men like Lord Robert Dudley, Dr. John Dee, Lord Howard of Effingham, and Queen Elizabeth herself.

The miniaturist Levina Teerlinc actually did live at the Tudor court working for both Queen Mary and Queen Elizabeth, and her father was indeed the artist Simon Benninck. Whether she had a brother or not I have been unable to discover, so I have taken the liberty of inventing one for her. She painted Elizabeth on several occasions, and Lady Catherine Grey, too. Dr. John Dee went to live in Mortlake near the church, where he had a vast library of scientific books, and the site of Mortlake Manor, once lived in by Thomas Cromwell, was eventually demolished and built on by the brewery.

Juliet Landon

Taming the Tempestuous Tudor

HARLEQUIN® HISTORICAL

Recycling programs
for this product may
not exist in your area.

ISBN-13: 978-0-373-30745-6

Taming the Tempestuous Tudor

Printed in U.S.A.

™ www.Harlequin.com

Juliet Landon has a keen interest in art and history, both of which she used to teach. She particularly enjoys researching the early medieval, Tudor and Regency periods, and the problems encountered by women in a man's world. Born in North Yorkshire, she now lives in a Hampshire village close to her family. Her first books, which were on embroidery and design, were published under her own name of Jan Messent.

Books by Juliet Landon

Harlequin Historical

At the Tudor Court

Betrayed, Betrothed and Bedded
Taming the Tempestuous Tudor

Stand-Alone Novels

The Widow's Bargain
One Night in Paradise
The Bought Bride
His Duty, Her Destiny
A Scandalous Mistress
Dishonor and Desire
The Warlord's Mistress
The Rake's Unconventional Mistress
Scandalous Innocent
Mistress Masquerade

Visit the Author Profile page
at Harlequin.com for more titles.

I owe a huge debt of gratitude to my daughter and son-in-law for making it possible for me to write in peace and comfort. More than that, my daughter's skills as an anger-management counsellor have been an invaluable source of advice on how Henrietta might have behaved, given her problems.
Thank you, Susie.

To Brian, I owe special thanks for his unfailing willingness to help a less-than-competent mother-in-law with the mysterious workings of a computer, even at the most inconvenient times.

I would also like to thank my editor, Linda Fildew, for her help, constant encouragement and friendship, and Tilda McDonald, whose work on the manuscript is so much appreciated.
They make historical-fiction writing such a pleasure.

Chapter One

January 14th, 1559—London

Chosen some months beforehand by Dr John Dee, Royal Astrologer, the day before the coronation had begun in the freezing dark hours, when the starry sky echoed to the din of every bell in every church tower in every ward of the city. As it grew light, the stands erected along the route of the procession took on a clothing of blues, browns and reds, with pink faces shouting above the clamour.

Henrietta sat with her seventeen-year-old twin stepbrothers, their cousins and Aunt Maeve, slightly envious of her own parents, who would be in Westminster Abbey tomorrow with other members of the aristocracy.

Cheapside seats, however, were the next best thing, for here the wealthy merchants and shopkeepers had decorated every surface with bright carpets hung from windows, shelves of gold and silverware, the coats of arms of the livery companies repainted for the occasion. Here was advertising as never before for the Drapers and Goldsmiths, Merchant Tailors and Haberdashers, Mercers and Fishmongers.

As far as the eye could see in both directions, a ribbon of colour threaded its way from the Tower in the east, past Charing Cross in the west, then round the bend of the river to Westminster, stopping at intervals to the constant blast of trumpets to allow for recitations and dances, songs and poems of praise for the young Queen Elizabeth. A crescendo of sound reached the stands and grew into a mighty roar as the waving became more frenzied. Through an arch of stone appeared a swaying mule-carried litter covered with shimmering gold cloth where, beneath a canopy carried by four courtiers, sat the new Queen, a vision of gold, white and silver, waving and smiling at the welcome.

From her vantage point, Etta saw the same bright copper hair as her own, splayed over the ermine-clad shoulders like a loose mantle of silk. She saw the same delicate skin and fine arched brows, the brown eyes that pierced the crowd as if she too was looking for one person in particular. 'Here,' Etta whispered into the noise. 'I'm here.'

As if she had heard it over the din, the Queen turned her eyes upwards towards Etta and, for the space of several heartbeats, exchanged looks of curiosity and recognition, telling Etta as clearly as words that her existence was already known about. Known, but not so far acknowledged. Then the glance slid away, leaving Etta as stunned by the recognition as she was by the radiant sight, the prancing white stallions and the gleaming forest of the halberdiers' pikes. For that moment, it had been like looking into a mirror where the reflection had a life of its own, alike in every respect except age. The Queen had been born twenty-five years ago, and Etta only twenty-one, and this was the first time their eyes had met.

Since she was a lively twelve-year-old, Etta had known something of her parentage, her sensible and loving step-parents deeming it only fair to explain to her how, from time to time, the father she had never seen, King Henry VIII, had taken mistresses. One of these had been her mother, the beautiful Magdalen Osborn, her stepfather's first wife who had died giving birth to her one and only daughter.

But despite their explanations, Lord and Lady Raemon had never been able to fill the deep emotional void inside Etta left by never knowing either of the parents who had given her life. To the sensitive and highly intelligent child, her natural parents were the shadowy and insubstantial figures about whom only their names and a certain amount of gossip had reached her ears, some of it carelessly dropped by her nurse, tutor or elderly maid who mistakenly believed that she would not heed it. She had heeded it, avidly. Throughout her most formative years her innocent coquettishness and occasional childish vanity had drawn remarks such as, 'She's taking after her mama, that one', or, 'That's an Osborn look if ever I saw it' which somehow Etta knew was not meant to be complimentary, for since she was scolded for these childish misdemeanours, it stood to reason that her mother's behaviour had been worse, in some way.

Nor did anyone realise quite how much anxiety Etta was absorbing from her step-parents' well-intentioned oversight to provide her with anything admirable in her mother's character to cling to. Was she really taking after her mother? How would she ever know? Her stepfather, Lord Raemon, would not speak of her mother at all; her stepmother had not known her, but it seemed to Etta as if all the world had known her father. Every now and then, some scandalous information filtered through the system to her childish ears about his various wives and their failures, about his two daughters and their unhappy lives about which she was both sad and grateful not to be in their shoes, as she might have been.

After Henry's death, his young son Edward and then his elder daughter Mary had reigned through eleven uncomfortable years of religious turmoil, and now the younger daughter Elizabeth had appeared at last with new hopes of tolerance. Lord and Lady Raemon's explanation of why King Henry had recognised some of his illegitimate offspring and not others, though making some sense to Etta, had done little for her wavering sense of identity. To have too many families with ties to royalty, they had said, would make the accession of his legal heirs more difficult. But although the royal rejection was not for Etta to contest, it added yet another layer of uncertainty, and some resentment, too, to her growing emotional insecurity.

'Did the King not want me?' she had asked her parents. 'Did I do something he didn't like? Was it my mama he fell out with, as he did with the two Princesses' mothers?'

'No, dearest. Nothing like that. Your mama died giving birth. The King was too sad to want to see you, I suppose.'

That, however, was not quite enough to settle the

questions, once and for all. 'Well, the new Queen doesn't seem to be in a hurry to see me, either,' she observed. 'I can't help but feel there must be another reason.' When she had expressed to her parents a hope that Elizabeth might send for her, even if only to put right her father's omission, Lord Raemon had not seen any reason why she should. 'It's early days yet,' he had told her. 'She's hardly had time to choose her ladies, never mind which relatives to recognise, and she's unlikely to acknowledge half-siblings so soon. Be patient, Etta.'

'I'm not asking to become her bosom friend, Father,' Etta had replied, 'but I long to go to court, just the same. All those interesting people surrounding her. Surely we must be alike in wanting that, wouldn't you think?'

'Alike in other ways, too,' her mother said, rather unhelpfully.

'What do you mean, Mama?'

'Your looks, my dear. From what I've heard, she's not one to welcome competition. Others might wish to exploit the likeness, but I doubt if she would.'

Etta had turned away, unable to argue the point. Only recently, she had formed a friendship with a persuasive young courtier who had obligingly recounted to her the glamorous details and doings of life at the late Queen Mary's court, fuelling Etta's interest and determination to become part of it, one day. With the death of that Queen, his interest in Etta had come to an abrupt end, and she could only assume that he had left the court or lost interest in her or, perhaps, been warned off by her father. She could not ask, for she had not told her father of her friendship nor sought his permission, but the idea of being given over for another woman was humiliating and it hurt.

As the tail-end of the cavalcade disappeared from view, the crowds merged and with them went all hope of catching sight of the young man, no matter how intently she looked. Like touching a scar to find out if it still hurt, Etta revisited the site of her wounded pride, telling herself that he had never mattered to her, really. She had tossed her brilliant copper hair behind her, even as her eyes had sparked with anger, and had accepted her Cousin Aphra's sympathetic embrace with no more than a sniff.

Only that morning, she and her step-parents had parted under a storm cloud when they had clumsily mentioned the delicate subject of marriage, signalling an end to their leniency over her choice of friends and her multiple rejection of suitors. 'Interference, Henrietta?' her father said. 'I'd have thought it obvious by now that what you call interference concerns your mother and me as much as you. As my daughter, you cannot continue to associate with any gallant young thing who takes your fancy. We are looking for something more for you than mere respectability.'

'Yes, Father. So is that why you warned Stephen Hoby off? I presume it was you, for I cannot believe there was any other reason for his disappearance.' If Etta was at a loss to know how both her father and uncle had discovered who she had been seeing of late, she was careful not to ask. Next time, she would be even more mindful of who she told. Her maid, Tilda, would never have spoken of it, she was sure of that.

Lord Jon and Lady Virginia exchanged glances.

They had known Etta would challenge them, but after long and arduous hours in preparation for the three coronation days, their stamina was wearing thin. It was her stepmother who replied, hoping to delay any controversy until later. 'Etta dear, we're all busy. We shall continue this conversation when we have more time. Now, you go upstairs.'

'Etta needs to know,' said Lord Jon. He used her full name when he was being serious, but the shortened name gave her a clue to his softening tone. 'Sit down a moment. We were aware of the young man you refer to, even though you never gave us a chance to meet him, but your mother and I thought it had better come to an end. Your Uncle George thought so too when he discovered that Hoby is heavily in debt to his tailors and probably hoped you might be able to help him out of it. A man who visits the moneylenders as often as he does is not the kind of friend a father wants for his daughter. Hoby may not have had marriage in mind, for all we know, but we thought it best not to wait to see what else he was planning. Now you have the truth of it. Go upstairs and we'll talk some more tomorrow.'

Etta had assumed that their friendship had ended to make way for another woman, but to learn that Hoby had been using her as a lifeline for his debts was, in a way, just as insulting. There was more she would like to have said, but this was not the time, and she knew any argument she could make would not appear at its most lucid. 'I'm sorry, Father.' Pecking them both on the cheek, she had gathered her skirts and gone to her room where her maid was still waiting patiently to dress her with not a single word of complaint.

Etta's step-parents had not found it easy to raise King Henry's illegitimate daughter, but the precocious and volatile Etta remembered little of those two motherless years before her stepfather's marriage to Lady Virginia. Yet, even from the start, they had soon identified the Tudor characteristics which, in childhood, had caused as much amusement as anxiety, and her nurses had been kept on the hop from morn till night as her physical and mental energies outran their efforts to keep up. She could behave like an angel, but there was also a wilfulness behind the smile that had more than once evoked such responses as, 'She's her mother's daughter and no mistake.'

'She'll have to commit herself to marriage,' said Lord Jon to his lovely wife, 'before...well, some time,' he added, lamely.

'You were going to say, before she runs into some real trouble?'

'Perhaps not that kind of trouble, exactly. I hope she has more wit than that. I just wish she'd be more careful who she favours, that's all.'

Jon was still the handsomest man Virginia knew, even at forty-six, and her eyes caressed him as she deliberated how much she could say to defend Etta's strong bid for independence. 'It's perfectly obvious now what her relationship to the Queen is, Jon. Anyone can see that she and Henrietta share the same looks, and she'll not be too keen on having Etta appear on the scene, will she? Can you imagine how sparks would fly?'

It seemed that neither Etta nor her parents could let the matter rest there, for the subject of her future was raised again a few days later when both parents attempted to explain that it was not so much that they wished to prevent her from making friends, but that she should now allow them to say who was suitable and who was not. Why now? 'Because of your relationship to the new Queen, dear,' said her mother. 'We shall have to be extra-vigilant whose company you are seen in. Surely you can understand that? Can you imagine the comments if the Queen's duplicate were to be seen in any but the very best company? That would hardly endear you to her, would it? Your freedom of choice must come to an end some time, my dear.'

'In other words,' said Etta, 'you're saying you intend to choose my future husband for me. Would you accept that, if you were me?'

'Heavens above, Etta,' said her father, 'we've been more lenient with you over most things than we have with the boys, but a woman's independence comes at a price, you know. Very few daughters of noble houses are allowed to choose their husbands. London will now be bursting at the seams with a younger generation of men eager to boost their careers and fortunes by marrying well. I'm not going to let you walk straight into the lion's den, young lady, to be pounced on by some well-dressed young cockerel with big ideas who thinks he can win you simply by making sheep's eyes at you. From now on, your mother and I will be saying who you are seen with. If you'd told us about young Hoby sooner, we could have saved you some heartache.'

On any other occasion, the menagerie of metaphors would have made her laugh, but when Etta made no immediate reply to that, Lord Jon turned to her. 'Well?' he said, aware that her silence didn't necessarily mean acceptance.

'This lion's den you refer to, Father. Would that be the court? As you know, I had hoped that the Queen might have sent for me, since she must know I exist. How could she not? As half-sisters, surely we could meet? Is that not what half-sisters do?'

Etta's mother tried to soften the edges of what she feared would come as unwelcome news. 'It's not as easy as that, darling,' she said. 'Our new Queen may not be quite as eager for your presence at her court as you are, you see. At the moment, she is the Queen Bee of the new hive. Now imagine how she would respond to an even more beautiful and younger queen bee in a hive swarming with handsome young men, watching them shower her with compliments in praise of exactly the same features as herself. Do you think she'd allow that? I don't. She won't stand for any rivals for her affection, Etta. She's a Tudor. You'd get the sharp edge of her tongue before you'd been there one day. I was with her when she was a child of five, when she was often with Anna of Cleves, the lady I was with for a time. I know her temper very well, believe me. You would not care for it.'

'And you really believe she would see me as a rival, Mama? Do you not think you and Father are making too much of this Tudor temperament?' Even as she spoke, Etta had to admit that her mother knew Elizabeth far better than she did and that she was not likely to be mistaken in this.

'Well, the truth of the matter is that we've had no

word of her mind on this. Until she sends for you, there's little you can do about it.'

'I'm sure you're right, m'dear,' said Lord Jon. 'If she doesn't send for her, the only other way Etta could be received at court is by marriage or with someone who's already accepted there and I'm not going anywhere near the place at the moment. Far too much going on, for my liking.'

Lady Virginia sighed and arranged the fur edge of her gown to cover her knees. 'Throw another log on, Jon, will you? If you so desperately want to see her personally, Etta, then you must marry a courtier. But you rejected the last two courtiers before you'd even seen them, I recall.'

Lord Jon dusted his hands off and kicked the log into the blaze. Etta stood up and shook out her skirts. 'But if I were to go to court, Mama, the choice would be so much more interesting, wouldn't it, than it is at present? I think I could do better than the Lord Mayor of Norwich's younger son, or Lord Torrington's middle-aged heir. They were the last two on offer. And I don't believe a title is an advantage, either. There are plenty of nobly born people at court without them.'

'Then what *would* be an advantage, young lady?' said her father, impatiently.

'Love, Father. If love was good enough for you and Mother, then it's good enough for me.' That, apparently, was to be Etta's last word on the subject before she walked to the door and closed it quietly behind her.

'God's truth,' said Lord Jon, 'she's behaving more and more like Elizabeth every day. We've been too soft with her, sweetheart.'

'But I think that was supposed to be a compliment, Jon dear.'

'Come here, smooth-tongued woman,' he said, holding out a hand.

'What?'

'This,' he said, taking her into his arms.

Etta's talk with her parents had given her some food for thought, and any mention of a love match was, she knew, as unrealistic as her dreams. The unpleasant truth about the young man's interest in money had certainly shaken her, because she'd thought herself to be better qualified in her choice of friends than anyone else. Evidently that was not the case. She had been misled by his exquisite manners and charm. It would not happen again. She adored her parents and had striven to please them in all other respects, especially so since she had learned of her royal ancestry. She had taken schoolroom lessons with the boys in an attempt to emulate the Princess Elizabeth's scholarship in so many subjects with the sole purpose of eventually making contact with her, on her own academic level. And no matter what reservations her parents had about the wisdom of this, she could not believe that anyone of Elizabeth's intelligence would regard her as anything but an asset, if ever the Queen chose to recognise her as someone worth knowing, on whatever level. Friend, confidante, just another relative, occasional courtier or however Elizabeth chose to recognise her, any of these would help in her quest to relate, physically, to one of her own kin. But her father's comment about not going anywhere near court, at present, did not bode well for any of the hopes she had nurtured for so long.

Next day, he had done his best to explain. 'Your mother and I know the royal court well enough, Etta. We both spent some time in the service of your father. I was one of his Gentlemen of the Bedchamber, and your mother was a companion to the Lady Anna of Cleves. But we were quite happy for our duties to come to an end. Edward's reign, then Mary's were too fraught with danger to make life comfortable, and I have no reason to believe that Elizabeth's reign will be any easier. That's why we never took you or your brothers there. Too many intrigues for my liking.'

Etta had accepted this, but had still enjoyed hearing about life at court from Master Stephen Hoby, who seemed to know all about it, who he knew there, what they wore, what new fabrics he had handled at the Royal Wardrobe and what the newest Spanish fashions were. It had seemed to her then that only at court would she ever meet a more interesting and engaging type of man who did more than praise her eyes. Surely the young Queen, with her amazing intellect and reputation for scholarship, would gather around her men who could converse with her on serious subjects.

Her parents' recent decision to find her a husband had been expected ever since the steady flow of suitors had begun to dwindle noticeably due, she was sure, to her reputation for rejecting them so quickly. So it was with some consternation that Etta realised that, this time, her parents were deadly serious and that her time of asserting her independence in this area was well and truly at an end.

Behind her step-parents' reluctance to understand her longing to meet the new Queen, Etta caught the vibrations of another kind of fear, that Elizabeth might exercise her right to dislike her. She had not needed them to point out to her that the sovereign was under no obligation to receive her with smiles of welcome, for the recent news that she was choosing fewer maids and ladies to attend her indicated some caution in the matter. As for conducting herself at court, her only education so far had been gleaned from listening to the experiences of others and from gossip when someone had breached the complicated codes of etiquette.

The next few days seemed intended to reinforce her longing to become a part of the royal court when she accompanied Lord and Lady Raemon and her brothers to the celebration banquets held by the various guilds associated with the Royal Wardrobe where Sir George Betterton, Uncle George, was a senior officer. So with banquets, jousts and masques, visits to the Abbey of Westminster to see the decorated interior and to Lambeth Palace to dine with the Archbishop of Canterbury, there were plenty of opportunities for her to meet gorgeously dressed men and women who reflected the latest fashions and spoke at first hand of life at court. With her parents close at hand to guide her through some of the complexities of names and titles, Etta felt that this was her sphere, even more so now when it had become obvious to all who saw her that the Queen had a close relative who rivalled her in beauty and grace. But for Etta, the experience of dressing in her finest clothes every day, being seen and admired, speaking with those who interested her as much as she did them, was enough to send her to bed each night longing to become an integral part of this enchanted and glamorous world.

Towards the end of that hectic week, she was invited to visit the Royal Wardrobe as the guest of Uncle George to see the Queen's coronation robes that had been returned for cleaning and, if it was needed, some mending. As her brothers had worked under Sir George for two years already, they took her with them by river to where the Royal Wardrobe was situated near Blackfriars, only a stone's throw from St Paul's Cathedral. The River Thames flowed conveniently nearby and Puddle Wharf was the landing place for cargo ships and wherries that plied the river constantly. From the jetty at Tyburn House, they were rowed downriver huddled inside fur cloaks against the biting wind and flurries of snow, Etta wearing her white fur bonnet and the matching muff she'd been given for her birthday, a little over a week ago.

On their arrival at the vast complex of buildings known as the Royal Wardrobe, Etta found that she was not the only one to have been invited to view the robes, for her Cousin Aphra was there too, and her brother Edwin who worked there under his father's eye. Other guests had accepted the invitation, some of whom she knew were wealthy merchants who supplied the Wardrobe with costly fabrics, furs and gems, silks for the embroidery, gold beads and threads. The twins, Michael and Andrew, went off with Edwin to the department where the tailors worked, while Etta and Aphra drew close together like sisters. As a four-

year-old, Aphra had taken the two-year-old Etta under
her little wing, acting as a mother hen to the mischievous child, and even now could not shake off the responsibility. 'Show me the coronation robes, Aphie.
I'm longing to see what she looked like,' said Etta.

'Father says it's been frantic in here for weeks since
the orders were given,' said Aphra. 'They even had
to stop the mercers from buying up the crimson silk
before the Queen had taken her choice. Of course,'
she added as they walked past ledger-covered tables
and the bent heads of clerks, 'it's not going to finish
now the coronation is over. Father says the Queen is
insisting on a completely new wardrobe, to be as different from the old Queen's as possible. And naturally,
when the Queen sets a fashion, everyone else will follow. Here we are, see?'

Through a wide archway, the room ahead was filled
with shimmering gold satin and rich velvets of purple
and crimson, piles of white ermine, tissues of silver
with pearls by the thousand, gemstones and gold lace
overlaying the twenty-three yards of cloth-of-gold. Not
one gown but four, for the coronation, then more for
the banquet and several changes for every day since
then, though some had still not arrived from Westminster and the nearby Palace of Whitehall. The cost
was phenomenal at a time when funds were low, but
the Queen's insistence on a rich show was as much a
statement of serious intent as vanity. Now Etta could
see in detail what had passed her by on that morning when all her attention had centred on the Queen's
recognition, the gold fabric worked with Tudor roses,
the gold-edged ruffles, the heavily encrusted tassels
of the ermine-caped mantle.

'These must weigh a ton,' Etta said, letting her fingertips brush along the fur. 'She must be strong to look her best through so many days.'

'Apparently,' said Aphra, 'she had to take to her bed after the coronation with a heavy cold. Some of the events had to be cancelled.'

'And no one to chastise her when she's late. Lucky lady. I wonder how much she paid for her velvet. Is it more expensive than the…?'

Aphra had moved out of earshot, her place taken by a tall gentleman who answered Etta's question without hesitation. 'Twenty-two shillings the yard, Mistress Raemon,' he said. 'And, yes, it is considerably more expensive than the satin, which can vary depending on colour and country of origin.'

Etta was taken aback. It was not usual for a stranger to speak before being introduced. She decided to dispense with formalities, however, for this man was interesting on several levels: for one thing, he knew about fabrics and, for another, he was perhaps one of the best-looking men she had ever met and well-spoken in a soft deep voice. Well dressed, too. Fashionable, but not excessively so, in a suit of good quality fabric, a beautifully tailored doublet that fitted perfectly across a deep chest and broad shoulders. 'Why should the price depend on the colour, sir? Are you telling me that some dyes cost more than others?'

'That is exactly what I am telling you, mistress. Dyes such as blue and brown are easy to come by, but dyes like purple, for instance, come from distant lands and are difficult to source and obtain. Some are got by a complex dyeing process, which is why the Queen reserves them for royal purposes.'

'Are you in the dyeing trade, then?'

'I am a mercer,' he said. 'It's my business to know about such things.'

'And how did you know my name?'

He smiled, revealing perfect teeth and showing a pair of laughing brown eyes that sparked with admiration. 'I could not help but know your name, mistress, when it's upon everyone's lips. Now we've had a chance to compare you, the sight of another woman with the Queen's looks cannot help but be the cause of some comment. I was present at the Guild of Mercers' banquet a few days ago, which you also attended with your parents, but you left before I could be introduced. Did your ears not burn?'

She looked away, laughing in embarrassment, though secretly she was excited to find herself the object of such interest. 'No, sir. I think you are teasing. Perhaps you could tell me more about the Queen's robes?'

So while the deep-voiced mercer told her of the Queen's artificers who made up her gloves, purses, hose, shoes and hats, showing her the heavily embroidered velvet bags specially made to keep them in, Etta constantly cast her eyes over his handsome head and masculine figure and wondered how she might develop this budding friendship without suffering the investigations her parents were set on imposing. He was probably of no particular importance, she thought, for her parents to have overlooked an introduction, and yet, to her, his knowledge of fashion and fabrics, his charming manner and obvious good breeding was of more importance to her than any titled good-for-nothing with more wealth than intelligence. But, of course, he would be married. How could he not be?

They had moved into an adjoining room where liveried men carried rolls of fabric on their shoulders between ceiling-high racks piled with bales of fabric, their labels dangling like tassels, the soft thud of cloth-rolls hitting the shelves, the faint perfume of lavender and spices. 'Did you not bring your wife with you, sir?' she asked, looking towards the open door.

His eyes lingered over her face as if deliberating how to answer the simple question, making her fear that it might not be to her liking, after all. When he replied, it was as if he knew exactly the purpose of her query, exposing her thoughts and linking them to his own. 'I have not yet taken a wife, Mistress Raemon,' he said. 'Perhaps you could help me to find one?'

She tried to search his eyes, but they were searching hers and she could not maintain her quest for a meaning. Long-lashed lids flickered like shutters to prevent him from seeing any sign that might expose her interest and, with an effort at the brand of nonchalance she used on such occasions, she moved away from him, speaking over her shoulder. 'I doubt it, sir. Perhaps you should look amongst the mercers' daughters. There are sure to be some available. Now, I must return to my cousin. She'll be wondering where I am. Through here, is it?'

She heard the soft laugh behind her, as if he were amused by her attempt at a dismissal, and it was no accident that she abstained from asking his name, if only to reinforce her uninterest. Except that she was far from being uninterested, for the sound of his laugh, his voice and the presence of him beside her stayed in

her mind all the way home and for the rest of that day.
Nor would she ask her brothers if they knew him, as
indeed they must have done, as perhaps Aphra did,
too. It looked to Etta as if, in that crowd of guests, not
one of them was willing to admit that they had noticed either the meeting or the unceremonious parting.

Partly to cling to her independence for as long as
possible and partly, she had to admit, to take another
look at the handsome mercer, she asked to pay another
visit to see the fine fabrics at The Royal Wardrobe,
for there were one or two she had forgotten the name
of, and perhaps Uncle George would sell her some.

'No, he won't,' said her mother, closing the lid of
the virginal and removing the music from the stand.
'It's all for the royal use, my dear. I thought you knew
that. It's bought in from the mercers and merchants,
and it's for her and the officers to say what's to be
done with it. But there's no reason why you should
not take another look, if you take Tilda with you and
be home in time for supper.'

There was a heightened sense of anticipation in the
river journey this time, though flakes of snow made
her blink and hold the fur more tightly across her chin.
Tilda's eagerness to see the robes was reason enough
for Etta's visit so soon after the first, but added to that
was the delicious feeling that she was still finding her
own friends in defiance of her parents who, although
having her happiness and safety at heart, could have
no perception of how much she valued her independence. If the sneaking thought entered her head that
her defiance was very close to deceit, then she pushed

it away along with the knowledge that they might well find out for themselves, as they had done before. She supposed Uncle George would see to that.

But Sir George Betterton was not there, though it was staffed as before by the liveried men far too intent on their onerous duties to pay Etta and her maid much heed. Over by the window, a group of men turned over some bolts of cloth, angling them to the light, and it was one of these who came to her immediately with a word of excuse to his colleagues. 'Mistress Raemon,' he said, lifting off his velvet hat with a graceful bow. Smiling, he replaced it. 'You hoped to find Sir George?'

She felt the breathless lurch of her heart betraying the nonchalance of her bearing, taking her quite unawares. He was every bit as handsome as she had remembered, giving her another chance to see the thick dark hair and the laughter in his eyes as they caught the small light from the window. It was at times like this, she thought, that staring ought not to be rated as bad manners, for if ever a man should be stared at, this fine creature was he. Suited in deep moss-green velvet, he proclaimed the gentleman down to the last discreet detail but, more than that, he had some indefinable presence that made women's hearts race. Etta realised that she was very glad they'd met again, quite by chance, of course.

'Not exactly,' she said. 'My maid wishes to see the Queen's robes. Mistress Tilda, this is… Master…er… I'm sorry, I don't think you told me your name.'

'My friends know me as Nicolaus,' he said. 'I would like to think you were both amongst them.'

'Master Nicolaus,' the two women whispered, dipping a curtsy.

Snapping his fingers towards two young men, he beckoned them over. 'Escort Mistress Tilda round the display,' he said. 'She wishes to see the Queen's robes. Tell her about them.'

Tilda went with them, happily leaving her mistress to look enquiringly at the man on whom her eyes had lighted as soon as they'd entered. He dipped his head as if to catch her thoughts. 'That is what you had in mind I hope, mistress?' he said.

'If that's what you wish to think, sir, then I have no objection.' Her slow, heavy-lidded blink delighted him.

'Your bonnet is wet with snow. Shall you remove it and lay it before the fire? And your cloak, too? Here, allow me to help.' On this day, she wore a one-piece gown of expensive London russet that showed no more than the high frill of her embroidered smock at the neck and wrists, though now her hair fell loosely about her shoulders until she caught it up with her hands and threw it behind her with a grace that appeared to fascinate him. She had done it before to great effect, this time allowing it to brush over his hands before they could move away.

'I came, Master Nicolaus, to remind myself of two or three fabrics I saw yesterday so I can order some, once I know how to call them. May I show you?'

'Certainly, mistress. This would be for yourself, would it? One must be careful, you see, not to overstep the sumptuary laws. I imagine the new Queen will be quite firm about observing them. Baudekin, for instance, has a distinct gold thread running with the silk, and although she wears it, very few others are allowed to.'

'I doubt if the Queen will ever see me, sir. It was not the baudekin I saw, but this one, I think. Is this what they call popinjay?'

He reached up and pulled it down from the shelf. 'The green-blue mix? Now, that would look well with your colouring. This one is silk. Feel the quality.'

'Will the Queen be wearing this?' she said, letting the silk flow over her skin like warm water.

'My understanding is that the Queen will be wearing only black and white, Mistress Raemon. She knows it becomes her, you see, and those mercers who supply the Great Wardrobe are already sourcing suitable fabrics to please her.'

'Only black and white? No colour at all?'

'Oh, I believe she will allow colours to creep in with the embroidery and accessories, of course. But her maids will all wear white and nothing else, it seems. It lessens our scope enormously. I hope you won't be following her lead in that.'

'You must have good contacts at court, sir, to have discovered so much so soon.'

'Indeed, mistress. Mercers must keep their ears to the ground if they want to have the fashionable fabrics in store as soon as they're needed.' He led her down the rows of shelving, obligingly pulling out rolls and bales, some of which had covers to protect them. And while they chatted about fabrics and fashion, both of them realised that this was not the sole purpose of her visit and that what they said to each other about the texture and pattern and softness had secondary meanings to do with hair and skin, beauty and availability, desire and attraction, strength and rarity. For Etta this was a new way to conduct a flirtation, and as she watched his strong elegant hands fondle the materials, she could almost feel the effect upon herself, warm and sensuous, silky smooth.

The January light was already fading, and Etta had found what she was looking for. 'I should return home,' she said, lifting a handful of sheer silk to her face. She could almost taste its beauty.

He was close, perhaps too close for a new acquaintance, but in the dimness it was hard to be aware of space. Turning, she found that he, too, was holding the same silk behind her head, easing her towards his lips while swathing her in its warm luxury. 'This is what you should wear,' he whispered, bending his head to hers.

'But it's transparent,' she said.

'Yes. As I said, it's what you should wear. But only for me.'

It was dangerous talk and she knew she ought not to allow it, for she had intended their meeting only to be an exercise in having her own way, making her own choice of friends. It would have been so easy to allow a kiss, but their friendship could never go as far as that. He was, after all, only a mercer. Unsteadily, she drew away, pushing at his chest to evade the firm bulk of his body. 'No, sir. This must not continue,' she said.

'I must see you again, Mistress Raemon,' he said.

'Well, perhaps you will, one day. Who knows? But now we must part. Thank you for showing me round. I hope you find a good wife who will be a help to you in your trade. I must return to my parents.'

'If that is what you wish, mistress.'

'It is, sir. There can be no future in our friendship. My father is determined to find me a husband very soon, you see.'

'And you are saying that he won't be looking for one amongst the mercers? There are some very eminent gentlemen amongst that company, you know. You must have seen some at the banquet last week?'

'Yes, I did, sir, but I think my father will be aiming rather higher than that. Thank you again, Master Nicolaus, and farewell.'

'The pleasure was mine, mistress. Will you allow me to give you a token, to remind you of our pleasant interlude? Here…a peacock feather. Will you take it?'

'Thank you, sir. I'll give it to my father for his hat.'

'Excellent.'

As it happened, Mistress Tilda was not so very eager to be found, and having been attended by two lusty young men for an hour, she did not notice her mistress's unusual silence on the way home, her own chatter sufficing for them both. Neither her brothers nor Uncle George and his son had been at the Royal Wardrobe during her visit, so the talk at supper skipped lightly over Etta's meeting as if she had been shown the fabrics by one of Sir George's assistants. She had no intention of mentioning Master Nicolaus or alerting her parents to yet another admirer of whom they would be sure to disapprove. A mercer, they would say. Respectable, but not quite what we're looking for, Etta. Which only went to show how wrong they could be, for he was by far the most interesting and exciting man she had ever spoken to.

Chapter Two

Beginning its life as a spring on the slopes of High-gate, the River Tyburn rattled gently down to the northern banks of the Thames near Westminster, where it was straddled by the gatehouse of the large residence called after it by Lord Jon Raemon of Risinglea. Tyburn House was an imposing mansion of decorative timberwork above stone foundations and surrounded by extensive gardens that sloped down to a jetty where wherries came to release their passengers. In the warm and welcoming hall where preparations were being made for supper, Etta presented her father with a snow-flecked peacock feather. 'For your hat,' she said, 'from the Royal Wardrobe.'

Lord Jon received the gift with a smile, turning it this way and that before handing it back to Etta. 'You shall stitch it on for me,' he said. 'It's a beauty. Tell me about your visit to the Wardrobe. Did you find what you were looking for?'

'Yes, Father. Very informative it was. I learned quite a lot.'

'Good. And was your Uncle George there?'

'No. Some buyers. Merchants, I think. That's all.'
Somehow, she felt that to speak Master Nicolaus's
name might break the spell of intrigue that had just
begun to surround him. And for the next three days,
that experience had to suffice as heavy snow covered London, when no travel except the most urgent
business was undertaken. At Tyburn House there was
plenty to occupy her in the preparation of scented
water for finger bowls and creams for chapped faces
and hands. There were household accounts to be
checked, lists to be made, visits to the nearby poor
folk, shirts and smocks to be stitched by the white reflected light of the snow. But none of this could prevent Etta's thoughts from revolving around the events
at the Royal Wardrobe, the dim warmth of the store-
room, the scents and shimmer of cloth, and a man's
proximity that was quite unlike the innocent familiar-
ity she had been used to. Asking herself why or how
he was any different, a host of answers came to mind:
his authority, his amazing good looks, his knowledge
and intelligence—all of which placed him on a higher
level than anyone else of her acquaintance. And, of
course, his manner of conducting a flirtation by anal-
ogy to that exotic merchandise. Had he practised that
on other women? Was she about to fall for his velvet
words? Was it his years that had given him the audacity to speak to her that way? Well, she thought,
nothing will come of it. A man in trade would never
be her father's choice.

After four days and nights of white-blanketed
lawns and rooftops, the overnight rain washed away
the snow and filled the River Tyburn up to its banks to
roar away into its powerful sister and to lift the boats

almost to the level of the jetty. 'Just what we needed,' said Lord Jon. 'Now we can receive dry guests instead of damp ones.'

'Guests, Father?' Etta said. There was something in the way he said the word that had an ominous ring, making her look sharply at him. A shiver ran along her arms as, in a sudden flash of awareness, she feared the worst. 'Anyone I know?'

'Not unless you know Baron Somerville,' he said, nonchalantly, walking away.

'When?' she asked her mother, later.

'The end of the week, dear. He'll be staying over one night, I suppose, now the days are so short. You'll like him.' Like. In the sense of *like to marry*.

'How do you know I will, Mama?'

'Why, love? Because your father and I do. Now, I have to go and speak to Cook.'

Their strategy of silence on the matter was hardly surprising, Etta thought, after her constant refusals to discuss the merits, or otherwise, of previous suitors. Obviously, they now believed that there was little point in supplying her with any details other than his name and title, when she would automatically resist. So, other than offering her the information that the guest was 'quite a few' years older than her and had not been married before, they remained annoyingly tight-lipped, which appeared to indicate that Baron Somerville's need to father heirs had so far lay dormant. Too busy hunting, Etta supposed. Or too shy of women. Or both.

Her cousin Aphra, with whom she had visited the Royal Wardrobe, was invited to stay with them that week. Greeting her, Etta quipped, 'I think I need some moral support.'

'Do you, Ettie? Why?' Aphra held a special place in everyone's hearts as the sweetest and kindest of women, fair and slender, graceful in thought and deed, serene and as steadfast a friend as anyone could wish for. Everyone knew that, one day, she would find a wonderful husband and Etta looked upon her as an elder sister. 'They've found a husband for you, haven't they?' Aphra said. 'Don't look so surprised. Your expression gave it away. Come on, it may not be as bad as all that.'

'I think it may be worse, Affie.' It was nothing new to Aphra to be the recipient of Etta's woes, but this time the only help she could offer was in her calming influence and companionship, and the advice to speak with her parents about her concerns. Predictably, the conversation was brief.

Knocking on the door of her parents' bedchamber, Etta entered at her mother's call, taking in the sweet aroma of last year's lavender and burning applewood. Half-dressed, they were both being pinned and laced into the various items of clothing, looking oddly lopsided. 'May I speak with you a while?' she said, sitting on the oak chest at the end of their bed.

Discreetly, the servants left the room. Her father's demeanour had not changed all morning from the determined expression he now wore and she knew that this time they would insist. 'Father,' she said, catching the anxious glance her mother sent in his direction, 'this time you're serious, aren't you?'

'We've made our choice, Etta,' he said, tying the

last of his points. 'You cannot expect us to change our minds. You must trust us to know what's best.'

'But if you thought love was the best reason for you and Mother to marry, then why not me, too?'

'Love?' Both parents' eyebrows lifted as they stared at her. 'Love?' her mother repeated. 'Etta, have you done something foolish?'

The temptation to pursue this line was almost overwhelming. 'No, Mother, I haven't. I just want some say in who I spend the rest of my life with. As you did.'

'As it happens, Etta,' said her father, 'that's what we want, too. You may not have given it much thought, but fathers don't usually give dowries along with their daughters to any man who declares his love for them. There's a lot of money at stake here and any father who throws that away on a young man's declaration of love is a fool. Your mother and I had got beyond that stage when we agreed to marry. I'm sorry if that sounds mercenary, my dear, but these are important considerations that parents must take very seriously. We've found a man with enough wealth to make that unlikely. The love will develop as you get to know each other. I expect.'

'Now go and finish your dressing,' her mother said, 'and try to take this with a good grace. We expect you to make yourself agreeable to our guest.'

There was no more she could say to them. All her personal preparations had been accomplished, hair washed and braided, skin scrubbed and perfumed, dresses chosen, pressed and mended, frills starched and gathered to perfection. She had chosen to wear a high-necked gown of deep-pink satin over a Spanish bell-shaped farthingale, the bodice making a deep vee at the front, stiffened by whalebone. Sitting down was only achieved with care, so now she stood with Aphra at the mullioned window of her room that gave them a view of the gardens with the great river beyond and the jetty where a small barge was coming in, its four oarsmen steering it skilfully against the tide.

'He's got his own barge,' said Etta, 'and his boatmen have liveries. That's serious wealth, Aphie. That'll be him, climbing out.' The small diamond-shaped panes of thick glass made it difficult to see any details, only that the manly figure leaping out of the barge did not quite fit Etta's mental image of a middle-aged aristocrat.

'He's tall,' Aphra said. 'Can't see any more. Shall we go down?'

Purposely, they took their time, lingering to catch sounds of greetings and laughter, Etta readying herself to show a confidence she was far from feeling. Her mind slipped back to her meeting in that dim store-room with the man who had made her feel womanly and desirable, when there had been no talk of wealth, dowries, bargains or filial obedience. Those had been moments she had kept safe in her heart, not even sharing them with Aphra. Now, she might as well forget them and face her real future.

He was standing with his back to the door as Etta and Aphra entered, accepting a glass of wine from his hostess, his tall frame matching Lord Jon's as only a few other men did. He had obviously taken great care to make a good impression, for his deep-green sleeveless gown was edged with marten fur worn over a doublet and breeches of gold-edged green velvet, slashed to show a creamy white satin beneath. As he turned to greet them, they saw gold cords and aiglets studded with seed pearls, and in his hat was a drooping peacock feather like her father's. He smiled, creasing his handsome face, making his eyes twinkle with mischief. 'Mistress Raemon,' he said, softly, 'your prediction was correct. We *have* met again, you see?'

A hard uncomfortable thudding in her chest made words difficult. 'Father, there's been a mistake. This man is not who you think he is. He was at the Royal Wardrobe when Aphra and I went there. His name is Master Nicolaus.'

Why were they all smiling?

Looking slightly sheepish through her smiles, her mother came forward to lead Etta by the hand. 'Yes, dear. He is also Baron Somerville of Mortlake. We know you have already met. That was intentional. Shall you make your courtesies?'

'No, Mother. I shall not. There is some deception here. Why did he introduce himself to me as Master Nicolaus? What is it that he's not told me that he should have? Be honest, if you please.' Her voice was brittle with anger and humiliation, and anything but welcoming. She had tried to make him understand that he was not the kind of man with whom she would form a relationship. She thought he had accepted that.

The smile remained in his eyes, though now tinged with concern. 'I have been honest with you at all times, mistress,' said Baron Somerville, reminding her of his deep voice and seductive tone, the reassuring words. 'My name is Nicolaus Benninck, from Antwerp. Recently, the Queen honoured me with the title of baron. I am one and the same person, you see. I believe you were kindly disposed to the one, so it stands to reason that you will feel the same about the other. How could it be otherwise?'

But the colour had now blanched from Etta's face as she made it plain what she thought of such reasoning. 'It may have escaped your notice, sir, that I am a grown woman, not a child of six to join in this kind of game. What is it you wished to gain from this deceit, exactly? Do you try the same nonsense with everyone you meet? Does your new title embarrass you so that you could not have spoken of it?'

'Henrietta!' her father barked. 'That's going too far. You are being discourteous to our guest. You should apologise at once.'

'The discourtesy is to me, Father. Tell Baron Somerville his journey is wasted. If a man is not honest enough to tell a woman of his status, on *two* separate occasions, then one must wonder what else he will keep from her. If I did the same, Father, you would have me locked in my room on nothing but bread and water.'

'You're taking this quite the wrong way,' said Lord Jon, crossly.

'On the contrary, Father. I find it patronising in the extreme to be fed misleading information as if I could not manage the truth. But that's not all, is it, my lord? Didn't you also tell me you were a mercer?' She turned to her mother, her eyes blazing with scorn. 'A *mercer*! I ask you, Mama, is it in the least likely you and Father would expect me to marry a *mercer*? Really?'

Her father's eyebrows twitched. 'Henrietta, you had better say no more. Baron Somerville is one of London's most successful mercers, a merchant of some standing, a freeman and alderman of the City of London, and the owner of several shops on Cheapside. Your mother and I have always had the greatest respect for mercers, otherwise we would not have been invited to their banquet last month. The mercers are one of the most influential companies, and one of the wealthiest. You yourself were impressed by the event.'

Still white with shock, Etta listened to this list of distinctions with a growing confusion, trying desperately to link what Master Nicolaus had told her about himself, which was very little, with what he might have said if he'd been trying to impress her. 'You didn't say you had spoken to my parents on that occasion,' she said to Lord Somerville. 'Why could you not have told me?'

'Because, mistress, I did not speak to them. I said I'd seen you there with them, but there was no opportunity for us to be introduced. Your father and I have spoken since then, and...'

'Yes, I see,' she retorted, 'and decided on a clever little plan to deceive me. The peacock feather. That was a sign, I suppose? Carried by me to my father. What a jest! How you must have laughed up your sleeves at that, both of you.'

'Etta,' said her mother, 'you have already said far too much. We expected some resistance to whomever we chose for you, but this is as much to do with names as much as anything else, isn't it?'

'No, Mama. It isn't. But never in all my born days did I imagine you would choose a *mercer* for me to live with, over a shop in Cheapside. I thought you had higher hopes for me than that, knowing of my ambitions. How on earth...am I...to...oh!'

Covering her face with her hands, she turned and ran to the door, fumbling with the latch until Aphra opened it for her, following her out and calling after her up the stairs, 'Etta! At least come and talk about it!'

But the door to Etta's room slammed and Aphra knew, as they all did, that her cousin felt betrayed. To Aphra's relief, their guest showed none of the signs of consternation one might have expected. As he smiled at her, she noticed that his teeth were white and even, his skin still glowing after the river breeze.

'We have not been introduced,' he said to her, 'but I hope you will take Mistress Raemon's place until she re-establishes contact with us.'

'Aphra Betterton,' she said. 'Sir George's daughter.'

'Ah, of course! You were there…'

'I was, my lord. And if I had known you then, none of this would have happened, would it? I blame my father for not doing his duty on that day.'

'He was busy, Mistress Betterton.'

'Blame me, Aphra,' said Lord Jon. 'I thought it might work. Indeed, your aunt and I were convinced it would. A bad start, I fear. But come, let's go into the parlour for some refreshment. Ginny, shall you go up to her?'

In the privacy of her bedchamber, Etta berated herself for a fool. Unable to see their plan as anything other than a ploy meant to deceive her, Etta was effectively blinding herself to any of the advantages. Knowing what the reply would be, Lady Virginia did not ask for admittance, but walked straight in. 'Etta darling, this won't do,' she said. 'Lord Somerville is a very attractive suitor.'

'Well I'm not attracted to him,' Etta said, keeping her back to her mother. 'Any man who can deceive me in such a manner is profoundly *unattractive* to me and I want no more to do with him and I'm ashamed and hurt…yes, *hurt*, Mother…that you and Father could think to marry me to a mercer. A tradesman.' The words fell out of her mouth in a torrent and ended in a squeak of fury, and Lady Virginia saw now that tears were getting in the way, a typical Tudor response that Lady Virginia had seen time and again in the five-year-old Princess Elizabeth. It would be interesting to hear, she thought, how the new Queen would react to anyone who tried to impose their will upon her in matters of the heart.

'Dry your eyes at once, Etta,' she commanded. 'This kind of behaviour will cut no ice with your father. You are a grown woman and this is most unbecoming. Whatever you feel, Lord Somerville is our guest and you must act accordingly out of courtesy to us all. Come now, mop your face, come downstairs with me and be civil.'

Etta realised that there would be more to it than civility. 'Mother,' she said, turning to show brown eyes sparkling with tears of anger, 'is he…are you… so determined on this…this union? Is this really the way you wish to make an arrangement?'

'Etta, the way we've made the arrangement is neither here nor there. All women must accept their parents' choice unless they are widowed and even then marriages may be arranged for them. It's what happened to me and it will happen to you, too.'

'You always told me that you and Father were in love when you married.'

'We were, in a way. But that didn't mean I was given any choice in the matter.'

'So you mean that Father will insist on it?'

'Yes, dear. There is no good reason to prevaricate any longer. Lord Somerville and your father have already entered into negotiations. That's all there is to it.' Her heart softened towards her beautiful step-daughter, so intelligent and sensitive, brimming over with vitality and expectations.

To have continued the talk of dishonour and treachery over dinner would have been unthinkable, for Etta had been well schooled in good manners and the arts of hospitality. Even so, she could not pretend that nothing had happened to change how she felt about the man, his deceit, his profession. Her deeply felt anger at the deceit overpowered the meal to such a degree that she tasted nothing of the roast meats and savoury sauces prepared with such care, and it was only because Aphra was there to converse with their guest that the diners managed without Etta's usually bright contributions. Politely, she spoke when she was spoken to, but since Lord Somerville made no attempt to coax her to say more on any subject, she found the meal miserably tasteless and tense.

There was still an hour of daylight left, though it was only mid-afternoon when they rose from the table. Etta had it in mind to excuse herself immediately, but her father had other ideas before she'd had time to speak. 'Henrietta, I think our guest would like to see the gardens with you before it gets any darker.'

There was no way out. Much too quickly, Tilda brought her woollen cloak, and since it seemed to have been taken for granted that their guest would soon be one of the family, no escort followed them out on to the paved pathway leading to the herbier. With the intention of walking quickly to avoid any attempt at conversation, Etta marched away down the path between low hedges of hyssop, lavender and thrift, brown-spiked and tangled grey, reflecting her mood. But there was to be no evading the long stride of her companion who, without her knowing quite how it happened, managed to steer her into the trelliswork *allée* covered with the winter stems of honeysuckle and climbing roses. Shielded from the house, Lord Somerville wasted no time in bringing her contrariness under control, catching her beneath one arm and swinging her round to face him.

Momentarily off balance, all her resentments, hurts and loss of face rose up to the surface and, with all her pent-up energy, she aimed a blow at his head which, if it had connected, would certainly have hurt him. But he was too quick for her. He had noted how her anger had simmered throughout the meal and how that, before too long, something would explode. In the blink of an eye, her wrist was caught and held away into the small of her back, his grip so painfully tight that no amount of twisting or writhing would dislodge him or prevent her other wrist from joining the first.

'Let me go!' she snarled. 'Let me *go*! I do not *want* you. Not now or *ever*!'

'Yes, I know all about that. Saints alive, woman, I never met anyone with so many preconceived ideas about men as you. And when you find a man you like, you're prepared to dislike him because he's even better than you thought he was. What kind of nonsense is that?'

'It isn't nonsense,' she said, pulling against his restraint. 'I'm prepared to dislike you, sir, because of your deceit and because I told you of the reasons for our mismatch well before this. You lied to me about—'

'No, I didn't. I spoke only the truth, mistress. If you put your own slant on it, that's your fault, not mine.'

'So why could you not have told me who you were, instead of…?'

'Shop-owner, ship-owner, mercer and merchant. I am proud of what I do, mistress. I have not lied to you, but nor did I tell you everything, either. What man would be flattered to know that it was his wealth and status that won the heart of a woman, rather than the man himself? Fathers may arrange marriages for their daughters along such lines, but I don't entirely fall in with that principle. And don't pretend you were not interested, because I know differently.'

'In a wily knave like you, my lord? Never. I would rather—'

Whatever her high-flown protest was to have been, it was cut short by his kiss, hard, thorough and long enough to make her forget. Wedged with her head on his shoulder and unable to move away, she could only wonder at the change in him from soft-spoken courteous gentleman to this, as if the sudden revelation of his title had endowed him with an authority of a far more potent kind. If this change had any direct link to the change in her, too, then she conveniently forgot it. It was, however, a side of him she had not expected and one which, if the truth be told, she found exciting, for it suggested that she could protest all she liked but would still be as desired as she was before. 'Let me go,' she said, not quite as emphatically as she had intended. 'If you think I appeared to be interested in you, my lord, you are mistaken. I was more interested in what you had to tell me about the fabrics That's why I returned—to take another look at them.'

His hold on her relaxed. 'And look where that got you, mistress,' he said. 'Was it worth all the effort?'

'No, it certainly was not, my lord. How could you ever have believed I would take kindly to being manipulated in this way?'

'I believed your father when he assured me it was probably the *only* way, mistress. He still does. But if you'd come down off your high horse, you'd see the advantages rather than the hurt to your pride. Recall, if you will, how you enjoyed talking with me about fabrics and the exotic places they come from, and about the latest trends in fashion. I could show you much more than that: the warehouses, the furriers and cordwainers for your leathers, the shoemakers, the very finest tailors.'

Her stony expression almost softened at that, but there was yet another cause to keep her anger simmering, too good not to use as ammunition. 'I wish to attend the royal court,' she said. 'Of what use would finery be if I could not show it there? I believe the Queen knows of me, my lord, and it is my dearest wish to meet her.'

Placing an arm across her back, he moved her along the *allée* and out into the knot garden where a tiny wren flitted beneath their feet into the foliage. 'It's not quite as rosy as that, mistress. Surely Lord and Lady Raemon have explained the position to you?'

'If you mean they have doubts about *her* wish to see *me,* then, yes, they have done their best to pour cold water on the idea. I'm not at all convinced.'

'Then I don't suppose I shall be any more successful, mistress. But I think you should be aware of the problems that would arise. The young Queen will not tolerate any competition, especially on a personal level. She has sent most of the late Queen Mary's women home and now retains only six maids. Her ladies are either personal friends or women the late Queen didn't like. What's more, even if I did attend court regularly, she would be unlikely to accept you simply because you were my wife. I understand that she enjoys having men around her, but she doesn't make any accommodation available to their wives. Nor will she feed them.'

'She would accept me. How could she not like her own half-sister?'

Their stroll along the gravel came to a halt as he turned her to face him. 'Listen to me, Henrietta. In many respects, you are alike and from a distance you could be taken for her, but anyone who's seen her at close quarters would see that she doesn't have your beauty. And that's the first thing *she'd* see. I shall not be taking you to meet her. That would be asking for trouble.'

'That's as roundabout a compliment as ever I heard,' she said, beginning to walk away. 'You paint a harsh picture of her, my lord, and a fulsome one of me. I refuse to believe she and I are so very different.'

Again, his hand caught a fistful of her fur cloak,

pulling her back to him. 'You have a lot to learn then,' he said, 'and one is that I don't flatter women as other men do to soften them up. The second is that your obstinacy and wilfulness are on a par with hers and that when I said it could be tamed, I meant it. You would do well to take my advice, Henrietta, if only to keep out of trouble.'

Etta glared at him with all the indignation of a thwarted young woman seeing for the first time that she would have to deal with a man as obdurate as herself. 'Tamed, my lord? You would prefer a pliant and obedient wife, then?'

'Yes, woman,' he said, holding her still by her elbows. 'I would prefer a pliant and obedient wife to a shrew. What man would not?' He bent his head to hers, looking deeply into her eyes with a piercing glare that made her blink. 'But you will not be twisting me round your little finger as you have been used to doing with your father. Your relationship to the Queen will not help you as much as you think. In fact, you may discover that you'd rather not be related. And, yes, you may glare at me like a tigress, Henrietta, but with me you've met your match. And tomorrow, we shall discuss our wedding plans.'

'No need to wait for tomorrow for that, my lord,' she said sharply, shaking his hands off her arms. 'That can be arranged in one word. *Simple!* The shortest possible ceremony with the fewest possible witnesses. There, how does that sound?'

She did not fully expect to be taken at her word on this, when everything she had said so far had been countered with some argument, and she had anticipated that publicity, grand guests and a show of his good fortune would be essential requirements for a man of his considerable standing and wealth. So when he agreed with her that a simple ceremony was very much to his taste, she realised with a nasty thud under her ribs that her retaliation had rebounded on herself instead of him.

'Excellent,' he said. 'I shall go ahead and buy a special licence to avoid all that time-wasting, if that's what you prefer. It's not cheap, but probably cheaper than feasts and dresses and all the trimmings. Worth it, to get things over and done with.'

Etta tried out what she hoped might be an impediment. 'But what about the Queen?' she said, frowning at his eagerness to comply. 'As a relative, surely I shall need her permission?'

'I don't see that that will be necessary, mistress, when she has not yet recognised you as her relative. Has she?'

'No. Not yet.'

'Well then, the sooner we get the formalities out of the way, the better. She's very unlikely to go searching for beautiful young female relatives, is she? In fact, quite the opposite, I'd say.'

This was not at all what she had wanted, or expected, but to say so was now impossible. By pretending to oblige her, he must know that he was acting to the contrary. And whose fault was that? 'It will take a while for you and Father to complete the formalities,' she said. 'There's the matter of dowries and jointures.'

'That's already in hand,' he said, setting off towards the house. 'Our lawyers are already drawing up draft agreements. I'm not difficult to please.'

'Already? What do you mean, *already?* When?' she yelled.

Ahead of her, he stopped and turned, his face a picture of merriment. Shaking his head with laughter, he came back to her. 'When?' he repeated. 'As soon as I saw you, Henrietta. At the Mercers' banquet. I spoke to your father the very next day. I know my own mind, too, you see.'

'And you had the audacity, my lord, to flirt with me at only our second meeting? Because you thought you were on safe ground? I find that behaviour disgraceful. Does my father know you went so far?'

'What, that I might have stolen a kiss, had I tried?'

'*Enough!*' she yelped. 'You are a knave and I neither desire you nor do I wish to marry you. I want nothing you can offer me. *Nothing!*' She would have dodged round him to walk away, but the pathway was narrow between hedges of box and, with one sidestep, he barred her way. Goaded beyond endurance by his trickery and his unyielding bulk, she pummelled his chest with her fists as she had not done since childhood fights with her brothers. 'Nothing!' she yelled. *'Nothing!'*

Easily, he caught her wrists and held them together on his chest, obliging her to stand close to him. 'Yes, you do,' he said, softly. 'Oh, yes, you do, mistress, though I know you'll not admit it. If you'd truly not liked the look of me, even a mere mercer, you'd not have returned for a second look, would you? You came to see me, not the fabrics, little schemer. And I have quite a lot to offer you. Now calm down, or do you want me to kiss you here, where we're being watched from the house?'

'No, I do not. Neither here nor anywhere else.'

Smiling, he let her go, retaining one of her hands in his. 'Good. Now walk with me up the path and show me the rest of the gardens, if you please.'

Like her royal half-sister, Etta had a pragmatic streak strong enough to influence those decisions and emotions that might have looked to the uninitiated like the perversity of an indulged and beautiful woman. Being aware of this, her step-parents intended to overrule their wayward daughter in the matter of marriage to Lord Somerville, once the peacock feather had signalled her interest. But for Etta, even through the humiliation of defeat, the bitter pill was made easier to swallow by knowing that this handsome creature was not to be compared to other young noblemen she had met, neither in manner, ability, intelligence or success in business. Nor would he easily be deterred from having his way, once he had decided on it. And in this particular, Etta was determined to test him to the limit, for he *had* deceived her, whatever excuse he gave, and he would not be allowed to forget. As for making love in the future, she was angry enough to hold out against him for as long as she could, for they had spoken neither of affection nor love and, as far as she was concerned, he had forfeited any right to expect it.

Her body, however, told her a different story, now she had tasted his kiss and felt the hard power of his arms. The man was despicable, unprincipled and arrogant, yet her conscience told her that, as his wife, she would have to call on all her reserves of will-power not to let him dent her armour. Or was it already too late for that?

* * *

With her parents and Aphra, Baron Somerville was totally at ease, showing no signs of the opposition that would have daunted men of lesser confidence. But as she sat in dignified silence, Etta was able to discover, through their interest in him, how much of the world he had seen. As a man of Flemish origin, a ship-owning merchant, he had travelled far and wide, even up to the ice-cold northern lands where waterfalls fell from the sky, animals swam beneath the sea, where lights danced in the night and jets of hot water spurted from the ground. In any other circumstances, she would have asked questions and shown an interest in the man she was to marry, but pride forbade this now and her eyes found other answers in their surreptitious examination of his thick, silky hair, his eloquent hands and the zest for life that shone from his eyes. As she watched, it became clear why he had packed so much into his thirty years, why he had won the admiration of his guild and why his business ventures had flourished on the back of his ambition. It came as no surprise to her to learn that an aimless life at court was to him a waste of time unless he could contact those men he needed. Perhaps, she thought, he saw her as a useful acquisition with her resemblance to the Queen, a way to attract attention to himself and to make contacts that might otherwise have taken longer. Everything about him added to her impression of drive and capability, even the way he had conducted this speedy claim to her hand, efficient even by her father's standards. Asking herself if she might have preferred a longer, slower wooing, she had to concede that her interest in him had been immediate, but that

she had made some serious errors by her pique and
overreactions. What this predicted for the next phase
in their relationship Etta hardly dared to think, in the
light of his considerable energies.

Nicolaus was not a man to be easily daunted by opposition, however, though opposition from a woman
was something unfamiliar to him. But then, he had
known that this one was different—as a successful
merchant, he had taught himself to look out for rari-
ties and Mistress Henrietta Raemon was about as rare
as one could get, with her looks and breeding.

The breeding, of course, was something of which
she was intensely aware and proud, and which, he
thought, must be why she wished to make contact
with her half-sister Elizabeth. Presumably, then, she
had set her heart on acquiring a courtier husband,
and although not exactly disappointed by this stance,
Nicolaus believed it was unrealistic and rather naïve
of her to set such an unnecessary target, especially
when her father had alerted him at the beginning to his
daughter's dream of finding a potential for love in her
future husband. Taking this hope seriously, Nicolaus
had suggested a way of finding out what was more
important to her, girlish romance or a courtier husband. For him to conceal his new title and any mention of his wealth and status from her at a trial meeting
had been his suggestion, meant to discover any sign
of attraction upon which they could base a relationship that would suit them both. Had he not been reasonably sure of the success of this plan, he would not
have suggested it.

His friendship with Lady Raemon's brother-in-

law, Sir George Betterton at the Royal Wardrobe,
had been the link by which he could make himself
known to her without any of the resistance her parents had warned him about. She was, they said, fas-
cinated by fabrics and fashion, as most women with
her connections were. What better, then, than an innocent invitation from Sir George to see the Queen's
coronation robes? From the first meeting, his experience with women had assured him of her interest,
not only in the materials of his trade but in himself,
as a man. Suspecting that she would return for a second look, he had arranged with Sir George for a little privacy and, because he was trusted, his precious
moments with her had proved to him that she found
him attractive. Her refusal to allow a kiss was no
great matter and her aversion to a mercer as a suitable husband had not deterred him either, thinking
that her attitude would surely be softened when she
learned what else he had to commend him. Perhaps
he had underestimated what a complicated character
she was. Perhaps his little deceit had been a step too
far? Or was it not only that she was a complicated
lady, but also an insecure one, too?

Her stepfather had made him aware of Henrietta's
parentage, which would account for her resemblance
to the new Queen, but since neither of her parents had
been known to Nicolaus, this information had not concerned him. It was only when he had met Lady Raemon at a later date, when she had mentioned Etta's
wish to attend court, that he had been made aware
of their concerns, wanting only to protect her from
what they saw as the inevitable malicious gossip of
those who had known that particular mistress of the

late king. Having been exposed to such wounding jealousies themselves, they knew what could happen to Henrietta if she was ever, as a young and innocent woman, brought into contact with court life. The fact that he, Nicolaus, had assured them of his lack of interest in this direction had been an added bonus to his suitability as a husband, though with Henrietta, it had been exactly the opposite. He was not only a mercer, of all things, with a home above a shop, but a most unlikely source of access to the Queen's presence, too.

Etta had not had the chance to explain to him exactly what lay behind this urge to make contact with her half-sister, but her reason of a mere relationship did not seem to him to justify a rejection of everything else he had to offer. If that was not a sign of insecurity, then he did not know what was. What did she want, apart from to see her sibling? What had that outburst been all about? More to do with a thwarting of her hopes, he thought, than with being the wife of a mercer.

Settling down into the warm feather bed that night, Nicolaus wondered if her lovely cousin Aphra would be of any help to him in explaining the deeper reasons for her unexpectedly violent aversion. He had felt Etta's body soften under his kiss, the way it had in his dreams. He had desired her from his first glance and knew he would have to make her his wife. Now, he saw that he would have to tame her to come to his hand, for she was of a wilder and more passionate breed than any he'd had dealings with so far. So much for her royal parentage. His last disjointed thoughts were of the peacock feathers. Such a boyish thing to do. No wonder she had not thought it funny.

* * *

The gardens at Tyburn House were not only extensive but also beautifully designed and kept in pristine condition throughout all the seasons. Few of Lord and Lady Raemon's guests were allowed to leave without first taking a look at the knot gardens and borders, the fountains, water courses, and Lady Raemon's delight, the large topiary hedges cut into the most fantastic shapes, lining the pathway to the orchard. Hoping to escape Lord Somerville's company before he returned home, Etta walked with her cousin along the path where a tall pudding-shaped tree would surely have hidden them from sight if they'd not first been seen by the tall figure of the mercer. For some reason which she could not name, Etta felt the thrill of excitement at his approach, for not even she could have faulted his appearance, the virile masculinity of his walk, the assurance of his bow as he swept off his hat, the proud reach of his arms as he replaced it. Etta knew she would not be allowed to get away with any more of her incivility, yesterday's furious objections having been dealt with quite pitilessly. A night of broken sleep and long periods of contemplation had told her that, this time, she would be obliged to accept, though perhaps not with the good grace her mother had commanded.

At his approach, Aphra disappeared with a diplomacy Etta did not appreciate. Even so, she retained a grain of satisfaction from knowing that, since supper last evening, she now knew much more about him than he had so far discovered about her. And she would have kept it so, had he not insisted on trying to redress the balance. 'Tell me about yourself, mistress,' he said, walking beside her.

She looked away into the distance where high shaped hedges enclosed them. 'I don't talk about myself to order,' she said, 'as some do.'

'Not even to the man you'll wed?'

'If the man I'm being obliged to wed could not bestir himself to find out more before he offered for me, then I'll be damned if I'll spell out my life story for his pleasure. Most men would have shown some interest before they made an offer.'

'I showed an interest, mistress,' he said, laughing. 'Ask your parents.'

'Then you know all you need to know, my lord. There is no more.'

'I see. Then you are content for me to find out for myself?'

'No, I am far from content. I thought you knew *that*, too.'

'Well, well,' he said. 'Most intriguing. Your parents told me you were fluent in French, Italian and Spanish. Is that what you mean by no more?'

'Don't patronise me, if you please. I'm not a child to recite what I have learnt for the benefit of my elders. Women seldom receive any credit for their learning, at the best of times, and it was not at my father's request that I joined my brothers in the schoolroom. It was my wish to find out if I could match the Princess Elizabeth's abilities. But so far I have not. I don't have her Latin and Greek yet, nor her Welsh. And I don't suppose I play on the virginal as well as she does, or dance. I doubt if I shall ever know now, shall I, my lord?'

He refused to rise to the bait. 'I find that quite re-markable,' he said. 'It's a pity, in a way, that you never had the chance to meet Lady Jane Grey. She was a scholar, too. Unlike her two sisters. They're feather-brained to a degree. Jane didn't dance well, though, and I'm sure you do.'

'Again, I'm hardly likely to dance before the court unless I can...'

'Go there, yes, Henrietta, I think I have the message now, I thank you. I can see we may be plucking on that one string until it breaks.'

'Yes,' she said, stonily. 'I intend to.'

'So how many children shall we have, mistress? Have you thought about that yet?'

'Oh, for *pity's sake*!' she cried, turning her head to avoid seeing his grin. They walked on in silence until Etta slowed and stopped, realising that her coldness was not going to help matters, yet it was the only de-fence she had.

'Etta?' he said. 'Look at me. Can we be friends now as we once were? Just as a start? It will make things easier for both of us if we can talk about this.'

Turning to face him, she tried hard to find the same sincerity he had shown before he'd revealed his con-spiracy to influence her decision. Her long silence signified the mental conflict still raging in her mind until finally she sighed with a slight shake of her head. 'As for being friends, my lord...that counts for little, doesn't it, when my future has been decided for me? I thought at one time that we could be friends, but you have lost ground since then and I shall need some per-suading that your integrity is what I thought it was. Don't ask from me any more than I can give, if you please. I have little choice, it seems, about becoming your wife, but you can hardly lay the blame at my door if you find you've bitten off more than you can chew. I am my father's daughter and I am being forced into this situation.'

'It was never my intent to forfeit your trust, Henrietta. Perhaps my determination to have you for my own, before anyone else, blinded me to the way it might be seen as underhand. But nor do I believe for one moment that I've taken on more than I can handle.'

Etta slid a hand to her cheek to cool it, knowing that he referred to her incivility. 'I have not been used to having a man other than my father telling me what I must do, sir. It will go hard with me. And you, too.'

'I think I know that, mistress, without you telling me.'

'But you've had women, I suppose? All of them compliant?'

'Yes,' he admitted. 'I've had women, but you are the first I've ever offered marriage to.' His hand moved through the shadows to touch her brow, then to trace a line down her cheek, his thumb brushing against her lips, feeling her tremble.

They parted slightly as something told her to stand firm, not to relent against this tender invasion, but the coldness she tried to summon was slow in coming and now the messages she was sending were the wrong ones. Etta knew how well he would be able to decode them. Placing a warning hand on his shoulder, she tried to hold him away, but it was too late and, before any words would come to her aid, she was being held against him with her face slanted across his.

The warmth of his mouth blanked her mind to everything except the thrilling sensation, and no matter that he'd had women before her, she believed in that moment that she was indeed the only one he had ever wished to marry. For those unfettered moments of honesty between them, each revealed to the other that desire would rise above all other conflicts, with or without their permission, for his kiss was persuasive. Had she not retained that indignation and hurt about being manipulated, she might have given in to the moment, the thrill, the newness of surrender. But she pulled away, moving back into the shadow of the hedge to hide her confusion, one hand covering her mouth. 'No,' she whispered, 'this is not…'

'Listen to me, Etta,' he said, easing her back to him. 'This *is* what we want. It's what we wanted from that first meeting. We both know it. But it doesn't mean your surrender if you don't want it to. You can fight me until you tire of fighting, but from time to time, sweetheart, we can indulge in a truce without shame to either of us. We shall be married within the week and think what a waste that would be if we were to spend our wedding night in useless animosities. That would be pointless. Is that what you intended?'

'It's my only weapon,' she said, looking away into the dimness.

'What? How can you say so, woman? You of the thousand pinpricks.'

'That's an admission, coming from you,' she said.

'Do your worst, Etta. I can handle you, but don't stifle what could be an endless capacity for loving, just to try to hurt me. Our new Queen may do as she pleases about marrying, but you don't have to emulate her in that, too. Be yourself.'

'Is this meant to…?'

'Oh, I know what you're thinking, that I want a submissive wife in all things. But, no, that's not what we're talking about, is it? I'm talking about you denying yourself to get back at me. You were made for love, Etta. Not just *that* kind of love, but compassion, empathy, kindness, generosity. I cannot believe that this recent resentment will last for ever. That's not the Tudor nature, is it?'

'How do you know that, my lord?'

'I'm learning every day. I think you could keep most men guessing as to which was the real Henrietta, just as the Queen does with her courtiers. But I'm getting to know you, sweetheart, and I'm better placed to discover every single facet.'

'Bad, as well as not so bad?'

'Yes, you need a strong hand. I can protect you. I can share all I have with you. Will you not do the same for me?'

Materially, she had little to offer him except what her father had decided she was worth in wealth and estate, but if he meant to know about all her vices as well as the virtues, she would show him exactly what he was taking on before she succumbed completely to his charms. 'What I have, my lord, is what you see and what you will eventually find out about. I am prepared to share with you my deep humiliation and anger, that's all. You think you can change me. Taming is what you call it. But I do not intend to change at any time in the near future, not until I have achieved something of what I have set out to do. Uncompromising that may sound, but it was you who wanted the connection, not me. I suppose my father will have warned you about what you're taking on,' she said, allowing him to hold her hand against his chest, 'and I'd be a fool to add anything more to his list. In fact, I dare say he's quite relieved for you to take responsibility for me. As for the rest, it's no more than you deserve, is it?'

Even in the dim light of that winter morning, she could see the dark slits of his eyes twinkle with a mischievous laugh. 'As you say, my beauty,' he whispered, bending his head close to hers, 'it will be no more than I deserve.' He touched her lips with his own before she could move away, then released her hand. 'Now, I must catch the next tide if I want to reach my home by midday. I want you and your parents to visit me at Cheapside, just to satisfy you that a mere mercer can reach your high standards. Bring your cousin Aphra with you, too. She might help to convince you of my suitability.'

'Please, don't say any more about that. My intention was not to insult you, or the mercers in general.'

'What was it, then? Is it that I'm not a courtier? Is that it?'

'Yes,' she whispered. 'I am no nearer to the royal court than I was before and I find that hard to accept, my lord.'

'Then let's shelve the problem for the moment, shall we? You may find that, eventually, there will be other things to occupy your time and energy, mistress.'

She would have been a dullard indeed not to have known what he alluded to, but she did not think that, in the circumstances, the prospect was very enticing. Nor, if she could help it, was it even feasible.

Chapter Three

'He kissed you, didn't he?' Aphra said.

'You can tell?'

Aphra chuckled. 'Well, there's nothing to see, exactly, but…'

'But what?' Etta peered into the mirror, touching her lips with the tip of a finger, feeling not only the firm pressure of his mouth on hers but also the hardness of his thighs, even through her farthingale. His arm had pressed into her shoulders, bending her into him. Not a tender kiss by any means. She ought not to have allowed it, but Baron Somerville was not a man against whom she was likely to win any argument, as her time in the garden had proved. He would hear her side of things but, in the end, he would retain the upper hand.

'You look as if you might be seeing eye to eye at last,' Aphra said. 'Are you?'

Etta scowled. 'Indeed not,' she said. 'Not as long as I'm expected to live over a shop. He wants us to go and see it. As if that will make any difference.'

'Just think of all those exotic fabrics and feathers, straight from the Orient and the Indies.'

'Aphie! You're not taking this seriously, are you? And anyway, where are the Indies?'

'I don't know, love. Sounds good, though.'

Etta was glad of her cousin's company at a time like this when her deepest thoughts had begun to conflict with the impression she was trying to give of being resolute, strong-willed and still deeply frustrated by recent events. If the truth be told, her first experience of being held so forcibly, of being overruled, kissed without her permission and made to listen, had dealt a serious blow to her attempt at a frosty and implacable manner, and now she felt confused by a riot of new feelings brought on, she knew, by the man's powerful and shocking closeness. Naturally, with his experience, he must have known how it would affect her, an innocent. He had been places, met people, done things, had women. That thought in particular made her frown. 'He's had women, Aphie,' she said.

But Aphra was looking out of the window, her lovely face suddenly lit by an excitement she tried hard to control. 'It's Ben!' she said, breathlessly. 'I can see it is. He has someone with him. I must go down, Ettie. Come!'

Instantly switched to a different channel, Aphra dismissed Etta's potentially interesting snippet of information to focus on their newest guest, their uncle, Dr Ben Spenney—Dr Ben, as he was known to the family—was the half-brother of Aphra's mother and Etta's stepmother, and was now an eminent apothecary whose home at Sandrock Priory had been left to him by his father, Sir Walter D'Arvall. Sir Walter and his long-suffering wife had been allowed to buy the priory after the closure of the monasteries over twenty years ago, spending a vast amount of money and effort on remodelling it for domestic use. Now, it was occupied by Dr Ben and his household, amongst whom were several young students of medicine from various parts of Europe come to study in England. He was a gentle and scholarly man, not unlike the monks with whom he'd been raised, and his family doubted he would ever find time to marry. In spite of the disparity in their ages, Ben and his niece Aphra had always held an extraordinarily deep affection for each other, though this had never been actively encouraged because of their close relationship. It was no secret to the family, but nor was it a subject ever singled out for comment, even by Aphra's younger brother Edwin or the twin cousins with whom he worked. Now, as Etta saw the sparkle in her cousin's eyes and the quick flush of colour to her cheeks, her heart ached for Aphra, whose special affection for Ben could never be allowed to flourish.

Downstairs, by the roaring log fire, the delight at seeing Dr Ben after an interval of several months was truly genuine, Sandrock Priory being miles away in the Wiltshire countryside within visiting distance of other second homes belonging to the D'Arvalls and Bettertons. Far enough away from London for the air to be sweet and pure. Dr Ben's companion was quickly made welcome. 'Master Leon of Padua,' said Ben. 'One of my very brightest students. I'm taking him with me to lecture at the Apothecaries' Hall. For the experience,' he added.

Master Leon, a well-made young man with large dark eyes and a skin that could only have been burnished by an Italian summer, wore a sober gown of

dusty black over a grey-brown wool tunic and a flat
cap that had seen better days. His manner and speech,
however, suggested that his education had been exceptional. 'Dr Spenney,' he told them, 'is either trying to offer me the experience or show me how little
I know and how much I have yet to learn.'

They laughed, but Aphra said, 'How little you
know about what, sir?'

'About the curative qualities of plants, *madonna*,'
he said, smiling.

'But any housewife knows which plants heal. It's
part of a woman's training,' she said. 'We have recipe
books that are generations old.'

'Aphra,' said Dr Ben, gently, 'stop teasing. You
know what he means.'

The glances they exchanged seemed to imply much
more than words, and the laugh that rose in Aphra's
throat was of a kind not often heard by the others. But
his half-sister, Lady Raemon, who also had a special
fondness for Ben, suspected that the real reason why
he had chosen Master Leon to accompany him was to
meet Aphra, and it was not long before the two were
gently sparring about which plants were native to their
respective countries. Etta joined in, then took them
both to inspect the herb garden. So it was quite by
chance that they missed the arrival of two more guests
in the same barge from further down the river, Baron
Somerville and Sir Elion D'Arvall, the eldest son of
the late Sir Walter, and elder brother to Lady Raemon.

Sir Elion D'Arvall had once aspired to a senior
position in the royal household, having assumed that
he might be offered the post as King's Cofferer on
the death of his father. But with the change of sover-

eign had come a change in many other departments
and Sir Elion had been overlooked, only to be instantly recruited by William Cecil, advisor on finan-
cial matters to the young Princess Elizabeth. Now she
was Queen at last and Sir William made Secretary of
State, Sir Elion had become an extra pair of ears and
eyes both in England and abroad, acting as diplomat
in the courts of Europe. It was inevitable that he and
Baron Somerville would one day arrive together, having often met while on business abroad. 'Where was
it last, Nic?' Sir Elion said, passing him a handsome
silver-lidded tankard. 'Antwerp, wasn't it?'

Lord Somerville took it from him. 'I was doing
deals with silk merchants,' he said, remembering with
a smile. 'I've learned a lot since then.'

'And now you're to marry the lovely Henrietta.
Well, you'll have your work cut out there, lad, and no
mistake. Brave man, eh, Jon?'

Lord Raemon twitched an eyebrow in Somerville's
direction. 'He knows what he's doing,' he said, laconically. 'I've warned him. Don't blame me.'

'Shame on you both,' said Lady Virginia. 'Henrietta's a lovely young woman and intelligent, too. If she
has both of you running round in small circles, you
can blame each other for forcing her hand.'

'What's this about?' said Dr Ben, looking from one
to the other. 'Surely you didn't think you could make
Henrietta's mind up for her, did you? Was that wise?'

'It was the only thing to do, Ben, if we didn't want
to spend the next twenty years failing to see eye to
eye on the subject. She'll come round,' said Lord Raemon, 'once she gets this latest bee out of her bonnet.'

'Which bee?' said Ben. He looked at Somerville for

enlightenment and was told of Henrietta's insistence that, because she had Tudor blood, and looks, the new Queen would automatically want to know her. 'I see,' said Ben. 'So if her father won't oblige and her future husband won't oblige either, who d'ye think she'll try next to make it happen? Three guesses.'

Sir Elion shook his head. 'Oh, no,' he said. 'We don't need three, do we? Any moment now, my niece will be in here to request a quiet word in my ear concerning a matter of courtly introductions. Do I have it right, Nic?'

'That's about the sum of it,' Somerville said. 'She's not going to take no for an answer from any of us, anyway. We need a strategy.'

'I think you need to be careful,' said Ben.

'I think you need to be *very* careful,' said Lady Sophia, Sir Elion's wife. 'She doesn't know the ways of the court as well as I do. She'll be hurt.'

'Not by any of us, my lady,' said Lord Somerville, gently. 'And anyone else who tries will have me to deal with.'

Sir Elion was familiar with personal disputes between couples whose marriages had been arranged for them, having helped to smooth the stormy path of his sister Ginny's marriage to Sir Jon Raemon, as he then was. So he was not surprised to learn that their Tudor stepdaughter meant to have her own way in one direction if she could not have it in another and, knowing the Queen's mind better than any of them, was able to see where the biggest dangers lay. When his friend Lord Somerville asked him how the new Queen fared once the excitement of the coronation had died down, his reply came as something of a shock. 'Oh, it's all about Lord Robert Dudley now,' he said, witheringly. 'Since she made him Master of Horse, you'd think a crown came with the job.'

'What?' said Ben. 'He thinks he'll be made king?'

'There's a lot of talk,' said Sir Elion. 'And not all of it innocent, either. Ah, here come the ladies. Congratulations, Niece,' Sir Elion said to Henrietta.

'Thank you, Uncle. Commiserations are in order. May I have a word in your ear, before we leave?'

'Certainly, love. About how to cope with mercers, is it?'

And so they laughed and teased each other before the roaring fire that took up half the wall, the logs sizzling and spitting and smelling of last year's apples.

Obligingly, Sir Elion made himself available to his niece, his answer formed well before her enquiry was delivered. 'Will you be returning to court any time soon?' she said.

'Not before the wedding, I think. Will that be here?'

'Yes, I expect we shall be going straight to Cheapside afterwards, but I want...well, the truth is, I want to find a way of seeing the Queen and I thought you might...?'

'You mean, just to see her, or to have her see you? I can tell you now, Etta love, that if Somerville won't take you, then I don't see how I can.'

'I simply want to see her, just to take a look. I don't expect to be presented. Not until she wishes it, that is. That may take some time.'

'And you want me to take you there? Is Somerville supposed to know about this? Because I shall not be doing anything unless he knows, Etta.'

'Uncle, if he knows I'm with you, he won't object,

will he? And it will be all right for me to walk in with you, because you're known there and I'm your niece. That won't be against the rules, will it?'

'Not as long as you abide by them, Etta. I can't afford to get on the wrong side of court protocol when I earn my living there.' Sir Elion saw this conversation taking a rather different course from the one discussed earlier, but what she was proposing sounded relatively innocuous, compared to what her father and future husband had anticipated as a head-on confrontation with their sovereign.

'I know that, Uncle Elion. I would not do anything to embarrass you.'

'Of course you won't, m'dear. Shall we be invited to the wedding?'

Etta shook her head and looked away. 'No,' she said, 'I doubt it. Lord Somerville prefers us to have a very modest ceremony. Only Mother and Father, that's all.'

'Oh, my dear,' her uncle replied, taking her hand. 'I'm sure he has his reasons. But give it time. You'll get to know each other eventually. He's a very astute man, you know. The Queen made him a baron at the same time as she knighted William Cecil, my master, and Baron Hunsdon, her half-brother. Somerville sent her money when she was still Princess Elizabeth and without a bean. When Queen Mary released her from imprisonment, she was in a sad state, poor creature. She doesn't forget those who've shown loyalty to her in the past.'

Etta was deeply impressed by her uncle's glowing tribute, causing her to wonder why, when he had told them so much else about his adventures in trading,

Lord Somerville had said nothing concerning his generosity to the woman she wanted to meet. She could not help but speculate whether the Queen's memory would extend to herself, at whom she had looked so intently on her progress through Cheapside. But now there would be much to attend to in the next days, the preparation of her clothes and the packing of all the dear childhood possessions she hoped would be given a place in the house on Cheapside above the mercer's shop. Aware that she had misrepresented Lord Somerville to her uncle over the wedding ceremony, she was now obliged to accept the results, stark as they promised to be.

To her surprise, and disappointment, too, Lord Somerville did not avail himself of the chance to speak to her in private, apparently finding the conversation more interesting with Sir Elion, Dr Ben, Master Leon of Padua and his hosts. She could not really blame him after her coldness of the previous day, though now she began to see that he felt no particular need to make himself agreeable to her if she did not intend to do the same. She wondered, after he and Uncle Elion had returned home in the barge, whether what she'd said about the wedding would 'accidentally' come to his ears, which only reinforced her regret that the most important day of her life would hardly be distinguishable from any other. Quite capable of blaming herself for this state of affairs, she wept quietly into her pillow that night as Aphra's comforting hand moved gently over her back.

Pretending a total lack of enthusiasm for the visit to Cheapside, Etta climbed into her father's barge which

was to take them down river as far as Puddle Wharf,
after which there was nothing for it but a rather dirty
and noisy walk up towards the great cathedral of St
Paul's. Beyond that lay the broad sweep of Cheapside
from where she had witnessed the coronation procession, though now the stands had been dismantled, the
shopfronts denuded of tapestries and carpets, bun-
ting, and showy gold plate. With her were Aphra,
Lord and Lady Raemon, and Etta's maid, Tilda, also
Ben and Master Leon, whose appointment with the
apothecaries was that day, those two talking quietly
together about what to expect. Huddled against the
sharp river breeze, Etta watched the passing wherries
bearing passengers clutching at their clothes without
the benefit of a canvas awning.

Threading their way through the noise and bus-
tle of Cheapside, avoiding delivery wagons and stepping over muddy cobblestones, the five guests of Lord
Somerville found at last the gilded Sign of the Bridge
hanging outside an extensive five-storey building.
The front of this was almost entirely made of dia-
mond-paned glass windows with intricately carved
mullions between, carved wooden friezes decorated
with shields and curved brackets holding up the jutting
storey above. Carved doorposts had polished galleons
over a stack of merchant's symbols, hardly an inch
undecorated. The windows on the ground floor were
especially large, allowing customers to see the wares
by daylight. It was one of the largest and most impressive shopfronts on a wide street known far and wide
as the most fashionable thoroughfare in the City of
London. Etta's mother said what she herself was trying hard not to think. 'Well, my dear,' she murmured,

'if I had to live above a shop, I think I might choose one like this without too much heartache. Just take a look at this doorway, Jon. Can we have one like that?'

'Yes, love,' he said, unsmiling. 'Remind me to cash in your dowry, will you?'

A liveried apprentice stood to one side to let them pass. 'Finest taffety and cambric, mistress,' he called, 'in the Queen's favourite colours. London fustian and Naples serge. New stocks, best prices.' Eyeing Tilda, he gave her a cheeky wink and opened the door. The clamour outside was cut off as it closed behind them, the interior of shelf-lined walls muffling all but the low murmur of customers and well-dressed assistants, the latter throwing ells of coloured silks across the counters, billowing it like sails, gossamer-fine, twinkling with metal threads. As if from nowhere, Lord Somerville came forward to greet them, bowing gracefully and giving them time to observe his restrained but elegant suit, a tan doublet with a high-standing collar of soft kid and a pleated neckband, tiny gold buttons and gold-edged slashes on the sleeves. The peacock feather was missing from his hat; in its place, a gold enamelled badge of the Mercers' Company.

Greeting them in turn, he lingered over Etta's hand, smiling into her eyes as if to draw an answering smile from her. He lowered his voice for her alone. 'I'm glad you came. I hope you will approve of what you see here and the living rooms above. Not as extensive as Tyburn House, but by no means uncomfortable.'

Etta knew the general plan of this kind of shop where business was conducted at street level, cellars and storerooms below, living quarters above. Everything about this shop spoke of quality, rarity and wealth. How could she not be impressed? Being cautious not to show it, Etta modified her praise by a question. 'Is the shop door the only access, my lord?'

'No, mistress. Our comings and goings are kept private through the side door. Come, allow me to show you where I live.' A carved oak staircase led past panelled walls where portraits of his Flemish ancestors stared at them darkly. The ceilings were of the latest white plasterwork moulded with wreaths and symbols of the wool trade from which hung heavy chandeliers holding dozens of beeswax candles to light the way. Upstairs, polished wooden floors and tapestry-hung walls led their appreciative gaze towards huge plate cupboards with displays of silverware and exotic glass, polished tables with richly carved bulbous legs, stout chairs, stools with sheepskin cushions and glowing Turkey carpets. From the inside, the glass windows almost filled one wall. A handsome marble-and-wood fireplace on an inner wall held a roaring fire, its light shining through a set of engraved glasses next to a silver-lidded jug. 'Joseph!' Baron Somerville called into the next room. 'Wine for our guests, if you please.'

A pleasant young man appeared at once, pouring wine and handing it round as their host answered his guests' questions about how long, how far, how convenient it all was, already seeing Etta as mistress there, approving, satisfied. She had not known what to expect, but now the phrase 'living over the shop' was already taking on a different meaning from her first shocked protest.

The warmth of the wine, a delicious malmsey, percolated through her veins, softening the hard edges of the pessimism she had brought with her, her determination not to be affected by anything he could show her. But this was the first time she had seen him on his own property in this sumptuous setting, at ease with his own surroundings and every inch the successful merchant who would know to the last detail exactly where every item had come from, how much its value and, probably, how it was made, too. Hardly contributing to the conversation, she listened to his deep well-modulated voice and watched his face, his expressive hands, and once when he turned to smile at her, she knew that he sensed the reason for her reserve and saw what she was thinking. Later, he took them into the other rooms, many more than she had supposed, a dining parlour, his office where Joseph sat amongst sheaves of papers and strong boxes, letter racks and inkpots. There were kitchens below, storerooms, larders and pantry, servants' quarters and, above these, several well-appointed bedchambers, one of which was furnished in the latest style with hangings of pale-blue velvet brocade that must have cost a small fortune. For a house above a shop, it was more than adequate, though it could not be compared to either Tyburn House or to Lea Magna, Sir Jon's country house where there was a complex of outbuildings and stabling for forty horses. Whether he had other properties in England she was determined to show no interest, although for all she knew, her parents might have discovered something. Aphra squeezed her hand. 'Like it?' she said.

'No garden,' Etta said. 'How am I going to manage without a garden?'

Her criticism was overheard from the other side of
the room, making her suspect that Baron Somerville
could lip-read. 'By the time you come to live here,
mistress,' he said, 'there will be a garden.'

She had been made to feel very uncivil. Even Aphra,
her dearest friend, looked at her in some surprise.
'Yes,' Etta said. 'That would be good. Thank you.'
She turned away to hide her blush, still struggling
against conflicting emotions. She had braided her hair
up again that day, intending to deny her future husband the pleasure of seeing it loosely splayed over her
shoulders. It was a small gesture of defiance that gave
her little reward, for the memory of his close admiration at their first meeting would not leave her and,
between wondering how she could manifest her displeasure at the way this marriage business had been
so hastily arranged, a thrill crept under her skin whenever she was near him. And to be near him every day
in this beautifully appointed house would surely test
her opposition to its limits, in the weeks to come.

A set of miniature paintings on the wall of the
front parlour caught her attention by their exquisite
detail and rich colour. The faces of the sitters were no
larger than her thumbnail. Seeing her cousin's interest, Aphra asked about them.

'Some of them are by my father, Simon Benninck,'
Lord Somerville told them, 'and these three are by my
sister, Levina Teerlinc.'

'I've heard of them both,' Aphra said. 'So you are
Simon Benninck's son? Are they both in Antwerp,
still?'

'My father is no longer with us, alas. But he taught

my sister. She lives at Whitehall Palace. I go there to see her whenever I can.'

Striving to keep the curiosity out of her voice, Etta immediately saw the connection and could not resist her own question. This might be the link she was looking for. 'Whitehall? The Palace? Near the Queen?' she said. Her parents came to look. There was a limit to the questions she could ask about this interesting relationship. Perhaps they would ask some.

'Yes, indeed. She is one of the few ladies from Queen Mary's reign to be retained by the Queen. They've known each other for years, you see, and Levina has painted her portrait already when she was Princess Elizabeth. She's working on her coronation portrait at the moment, I believe. The Queen saw no reason to dismiss her when she likes what she produces and Levina has nothing to go back to, in Antwerp.'

'So she is widowed?' Lady Raemon asked.

'Indeed, my lady, but very content with her rooms at the palace. She knows everyone there. She's painted many of them, too.'

'Commendable diplomacy,' murmured Etta's father.

Commendable connections, too. How soon shall we be paying a visit to Mrs Teerlinc, I wonder? 'Beautiful portraits,' Etta said, seeing a faint ray of optimism for the first time.

With the arrival of the special licence signed by the Bishop of London, the wedding coincided with the greyest day February had to offer, timed so early that everyone was out of bed before daylight. This

was so different from the wedding about which she
had daydreamed for years, and, as the reality of the
situation took shape, she almost managed to convince
herself that her wishes were being ignored and that
this hurried, mean, unromantic performance was entirely Lord Somerville's fault. Dressed in her most ser-
viceable clothes, she made her brief vows in a voice
tense with the simmering disappointment of days during which she had directed her packing from dawn
till dusk while, at each supper time, the conversation
had revolved around matters of local interest and no
questions asked about her feelings or thoughts. Baron
Somerville had no need, she told herself, to interpret
her word 'simple' quite so literally and not a word
from him of persuasion to make her day special in
some way.

Just before the ceremony, her mother had tried to
console her with carefully chosen words about duty
and love growing out of respect, and time healing
rifts, and had said how much they would miss her.
Lord Jon's attempt at consolation was more robust,
reminding her what a good match this was. But by
this time, self-pity had turned to deep offence, and
after a brief breakfast of ordinary porridge, she had
boarded Lord Somerville's barge with neither smiles
nor tears to waste on those who had connived to dictate the course of her life. She had, however, said a
tearful farewell to Aphra.

'Well, Lady Somerville,' said his lordship, covering her knees with a rug. 'Was that simple enough for
you?' It was clear he did not expect an answer and her
silence went unremarked as they pushed off into the
middle of the river, the company including Tilda and

his man, Joseph. But to her surprise, the barge headed upstream instead of towards London's Puddle Wharf, forcing a question from Etta about their destination.

'Mortlake, my lady,' Somerville said. 'It's near Richmond.'

'Richmond? Mortlake? We're stopping there overnight? You didn't tell me that.'

'You didn't ask, did you? Too busy nursing your woes. Mortlake Manor is our Surrey home. It belongs in royal hands, but I have the lease of it. That's where we shall live.'

'So we shall not be going to London? Not to Cheapside?'

'Not for a while. Well, not you, anyway. I shall have to attend to my business there, but I take my barge downriver. It's much quicker by water.'

Etta hunched into her cloak, frowning. Yet another deception. Another setback. This was not what she had expected but then, neither was Mortlake Manor, a magnificent place built of red-patterned brickwork and timber, approached via a wide wooden jetty and a gravel pathway to the front porch, wide enough for an elephant. To one side, beyond the great house, was a spread of outbuildings, sheltered by elms where noisy wheeling rooks settled in for the night. Smoke rose white into the darkening sky from tall clusters of chimneys, dogs barked in welcome, men shouted orders, running towards their master and new mistress, lighting lamps, opening doors.

The deep disappointment Etta felt at not going to London first was weighed against the need to come to terms with this enigmatic man and the life she would be expected to lead with him. She had so far made no effort to please him, and when the chance had been offered her, she had refused to take it. Since then, he had made it almost impossible for her to thaw by remaining beyond her reach. Was he now offering her a second chance to make herself affable, or did he mean it when he implied that work would come first for him? Could she bring herself to share his bed? Would he wait for her to thaw? Could he afford to, when consummation of the marriage was such an important part of the contract? Pragmatic as usual, Etta's common sense reminded her that she was unlikely to be taken to London as long as her frostiness continued, for she had seen how he could carry it further, and to greater effect. Catching his eye, she received his smile with a blink of acknowledgment. 'You said nothing of this, my lord,' she said.

'I wanted to surprise you. Wait till you see inside.'

If she had been impressed by his house on Cheapside, she was even more affected by the richness of this interior glowing with mellow colour from tapestried walls, gleaming glass and silver, polished furniture and panelling, tables carpeted with bright eastern rugs, cushions and curios. Her parents' houses were well appointed, but this reflected a man's journeys through foreign lands, his ambition, success and portable wealth, and that when her father had reminded her what a good match she was making, he had known what he was talking about. On the other hand, she wondered if her father had bothered to mention to Lord Somerville that she was also a good match. Or had that small detail escaped him?

'Well?' he said. 'D'ye think you could be comfortable here?'

'This is a beautiful house, my lord. I was unsure what to expect after—' She broke off, aware that, in her tiredness, she was close to revealing too much about her last few miserable days. Tears were close to the surface and confusion dried up any generous words she might have used.

'Shall we talk about it later?' he said kindly, keeping hold of her hand. 'I think we may have some catching up to do, don't you? This is the day of our wedding and there is still time to redeem it, if you wish.'

It was obvious to her by this time that their arrival had been planned some days ago, and that if she had shown any kind of interest, she could have discovered it for herself. Servants were everywhere in evidence, the enticing aroma of food wafted along passageways and all the luggage which had gone ahead of them had been unpacked and set about the place, clothes in chests, personal belongings arranged. Her own large bedchamber was sumptuously furnished with cushioned chairs, carved tables inlaid with ivory and a huge bed curtained in the colours of spring with a matching silken bedspread heavy with gold fringing. Reflecting light from dozens of candles, the white plasterwork ceiling was a maze of pattern more recent than the low beams of Lea Magna. This place, she thought, was a palace.

Left alone, she and Tilda began the transformation into a dress more worthy of her first supper as Lady Somerville, a gown of dark-green velvet with white fur around the high neck and over-sleeves, paler green undersleeves with gold embroidery, a gold mesh caul for her hair, studded with pearls. The simple gold wedding band felt as strange as it had when he had placed it on her finger that morning, since when she had not been able to forget it was there. Tilda saw her examining it and took her hand in comfort. 'It'll be all right,' she whispered. 'It's for the best, isn't it?'

'I suppose so. I'll go down, Tild. Shall you wait up for me?'

'Yes, if you want me I'll be in that little room over there,' Tilda said, pointing to the corner. 'There's a bed in there just my size. Come, m'lady. This is not like you. You're not afraid, are you?'

'Too late for fears, Tild. It's just that this man is... well...'

'Different? Not a boy, but a man? Better that way. He'll know what he's about.'

'Yes, I only wish I did. I'm not afraid, just mixed up.'

'About your feelings for him? But you like him, don't you?'

'I don't intend to fall in love with him, Tild. Not yet. It's all happened too fast for me.'

Tilda smiled and said nothing to that. Love would not wait on convenience. She might have added that, in her opinion, her mistress was already part way there and that the next few hours would tilt the balance one way or the other, if only she would put away her grievances.

This was Etta's second experience of observing Somerville on his own ground, hearing how he spoke to his servants with quiet authority and how eager they were to please him. Giving a last order to his house steward, he received her with an outstretched hand at the bottom of the grand staircase, affording her a leisurely view of his dull gold suit of figured brocade from which jewelled aiglets winked in the candlelight. Framed by a white gold-edged frill around his neck, his tanned skin and dark hair gave him, she thought, the air of an adventurer, needing only a gold ring in one ear to complete the effect. She saw how broad were his shoulders accentuated by slashed pickadils, how deep the chest, how shapely the fine legs encased in smooth jersey hose and how strong the hand that supported her down the last step. She had placed a wide gold band there only that morning.

His eyes held an obvious admiration as they moved over her, drinking in the willowy grace of her bearing and the amazing brown eyes that still looked on him with a hint of resentment. 'Your taste in dress is faultless, my lady,' he said. 'I cannot ever recall seeing a woman look more lovely in that colour.'

'And I think, my lord, that you would have thought twice about offering for any woman who could not share your love of fabrics. Wouldn't you?' She was aware how clumsily she had accepted his compliment and was instantly sorry.

'Twice? Three times, perhaps. But then, I didn't have to, did I? I offered for you before we met. That was enough. It was not your sense of style I wanted most.'

'Are you as certain about everything you want, my lord?'

'A merchant has little time to deliberate, usually. He has to make his mind up quickly before others snatch up what he has his eye on.'

'A risky business, then.'

'Not if he knows what he's doing.'

Etta could have argued along those lines when his

scheme to win her had suggested a certain over-confi-
dence, but they were entering the dining parlour where
the ambience was too cosy and intimate to spoil with
bickering, and the aroma of roast meats reminded her
of the day's deprivations. 'I know you wanted simplic-
ity,' he said, 'and so far I've done my best to oblige.
But here, it's all about the modest company rather
than the fare. I didn't think you'd appreciate musicians and trumpet fanfares, or speeches and silly jests
about newly wedded couples, so it's just you and me.
Alone. Is this what you had in mind, my lady? Do we
need company?'

Pride prevented her from saying what she would
have preferred, a crowded supper table with smiling
faces all round, music, happy banter from those she
loved and the support of her family. She would have
liked his friends to be there, too, if only to show them
how well she could manage, how civil her manners
and conversation, and what a good mercer's wife she
would make. So she made no reply to his impossible
questions but wrote him down in her mind as uncompromising and much too perceptive for her comfort.
She would have preferred some kind of persuasion.

The meal could not be faulted, however, for although they ate alone, the variety and quality of the
dishes presented by silent young men was worthy of
any wealthy merchant's household. Poultry, game and
fish served with spinach and onions, leeks, spiced
baked apples dressed with parsley and lemons, pas-
tries and sauces enough to cover the long table with
white-glazed dishes from Antwerp, the wine in Venetian glasses engraved with the initials N.B. As she cast
curious glances over the room, she noted how many

items were of foreign origin, not only the tableware but the tapestries from Brussels, more portraits of his Flemish ancestors, coffers from Italy, shelves of brass instruments and a revolving globe.

'I know,' he said, recognising her interest. 'It's a masculine kind of room, like the rest of the house. It needs a woman's influence.'

'Does your sister advise you on such matters? Does she visit you here?'

'Occasionally. She and her husband were once regular guests, but Willem died last year and since then she has preferred to stay with her friends. I'm sure she'll come if she knows you'll be here.'

'But surely we shall be going to London soon, won't we?'

'Eventually. There's no hurry for you to go before you've learned how to manage this place. One thing at a time.'

The sudden straightening of her back coincided with the turn of her head away from him, but not quickly enough to hide the annoyance she felt at his plans for her immediate future. To her, there *was* a hurry, and whilst managing his household was an inescapable duty, it was by no means her sole aim in life. While she was here at Mortlake, perhaps for months, the royal court would remain unmindful of her and the Queen would conveniently forget that moment of recognition while others wheedled their way into her favour.

But as if he had read her mind, he reached out to lay his large hand over her wrist before she could move it away, obliging her to look at him, to hold his eyes as he spoke. 'I know what this is all about,' he said.

'I know you wish to visit Levina at court and why. I know you also hope to gain an entry with Sir Elion, somehow. But if you get there at all, my lady, it will be with me and no one else. For now, I suggest you put it out of your mind until the time is right. Just be patient, Henrietta. You will find plenty to keep you occupied as mistress of the house, and you'll be able to make visits to Cheapside to choose fabrics for a new wardrobe. I want my new wife to be the best-dressed lady in the Guild. You already have a head start in that.'

'I do?'

His hand released her and moved upwards to describe the shape of her face with the backs of his fingers, sending a shiver of excitement across her chest. 'Yes,' he whispered, 'you do. Most of the mercers' wives are middle-aged and, although they have the means to dress well, none of them have your style or your looks. You will have to use all your diplomacy, sweetheart, not to eclipse them entirely. Can you do that?'

At the lure of a new wardrobe, Etta's earlier vexation dwindled beneath a mound of velvets and samite, taffeta and brocade, kid gloves and shoes with buckles and bows, embroidered sleeves and farthingales as wide as doorways. 'Yes,' she said. 'I suppose a married lady must have discretion, at the very least. There will be no trading of insults from me, my lord. I've heard them. I shall do nothing to make you ashamed of me, as some husbands are.'

'Then we've already made some progress, Lady Somerville. Tomorrow, I shall show you round your new home for you to see what you are mistress of. But for now, let me show you what I have for you, in here.'

Leading her away from the table, he took her by the hand into an adjoining room where lutes hung on the wall. Over by the panelling stood a richly decorated virginal, the keyboard instrument upon which Queen Elizabeth was so accomplished. 'My wedding gift to you,' he said. 'Shall you try it out?'

After the trials of the day, the newness of her surroundings and situation, Etta was relieved to spend the rest of the evening making music on an instrument she had been sure would be missing from her life, for she had had to leave her mother's virginals behind. Lord Somerville's lute-playing, polished and sensitive, demonstrated a skill that made her strive hard to match him and it seemed to her that he had chosen a perfect way to soothe her irritations and to find that sweet compatibility they had shared at the very beginning of their relationship. When it became impossible for her to stifle her yawns, he laid down his lute and led her from the cushioned stool, saying nothing as he walked with her upstairs to her room.

In the candlelit bedchamber, Tilda rose from her chair as they entered.

'I'll be back shortly,' Lord Somerville said.

'No,' said Etta.

Master and maid looked at her for confirmation. Which of them did she mean? 'Mistress?' said Tilda.

'I'll send for you in a moment. Leave us,' Etta said to her.

Waiting until the door had closed, Somerville came closer, thinking that perhaps Etta had another way to proceed. 'You want me to undress you?' he whispered. 'It's all right. Just nod, if that's what you want.'

'No, that's not what I want,' she said, stepping backwards.

'Then what?'

'Nothing. I'm sorry…but…nothing. I can go…have gone…so far with this charade, my lord, but I can go no further. We must sleep alone.'

He was very still, half-expecting her to elaborate. But when she remained motionless, looking around her as if she were lost, he folded his arms and leaned against the door. 'Alone,' he said. 'I see. So you have decided to use this as a bargaining tool, have you? I don't get to share your bed until your anger wears off. Or is it until I promise to take you to court? Do I have it right? Is that what it's about? Does it not occur to you that using your body as a reward is a dangerous way to proceed? It could backfire, you know, and what would you use then, I wonder?'

'Yes, I do know that. But I have done everything I was obliged to do so far, with no choice in the matter. This is the only issue about which I am able to assert myself, my lord, though of course if your penchant is for unwilling women, then there's little I can do about that except to suffer in silence. Is that what *you* want? You have tried to redeem the situation, I'm aware of that, as you would offer trinkets to a fractious child, but the plain truth is that I have offered you not the slightest encouragement from the start and I see no reason to change that, not until I see something in this arrangement for me. I have pleased my parents, and I assume that everything has gone according to your plan, too. But as I've said, I can go no further at present. Going to bed with you is asking too much of me, my lord. I'm sorry.' She spread her hands, helplessly. 'I need more time for this part.'

'Take all the time you need,' he said, unconcerned. 'The Queen's reign is only just beginning and I expect she'll be on the throne for quite some time. Goodnight, my lady. Sleep well. Alone.' Abruptly, he unfolded his arms, swung the door open and left her standing in the middle of the room, shaking, feeling a hard lump of unhappiness rise in her throat.

Holding her face in both hands, she took deep lungsful of air to prevent the tears of self-pity from diverting her reasoning, as they surely would, the reasoning telling her that, whatever the rules of matrimony, in her eyes this man had no right to the use of her body. Would she have behaved differently if her wishes had been granted in some small way? Perhaps, because then her heart would have been softened and she would have had something concrete to hope for. But to reveal that his own sister was a friend of Elizabeth and that he visited her at Whitehall Palace, then to bring his new wife to live here, miles away instead of close to court, was not only perverse but seemingly intended to delay for as long as possible any chance of seeing the Queen. He knew of Etta's urgency, but obviously had no concept of the reasoning behind it. A whim, he would be thinking. Just a woman's fancy to make contact with a relative for the sake of the royal connection. Too difficult. Too dangerous. Elizabeth doesn't care for competition. What nonsense! It was not about competition. It was not about being one of her ladies, or a personal friend. It was about finding just one connection to her own family, someone of her own flesh and blood, to find out what else they shared apart from looks. Could they be alike in other ways, too? She had to know. Her need for identity demanded it.

She called for Tilda and, in the silence of barely controlled distress, suffered an undressing that might have been so much more interesting, under his hands. She would not think about that. What she had never known, she would not miss, though she realised that, in spite of his unconcern, he must have been particularly puzzled and hurt by her rejection. Especially, she mused, after the beautiful gift of the virginal and all his attempts to make her comfortable except in the one area that mattered to her most. After she had examined her motives for the hundredth time, she still felt justified in holding herself back on what ought to have been the happiest night of her life. The problem now was that, as he'd pointed out, this policy could backfire, for as long as she denied herself to him, he could also deny her any hope of reaching her goal. What a wedding night this had turned out to be.

Ought he to have expected this? Somerville poured himself a glass of wine and studied its blood-red reflections by the light of the fire. His room was warm and comfortable and more like a study, but he had not expected to be here on this night. He ached with desire for her. She was stunningly beautiful, more so than Elizabeth, and clever, too, and there would certainly be some skirmishes between them if he were to retain control of events, and of her. But how to do this without crushing that vibrant spirit? He knew that Lord Jon and Lady Raemon had told her of her parentage, which was only right and proper, but they had con-

fessed to withholding information about the notori-
ous Magdalen Osborn, the wealthy mistress of King
Henry, who had ridden roughshod over everyone in
her way, including Lord Jon himself. Their concern to
protect her from vindictive courtiers was understandable. But what if Henrietta had inherited her mother's
ruthlessness? What if, after this unexpected streak of
defiance, he himself had unleashed in her a weapon
too powerful to keep in check? With good reason,
Lord Jon had kept her away from court, but now she
had the bit between her teeth and he, Nicolaus Benninck, would have to guide her through the dangers
without causing too much damage, either to herself
or others. It was at times like this when he wished
his generosity to the young Princess Elizabeth had
been forgotten, for now he was in her favour, and his
sister too, he could not stay away from court for ever
without causing deep offence. And that he could not
afford to do. Nor could he afford to offend his wife
indefinitely, either.

All the same, Henrietta had never been so much at
ease with him that she could explain exactly this need
to meet her half-sister. It was, to be fair, too soon for
her to trust him with the workings of her heart. Was
it simply a woman's whim that would fade with time?
Or were there other things that would eventually fill
her thoughts instead? Well, he told himself, replacing
the glass, for that to happen, things would certainly
have to go more smoothly than they had on this night.
'Ah, Joseph,' he said as the door opened, 'I shall need
your assistance to go through some of these papers.'
He indicated a pile of letters on his desk. 'Come on,
man. I don't pay you to stand there looking aston-

ished.' It was only then, as he filled his glass up again
with the rich red wine, that the thought occurred to
him that she might have been using her anger as an
excuse for something else she was reluctant to mention. Her monthly courses. If so, that would be yet
another inconvenience for her. The date. She had not
been allowed to choose that, either.

Chapter Four

In the fading light of the previous day, Baron Somerville's manor house at Mortlake had seemed to Etta very much like Lea Magna in style and size although the interior, lit by dozens of candles, had revealed more about its prominent owners than she had wanted to ask, at the time. The influence of the present occupant was in evidence everywhere she looked, from the silk-covered chairs to the foreign tableware and the substantial library of scientific books. But, she wanted to know, who was responsible for all the ecclesiastical-themed heraldry?

They stood side by side in the great hall in which no surface had been left undecorated on chequer-patterned walls, plasterwork ceiling or tiled floor. Around the tops of the panelling, a deep frieze held a succession of heraldic shields. 'The Archbishops of Canterbury,' Somerville told her. 'They've been using this place since the eleventh century. In fact, nine of them died here. So all those arms up there, as you can see by the mitres, belong to them.'

'And after them?'

'Oh, your royal father put a stop to all that. He took it into his own hands when he dissolved the monasteries and gave it to Thomas Cromwell, his Minister of State. But by that time it needed bringing up to date. Cromwell had it enlarged, but sadly, he didn't have much time to enjoy it. Then the King gave it to his last wife, Catherine Parr, and she used it for a while. It still belongs in royal hands, but Elizabeth has given me the lease of it.'

'I see. So it's Baron Somerville of Mortlake's now.'

'Quite a mouthful, isn't it?'

'And do you have plans for it too, my lord?'

'I have plans for everything I own, Henrietta,' he said, taking her hand. 'But I want you to take a critical look at the place and tell me what it needs to become a family home.'

'A family home? Why, are you...are we...?' She frowned into the long beam of sunlight slanting across the hall floor, rainbow-coloured by the stained glass. 'Surely not so soon?'

'It's bound to happen eventually,' he said, pulling her hand out wide to make her face him. 'So what's the problem? Is this a bad time of the month for you, or is motherhood not on your list of needs yet?'

Put like that, it sounded coldly unromantic, her hesitation revealing to both of them that this was a subject about which she had given very little thought. To be truthful, she had not thought about it at all until this moment. Now, in a flash, she saw how motherhood would seriously interfere with her plans for a life at court, such as they were. 'No, my lord, it's not that time of the month for me, but nor is motherhood on my list of needs. I would find it very inconvenient, so soon.'

'Inconvenient? I assumed every woman would hope to bear children and to have a happy family life.' Dropping her hand, he walked away towards the screened passage, and she saw how much her thought-less words must have wounded him, especially after their chaste night apart. He would know by now what was at the top of her list.

She walked fast to catch up with him. 'My lord,' she said, 'don't say that. Please. I cannot help the way I feel. Give me time. It's all happened so suddenly and my hand is being forced in all directions. Not this one, too. Please?'

He slowed and stopped, his handsome face suf-fused with disappointment. 'I am not a magician, Hen-rietta, nor shall I make use of any method of avoiding conception. I made no secret of the fact that I want a family. It's one reason why I chose a wife and I was stupid enough to think that, if I could interest you in making love, as I have failed to do so far, you might begin to forget your close relationship to the Queen and forge one with me instead. Now I see that, to please you further, I must sleep in my own room. Per-haps you'll be good enough to let me know when the inconvenience is past.'

His thorny words twisted painfully into her heart as she watched him walk away. He was right and, in putting her own desires first, she was not being to him the dutiful wife he expected, but how *could* he expect such a thing from her when he knew of her priori-ties beforehand? Was it fair of him to use this against her? She would try to be a dutiful wife in all other things, but he must not expect so much from her that she was still not ready to give. As for them sleeping alone, she did not think that would discomfort her as much as it would him.

Echoes of men's voices reached her from the courtyard. Guests? Already? Keen to perform her duties as a hostess, if not in other departments, she followed her husband to the porch and was just in time to see him in a hearty embrace with what looked at first like an elderly wizard whose long snow-white beard made a stark contrast against the flowing black gown that reached the cobbles. Over Lord Somerville's shoulder, the guest's twinkling blue eyes espied her, creasing with pleasure into his rosy child-like complexion. 'Ah, my Lady Somerville, so it's true what they told me.' Disengaging himself, he came towards her as if she were the one he'd come to see. 'You are indeed every bit as lovely…oh, dear…I forget myself. How churlish. John Dee, my lady. Your husband and I have known each other for years. He sells me his offcuts for my gowns at a bargain price,' he added, teasingly, knowing he'd not be believed. His voice held the delightful musical lilt of the Welsh.

'You are welcome, Master Dee,' Etta said, realising that her first assessment of him as an elderly man was wide of the mark, despite the white hair. 'Do you live locally?' Laying her hands upon his outstretched palms, she suffered a hairy kiss to her lips, as was the custom these days, feeling the warm grip of a young and enthusiastic personage, dynamic, yet spiritual, too. It was easy to see why her husband was so pleased to see him.

'Ah, no,' he said. 'I came up by boat on the tide

from the city. One day I shall live here, when Nic
finds a little cottage for me.'

'When I know you're serious, my good friend,'
said his lordship, 'I shall build you one. Now, come
inside, and don't think I'm persuaded you've come
to see my library when I know full well you've come
to take a look at my wife. You'd not have believed it
otherwise, would you?'

Men's laughter, men's teasing about why he had
not married sooner, making Etta blush while thinking heaven that this man's timely arrival had stepped
into a breach that ought not to have happened. They
seemed to want her with them, so while they sat com-
panionably together to drink ale and eat plum cake
with cream, she learned that this was none other than
the Dr John Dee who had advised the new Queen
on the most auspicious date for her coronation. As
a young princess, she had often consulted Dr Dee
about her horoscopes and now he was welcomed at
court as a man of great learning and wisdom, for all
his thirty-odd years. Brilliant mathematician, astron-
omer and astrologer, geographer and alchemist, there
was little this man could not turn his hand to, either in
this country or in the rest of Europe, and Etta found it
no hardship to sit in his company with her husband,
listening to their shared knowledge. There was, she
discovered, something very attractive about her husband's modest scholarship which, though not on a
par with John Dee's, added another veneer of interest
to his many-faceted character. Was she being a fool
not to try to please him in every respect? She knew
the answer to this, but pushed it away to the back
of her mind. She noticed that their conversation had

become more specific, more intense. She listened to their carefully chosen words. 'I have them safe for you, John,' her husband was saying. 'They're waiting in the warehouse.'

'Does anyone know?' The blue eyes held concern.

'No one over here. Don't worry, I'll get them to you within the next few days. Now, you must come and sup with us.' He took Etta's hand, lovingly, smiling at her as if no harsh words had ever passed between them.

'Yes,' she said. 'We shall be taking our meal in an hour or so. Why not join us, Dr Dee? That will give you both time to talk books.'

'Thank you, my lady. That is what we were talking about.'

'Oh, I see. And you have concerns about some?'

Her husband squeezed her hand. 'This is not for public consumption, Etta,' he said, 'but we were talking about Dr Dee's latest almanac that I'm having printed and bound in Antwerp for him by a friend of mine. I've brought them over on one of my ships along with a consignment of luxury wares.'

'Well then, that's as good an excuse as any for us to make an early visit to London, isn't it? But why have them printed in Antwerp, Dr Dee? Is there not an easier way?'

Both men spoke at once, mincing the explanations into a jumble.

'It's quicker than…'

'It's cheaper in the long run…'

'Yes?' Etta said. 'Why is it quicker to have a book published abroad? Is that what you said, Dr Dee?'

The sharp blue eyes darted towards his host before

he explained. 'In England,' he said, 'our last queen established a Stationers' Company who make it impossible to publish any book without their approval. Queen Mary was keen to stop Protestant literature being circulated, you see. So it can take months or even years for them to decide on what can and what can't be published, by which time the information in my almanacs is partly out of date and, even then, they may decide it's not in the public interest to pass it.'

'Because,' said his lordship, 'the readers they employ don't understand a word of it, so I take the manuscripts over to Antwerp, and have the books sent back in bound copies, and as long as Dr Dee sells them privately only to his friends and followers, the Stationers' wardens are unlikely to find out.'

'And if they did?' Etta said.

'If they did, all those years of work would be confiscated,' he replied, 'and we'd both have heavy fines to pay. I'm more concerned about the work than the fines.'

'But you also said it was cheaper.'

'Paper,' said Dr Dee. 'No one makes it over here. It's made on the Continent, so it's cheaper to have it printed there too. And in England, the only company who have been granted the monopoly on the printing of almanacs and prognostications, which is what I do, are Watkins and Roberts, so if *they* don't agree with an author, they're not going to publish his work. Nobody else holds the licence to print scientific works of an experimental nature. The Stationers' wardens think it's the work of the devil. I would not stand a chance, Lady Somerville.'

'But surely,' Etta said, 'now you have the Queen's favour?'

'The Queen's favour,' said Dr Dee. 'Yes, sincere enough at the time, but not to be relied on too heavily, I fear. Her Majesty promised me riches as a reward for my computations on her coronation day, but I have yet to see a sign of them. Mind you,' he hastened to add, 'don't mistake me, dear lady. She is an angel. A Diana. The moon and stars combined.' His eyes lifted into his neat white eyebrows and his hands came together as if in heavenly supplication.

Etta did not think his dramatics were anything but the genuine expression of adoration, so she took the chance to find out more. 'You have obviously made an impression on her, Dr Dee, and she on you. Did you find her gracious?'

'Gracious in the extreme, my lady. Quite delightful and very well informed. She talked with me on a variety of matters. So easy in her manner. So very kindly.'

Etta looked sideways at her husband as if to say, *There you are, you see. Who says she's difficult to please?* 'And do you think she might look kindly upon me, if my lord were to introduce me to her? Or you yourself?' she said, ignoring the sharp movement of her lord's hand upon hers.

Dr Dee's reply was quite emphatic, for she would discover that the dear man had an opinion about everything under the sun, even when he had few facts upon which to base it. 'Of course she would,' he replied. 'How could she not love you like a sister? Such a dear, intelligent lady. I saw her dance the galliard, you know. Never seen anything like it. What energy and grace. Did you dance it at your wedding, Lady Somerville?'

'Ah, no,' said Etta, wistfully looking towards the tapestried wall where, in a Flemish country scene, the Rite of Spring was in full swing with a banquet and some debauchery going on in the background. Leering satyrs and goat-legged creatures played on pan pipes and drums. 'No, no dancing. No anything, really. Do you chart horoscopes, Dr Dee?'

'Indeed I do, my lady. I would deem it an honour to chart yours, if your husband will allow?'

Keeping hold of Etta's hand, Lord Somerville stood up, pulling her with him. 'Yes, by all means do, John. Neither of us will disagree with a prediction from the Royal Astrologer. Come. Shall we go into the library? I have a new astrolabe to show you.'

Even so, Etta managed to avoid the issue of the horoscope when the last thing she wanted was to hear when it would be appropriate for her to become pregnant, which he might be tempted to mention. She didn't need Dr Dee's help there. So by the time he had to take the wherry back to London, he had drunk enough Rhenish wine to make him happily forgetful. Later, she anticipated some kind of admonishment, to remind her of her promise to do nothing to embarrass him, but he seemed not to have been seriously affected by her indirect reference to their simple marriage of one day, or by yet another attempt at a court invitation.

She had not been idle during Dr Dee's stay and, while the February sun shone through the windows, she and the house steward toured the rooms set round three sides of a courtyard. Some of them had been extended and enhanced with extra windows, fireplaces and passages connecting in all directions to the upper and lower storeys. It was now easy for her to find the improvements made by Thomas Cromwell and to see his arms as the Earl of Essex blazoned on so many surfaces. Sure that the house steward would pass on her useful comments, she made small suggestions that only a woman would think of, more cushions on chairs, more tables, a change of bed-hangings and some smaller beds for her uncle's children who would surely visit on their way to and from London. Cromwell's bed, used also by Henry's last queen, was large enough for a child to get lost in.

That evening, in an attempt to show her pleasure at his gift, Etta played on her beautiful virginal, admiring its tone and the pale-pink-and-white roses painted on the woodwork. When it grew late, she wished her husband a courteous goodnight and went to her room, wondering if he might follow. For several hours she lay in her bed, listening for the sound of the door to open, knowing that it would not, for not only had she spurned him, but had also revealed that the sound of children in the house was not on her list of priorities.

Racked by her own selfish motives, with sadness for the pain she was causing, with guilt at not being a true wife and anger at this ridiculous situation, she threw a rug over her nightgown and tiptoed out of the room into the passageway where the flickering candle threw a pale light ahead of her. Even now, she was unsure of what she wanted except to see him, to hear his voice, to see the desire in his eyes, the same desire that now stirred within her. Exactly what she was missing was still something of a mystery to her, yet she knew it meant having his warmth near her, his hands upon her, his kisses, too. Would he offer her a way out of this impasse? Or would he expect something more definite than an appearance at his door? In truth, she had no words to say what her heart needed, only that it ached for him.

Downstairs, all was darkness and silence, though a faint strip of light showed beneath the door to her husband's library, inviting her to investigate. The soft clack of the latch made him look up from his paperwork while, instinctively, his hands rearranged the documents to conceal his writing. 'What is it?' he said, softly. The single candle on the table cast his face into strange shadows, highlighting the grey squirrel fur that gaped down the front to reveal his bare chest. He saw where her eyes had been drawn. 'You should be asleep,' he said.

'I couldn't,' she whispered, holding on to the door. 'What are you doing?'

He cast a glance over his table of papers before deciding what to say, whether to accept or reject her attempt at capitulation, appreciating how poor the Tudors were at that. 'I have work to do,' he said, without elaborating.

'Can't it wait?'

'No. Go back to bed.'

The door closed as quietly as it had opened, though it was quite some time before his lordship picked up his pen and continued to write, using all his faculties to keep his mind on track and away from the picture of that beautiful body which, if he had not been so pigheaded, he could now be looking upon. Rarely had he turned down such an offer from a woman, and now, when it really mattered, he was determined to win this battle of wills, perhaps to his cost rather than hers.

Once so sure of getting exactly the kind of attention from a man she desired, though never the kind she now desired from her husband of two days, Etta had no one to blame but herself. Instead of weeping with anger or humiliation, she mulled over the situation yet again by candlelight, believing she knew which of them would be hurt most by this stand-off, even though she had no experience to tell her what she was missing, exactly. She had seen the tanned vee of his chest inside the squirrel fur and the thick muscular column of his throat, his bare wrists and forearms, which she had not appreciated could be so attractive, if that was the word to use. But just as significant had been his attitude towards her that day when, after her latest refusal to please him over the issue of children, he had been courteous to her in every way, both during Dr Dee's visit and afterwards.

Tempting as it was to assume he was unaffected by her waywardness, it was more than likely, she thought, that he was better at concealing his feelings than she was. Not only that, but he could play the waiting game better, too, for although he had made his desire for her known, he was prepared to wait for a more positive sign than a simple appearance in her nightgown, asking what he was doing. Apparently, she would have to do better than that to break the impasse, as she would also need to overcome her preference not to become pregnant.

It was not so much that she disliked the idea of bearing his children. Far from it. But not yet, not until she had fulfilled her greatest wish to make some kind of connection with her half-sister that would cement, however tentatively, the physical bond that had been missing all her life. As a woman, her need of a family was as strong as his, but to establish her own roots must come before planting new ones. At the same time, the urge to sleep in his arms and to exchange loving was like the promise of a heaven she had never experienced. It was time, she thought, blowing out her candle, to ask herself some more serious questions before her husband began to look elsewhere, as men did. As her natural father had done.

Etta's remarks to Dr Dee about a possible introduction to Elizabeth's court had not been lost upon Lord Somerville, who was by now convinced that she would try every device to have her own way. In one respect it was no more to him than a clash of wills, but the very real dangers that awaited any starry-eyed innocent, especially one as lovely and desirable as Etta, were such that no husband would intentionally allow his wife to face them unless he had a very special reason. Hoping to distract her, at least for a few months, by discussing changes she might like to make to the house, then the extensive gardens where she could entertain in summer, he kept her occupied all the next day until the light began to fade. They had already compiled a list of tasks, and Etta had made some useful suggestions when the courtyard was suddenly filled with the clamour of arriving guests, shouts of greeting mixed with groans of weariness. 'I hoped we might have made it in one day,' called Sir Elion D'Arvall, holding out his arms for his niece's welcome, 'but I couldn't get my beloved wife and children moving until well into the morning. I think they might have intended to stop overnight here. You don't mind do you, love?'

They had seen each other only a few days ago at Tyburn House when nothing had been said about an imminent return to London or the possibility of a visit. But Etta was glad to see them, even at short notice, and to put them up for the night, especially when it would give her the chance to show off her skills as a hostess. Having met the kitchen staff only the day before, Etta was well primed on stocks of food and the cook's ability to prepare an impressive supper within the hour. It was a huge success, after which his lordship was reasonably sure Etta would once again introduce the topic of her dearest wish while he and their guests were mellowed by wine, food and warmth. Sure enough, the subject was delicately broached, skirted round, and left undecided before Etta and Lady Sophia took the children up to bed, leaving Sir Elion and Lord Somerville alone to pick up the threads of Etta's argument without her interference.

'Nic,' said Sir Elion, 'I've known her longer than you have and I can tell you she'll not let this matter drop until she's seen for herself.'

'It's my duty to protect her,' Somerville said. 'You know what they're like there. They'll tear her to bits within the week. And you can see Elizabeth, can't you, taking one look at her and deciding that the competition doesn't please her?'

'You're thinking that won't be good for you and the business?'

'Of course I'm not, Elion. It's not likely to affect

my business one way or the other when I supply to the Royal Wardrobe, not the Queen directly. It's Etta I'm concerned about.'

'Her relationship to the Queen?'

'That, and the fact that there are those who'll remember Etta's mother. She knows only that her mother was beautiful and that Henry loved her enough to give her a child. Well, what else could her parents have said? But there'll be no punches pulled when she comes face to face with some of the other reprobates Magdalen Osborn had to do with.'

'But you'll be there with her. You can protect her from that.'

'In theory, yes. But there will be times when I cannot and that's when the damage will be done.'

'She's a grown woman, Nic. She'll have to hear a few home truths before too long and, if that happens because of her insistence, I don't see how she can grumble too loudly. In fact, I think this is the time to let her see what it's like there and to make up her mind whether she likes it or not. After all, there isn't the slightest possibility that Elizabeth will allow her to get too close.'

'No, I don't think she will, either. But Elizabeth's methods of sending off those she doesn't like can be brutal, can't they? So what am I to do? If I cannot prevent her going without holding it against me for the rest of her life and I cannot protect her from everything that happens there, what's best for her?'

'Is she holding it against you?' Elion said, meaningfully.

'Yes, she is.'

'Well then, I'll tell you. Let her have a new wardrobe, for a start. Elizabeth wears a lot of black and white, but recently she's begun to wear colours here and there. It's a reaction against Queen Mary, I suppose. Let Etta have some gowns for every occasion, a change for each day, the latest styles, but not enough to rival Elizabeth's. Tell her all you know about protocol and who goes before whom, what to say, how to say it.'

'How to grovel, in effect.'

'Yes, that, too, if she'll listen. Let her practise her languages and her music, card games, archery, and her dances, too. Elizabeth dances every day, you know. She rides, hunts…'

'With her admiring and ambitious Master of Horse.'

'Oh, him! Well, let Etta have a couple of good horses with the best saddles, so she won't be disgraced, and in a month she'll be ready for anything. Stop worrying, man. If she gets hurt, she'll have to pick herself up and start again. But you cannot keep her away for ever. That would be rather unfair.'

From one who had known her all her life, such unsympathetic talk was understandable, but Somerville's concerns were of a more tender nature, and the thought of Etta being hurt while living her dream sat very uncomfortably on his conscience. 'Yes,' he said, 'I think you may be right. You'll be there, too, won't you, occasionally?'

'I will. And you have your sister there, Mrs Teerlinc.'

'Levina. She's Willem Teerlinc's widow now, but she holds a special position as the Queen's miniaturist. I doubt very much if Elizabeth will ever send for Etta, even when she knows she's my wife. Officially, she doesn't recognise her.'

'Well, that's all right. You just present yourself and Etta when the Queen comes into her Presence Chamber and wait for her to speak. You know how it goes, Elizabeth will see you and decide whether she wants to speak to you. You may wait for months, or only an hour. I doubt she's ever kept you waiting long, has she?'

Somerville smiled. 'No, but you know how she feels about wives. And about husbands, too. They'll not force her hand on that, you know. I know more now about the Tudor temperament than ever I used to.'

'Hah! My niece is a handful, then?'

'Let's say we're both learning a lot.' Lord Somerville did not return his friend's smile. 'But you sound, Elion, as if you're keen for us both to be there. Is there something you've not told me?'

Sir Elion leaned forward in his chair, leaning his elbows on his knees. He looked at his hands, then let them droop into the space. 'Your nose is still as sharp as ever, Nic. Yes, there is something. Cecil needs you as one of his links.'

'Spies? The Secretary of State needs more spies?' Somerville sat up straight, alert and already suspicious.

'No, not exactly spies.' The hands flapped. 'Informers, more like. Traders in information. Nothing too deep. We've already recruited your sister.'

'*What?* You've dragged Levina…?'

'Hold it! Nobody's dragged her into anything. Levina is the Queen's friend and she's only too happy to help. She was not coerced, but she's in a very useful position, Nic, as one of the late Queen Mary's friends, now favoured by Elizabeth, meeting sitters every day, listening quietly while they gossip.'

'What d'ye mean by gossip?'

'You know…at ease…people open up to her…tell her what they've seen and heard at court…some of it useful, some not. But it doesn't do for Levina to be seen talking to me except for a *Good day to you, Sir Elion*, because it's known that I work for Cecil. So we need your help here. *She* tells *you* what she's heard…'

'About what? Treason?'

'Heavens, no. But the reign has just begun and people are still milling about, trying to find the safest faction to support, those who think Elizabeth is on the right track, those who want her married, those who don't, and so forth. These are the people Cecil needs to watch more closely. Levina could pass on any information to you, speaking in Flemish, perhaps, you then pass it on to me as your new uncle-in-law. Simple. No one would think anything of that. You leave it to me to sift out what's useful and what isn't, and you'd be doing Elizabeth another good turn.'

'She wouldn't know, would she?'

'No, she only knows what Cecil tells her about where information comes from and he doesn't tell her everything. Not yet, anyway. That's why I want you there with your wife, enjoying yourselves and visiting your sister. Easy.' Sir Elion clasped his hands and waited.

'M…mm,' Somerville said. 'Well, I suppose if Levina thinks it's safe, then I don't see why I couldn't help. That's negatively positive I know, but, yes, I'll start a move to Cheapside in the next few days. Will that do?'

'Thank you, Nic. And you can rely on my help with Henrietta at any time. And Sophia's, too.'

Somerville nodded. 'I might need it. What is Levina doing about this, meanwhile? Does she have a contact already?'

'She gets notes to me. But that's dangerous, Nic. I'd rather use you.'

'Is this why you're returning to London so soon?'

'It is, yes. These early months are rather fraught, as long as the lady changes her mind almost daily. In Parliament the other day, she let off a hail of warnings about how they need not think she was a soft touch. She would have her own way, or else.'

'Sounds like somebody I know,' Somerville said, smiling.

Not knowing anything of the conflict between Somerville's desire for a family and Etta's ambition to see the Queen, Lady Sophia had seen no reason not to tell her hostess, next morning, what Sir Elion had hinted at last night as they lay in a strange bed on the brink of sleep. Etta's wish was no secret to any of the family, but Lady Sophia had not thought it would be allowed to come between the newlyweds so soon, nor had she quite expected such a display of triumph and elation from Etta as she helped to prepare for the last few miles of their guests' journey. 'But let his lordship tell you himself,' Lady Sophia said, holding Etta's arm. 'You must pretend not to know. It will be his surprise.'

His lordship, however, did not give Etta the news in a nutshell, as their guest had done but, later that afternoon, casually announced that they would visit the

shop within the next few days to find fabrics for a new
wardrobe and, yes, they might even stay a few nights
so that the tailor could take measurements. About any
more plans he would not be drawn, using the excuse
for his vagueness that he had business that must be
attended to which might take some time. As for what
would happen here at Mortlake Manor, he was equally
unconcerned. 'The staff here are used to my coming
and going,' he told her. 'I like to be able to get away
from London at short notice.' Casually, he added, 'I
don't have rooms at court, either. They're very sparse
and uncomfortable, and I can easily reach Cheapside
from most of the palaces.'

'Does the Queen offer hospitality to many of her
ladies?'

'Those closest to her have suites of rooms. Those
who have duties are given a small room and to those
women she needs but is not keen on, she gives the
smallest rooms with no fireplace and a long walk
away. That's how it works, from what I've heard.'

'I shall be kind to all my ladies,' Etta said, 'when
I have some.'

'You need more than one? Yes, certainly you do.
A companion for the times when I cannot be there.
Do you have someone in mind?'

They were sitting together on a wooden bench
where the knot garden overlooked the river, where
small craft struggled against the tide that pushed the
water back against its flow. The low evening sun made
pink ripples bounce off the banks and reflect the questions in two pairs of eyes. 'The only one I'd like to
have with me is Aphra,' Etta said. 'May I invite her
to come, too?'

'Of course. Aphra would be the perfect companion for you.' He placed his arm across the back of the bench, touching the strands of red hair that spiralled down Etta's neck, twisting them round his fingers. 'You have done well,' he said. 'Five guests already, Lady Somerville. I wonder who'll turn up tomorrow.' His hand moved round to her face, easing it towards his own and tilting her head back to rest on his shoulder, his eyes searching hers for some sign of capitulation, almost drowning in the startling brown that changed to black even as he watched. Was she warming towards him, at last?

Etta had seen his desire grow as they talked and now she felt his hand upon her bodice move upwards to the exposed skin where the cleft of her breasts had held his attention. The warmth of his hand sent waves of pleasure rippling over her body, catching at her breath and holding it, waiting for the next intimacy as his head bent to hers. But surely this was not what ladies did, in view of those on the river, servants in the house behind them? Was this what any man's touch could do? 'No...not here,' she whispered. 'My lord, we can be seen.'

He took her by the hand, standing and pulling her up in the same movement, confident as never before that she was putting some of her grievances behind her. Many times he had thought of a long and leisurely wooing for her first time, but the desire blazing from her eyes and the mouth waiting for his kiss told him that her passion was already soaring with his own, mindless, impatient. His kiss was long and fierce, making up for all those times of denial, anger and petty revenge. Etta melted under his mouth, feel-

ing the surge of aching warmth in her secret parts that
made her cry out against his lips. 'Yes…yes! Where
can we go? Quickly, my lord.'

Without waiting for more assurances, he placed an
arm about her waist and drew her along as his strides
on the gravel pathway led her towards a distant corner
of the garden right on the river's edge where a small
banqueting house nestled between clipped hedges.
The last of the sun's rays caught the thatched roof.
A sprinkling of dry leaves littered the floor beneath
a central marble table where, with mouths already
seeking each other's, Etta was held upon the edge,
with all her senses flaring into life like a new-kin-
dled fire. She did not question what he did, but let
her mind follow of its own accord, follow his hand
that stroked the smooth skin of her inner thigh, his
command, whispered and breathless, to lift her legs
and clasp him, sure of her willingness. Overcome by
their shared excitement she obeyed, trembling with
desire and seeing nothing except the heat behind her
eyelids, feeling only that powerful part of him plunge
deep into the aching cavern of her body and, under
her hands, the unstoppable energy of his rhythm, the
fast pulse of being. The force of life itself.

She moaned, throwing back her head, feeling the
ripples of sensation flood into her with each of his
thrusts, melding her body with his in a way she had
never thought possible. Spontaneous, immediate and
all-consuming, this was no gentle or courteous coupling, but something primal that neither of them could
have ignored beyond that moment. If it took Etta by
surprise, it was even more unexpected to Somerville,
for he had not thought his new wife would respond

to him in this way after her vehement objections to marrying him. For her part, Etta had not known that there was any other way to do this other than in a bed, after a certain time of preparation and a slow build-up of desire, so when the peak of excitement came almost at once to blank her mind, the wail that echoed around that empty little room seemed to come from far away, from another world.

She heard his groan come with the last plunges, felt his mouth over hers, hushing her between kisses and breathless cries of wonder that came on the edge of laughter. 'What a woman!' he said, softly. 'What a *woman*!'

Etta felt his careful withdrawal as, for the first time, she became aware of the discomfort of her position. She could not speak nor, thankfully, did he expect her to, but with her feet on the floor once more she was held tenderly within his embrace, her nose nestling beneath his jaw, her heartbeats returning to their usual pattern.

'Are you all right, sweetheart? That was rough. It was not how I meant our first time to be. Did I hurt you?'

With her lips under his jawline, she moved gently over the skin with a flurry of nibbles. Then a soft but noticeable nip. 'Yes,' she whispered. 'You did.'

'Oh, my beauty. Forgive me. I should not have…'

'Yes, you should. It was not how I thought it would be, either, but it happened, didn't it? And perhaps that's the best way, after all. Unthinking.'

'Next time, we'll take it slowly, with all the trimmings. Can you walk? It's already dark. We shall not be noticed.'

'I can walk. Just.'

'Come here. Let me kiss you again.'

Rocked in his arms, it was on the tip of Etta's tongue to ask how soon they would go to London. But something warned her not to, that this was not the time, for he would surely think she was expecting a reward for her compliance. She knew that this was not the case, but would he? Yet the dark thought was still with her as they walked slowly back to the house that he himself might be playing some clever game which would ensure a pregnancy, just when it seemed his mind had been changed in her favour. He would deny it, certainly, and she must try not to think along those lines or impart any bitter taste to the unexpected joy she had just shared with him.

Chapter Five

After that, it was not to be expected that things would ever remain the same between them when each had recognised in the other a certain impulsiveness that could be kindled by no more than a look or a touch. Merchants were not impulsive beings, as a rule, yet this so-far-unseen side of Nicolaus nevertheless had its echoes in the way he had wanted to capture that brilliant creature on sight and decided there and then to make a bid for her, as he had on occasion bid for a rare diamond. He had already experienced her puzzling changes of humour and had done his best to resist their effect on himself and his plans. But now he had seen how quickly her fiery passion could be kindled, even when he might have expected the more usual reserve of a virgin. And although much had been missing from that encounter in the way of seduction, it had apparently excited her as much as himself. In some respects, that had perhaps been the best way to start, as she had said, for now there was a great deal more for them both to look forward to of which, as yet, she was quite unaware.

Etta, however, had most to lose by being swept into
what could easily become a frenzy of lovemaking, for
although that amazing experience in the banqueting
house by the river had aroused her curiosity about
what could be done *without* clothes, the risks of finding out were very great. As it happened, her immediate fears were suspended as soon as she reached her
room that same evening when she had to call Tilda
to bring her cloths. The energetic consummation had
served a different purpose from the one for which,
she thought, it might have been intended. He had been
quite clear about his wish for a family, and indeed
that was understandable, at his age, nine years older
than she. As for her, she intended to wait longer to
become a mother, until she felt the time was right for
her mind to be cleared of other concerns. After all,
making babies must surely be as much at the mother's
convenience as the father's?

That perfectly natural excuse was made to spin out
until the next one came along in the form of Aphra,
not alone but with Master Leon of Padua, who had
been sent by Dr Ben on some important business in
London. To accompany Mistress Aphra Betterton as
far as Mortlake were his instructions, then to proceed
into the city on the next day, not knowing that Lord
and Lady Somerville were preparing to do the same.
'Where do you stay in London?' Somerville asked
him at supper.

'I hope to be offered a bed at the Apothecaries' Hall
near St Andrew-by-the-Wardrobe, my lord. They're
interested in the unusual plants Dr Spenney grows
in his herb gardens, you know. His name is well re-

spected by apothecaries everywhere, these days. I'm
fortunate to be allowed to study with him at Sandrock.'

'Well then,' said his lordship, 'if you find their
hospitality not to your liking, there will be a bed and
board for you at the Sign of the Bridge on Cheapside.'

'Thank you, my lord. What does the bridge sig-
nify?'

'Bruges, in Flanders, my friend. It's my birthplace,
though now I work from Antwerp. Bruges has almost
as many canals and bridges as Venice.'

Etta listened to this exchange with interest while
realising, to her shame, that she had never asked him
this, nor yet any other thing about himself except his
experience of women, and that all she had picked up
about him had been from their talk with Dr Dee and
the scraps of information left over from conversations
he'd had with her parents while she had sat there,
stewing in her anger.

So this night, it was Aphra who shared Etta's bed,
chattering in hushed tones about all that had happened, leaving aside only those controversial details
about which Etta was still confused. Unwilling to
explain why she was allowing her determination to
make contact with her half-sister the Queen to over-
ride every other consideration, she dwelt instead on
the excitements ahead of them. She also wanted to
know if Aphra's opinion of Master Leon had changed
since their last meeting. 'He's very good looking,' Etta
said, 'and he obviously likes you. You should see the
way he looks at you.'

Aphra was still cautious. 'He's well enough, I suppose, and young. But I shall reserve my judgement

until I've seen how he looks at other women. One cannot tell the true mind of a man until one has observed him in the company of other women, can one? Oh… dear me…what am I saying? I don't mean your husband…no, not at all. I'm sure he would never look at another woman while he has you, Etta. You've had no chance to find that out yet and he's such a man of the world, but he chose *you* above…well…others.' Aphra floundered to a standstill like a woman wading through a bog, sinking deeper into trouble. Quickly, she changed the subject, but her concerns had provided Etta with more than enough food for thought about her lord's travels and contacts with beautiful women, about how many he had made love to, how and where.

She had not expected to be in the slightest way disturbed about the possible answers to such questions, but it was some time before she could dismiss them from her mind as she relived those shared moments of fierce passion, sure that, for him, they would not have been as exceptional as they had for her. Somehow, the thought of him holding another woman in his arms troubled her, while her fertile imagination clothed unknown foreign beauties in those diaphanous gauzes he had once held to *her* face while seducing her with his words. And now, she was insisting that he take her into the very place where women were at their most alluring, where they would be sure to compete for his attention, where she herself could not afford Aphra's cool detachment, or pretend not to notice.

Banning those thoughts, she talked instead of the gift she would make for the Queen, of how they would spend their days in preparation for a court debut, what colours, dresses, embellishments and headdresses, what jewellery and fabrics, hair-pieces and shoes, how they would respond when the Queen noticed them, as she would surely do, and how they must practise harder at all those accomplishments expected of them. They would hire a dancing master, too, well before being required to perform a galliard, a coranto or a volte. They would, of course, be expected to involve themselves in the domestic side of managing Lord Somerville's city dwelling, for he would have guests to dine, fellow mercers, merchants, neighbours and clients for which a table laden with good food was an essential. What a good thing, they said, yawning, that they had been well schooled in housewifery.

Etta's last thoughts, however, were of how it would feel to have her husband's warm naked body settling into hers, his strong arms, and of those stolen moments of frenzied desire that they would surely find almost impossible to repeat, once they were in London's hectic domain.

Cheapside, London

With her pen poised over a long list of requirements, most of them fabrics, Etta's query was aimed loosely at Aphra. 'So what's the difference between a yard and an ell?' she said.

'Very little, I think,' Aphra said, looking down from the stool on which she stood.

'Just leave it to me, my lady,' said the seamstress, taking the last of the pins from between her lips. 'You just write down what you want, what lining, what braids, and I'll put in the yardage. Now, mistress,' she said to Aphra, 'once we get a nice wide farthingale under this, you'll look quite splendid. I'll make one in plain canvas and one covered with shot taffety for best.'

'And a roll?'

'Oh, yes, you'll need a bum roll, too. I've left extra length in the train for that. Ready, ma'am?' She held out a hand to help Aphra down. 'And are we going to go for the wider ruffle round the neck? It's a very pretty style. Ruffles are sure to get wider, eventually, so you might as well lead the way.'

'Then I'll leave that to Lady Somerville,' Aphra said.

'Why not?' Etta muttered, scribbling. 'If we're going to make any impression at all, Aphie, it might as well be with a ruff.'

Privately, the seamstress thought Lady Somerville and her cousin would turn heads wherever they went, with or without a larger-than-usual ruffle. This was the second week she had attended the two ladies at the Sign of the Bridge, though she had worked for Lord Somerville before on several occasions, making his shirts.

The last two weeks had been hectic for everyone, with a new house to manage, servants to supervise, changes to be made to rooms for Aphra and her maid and, inevitably, a new wardrobe to withstand the royal scrutiny. Etta had been surprised by the size of the house behind and above the shopfront, large storerooms below ground, a large kitchen across the courtyard at the back, and many more rooms on several levels, all tastefully furnished and decorated in the latest style. Expecting to be visited by many more of her husband's colleagues, friends and clients, she had worked hard to acquaint herself with the daily routine of a merchant's life, being prepared to entertain at a moment's notice, striving to look her best while admitting to herself that she had no good reason not to.

The exciting spontaneity of that episode at Mortlake Manor had not been possible here above a busy shop, especially with Aphra never very far away. Lord Somerville's days were taken up at the warehouses of the Steelyard, the Royal Wardrobe, or in his counting house, arriving home quite late on some evenings. She had not grumbled at his absences when each day was so full, but could not help anticipating his return when he would want to know how their preparations had progressed, what fabrics they had found on the shelves, what new dance steps they had learned and how the Queen's gift was coming along. She had managed to make tiredness and a headache two poor excuses to avoid lovemaking for as long as it was possible, but the time came when, as she and Nicolaus admired armfuls of silk and soft velvets brought back from the warehouse, she was reminded of those occasions at the Royal Wardrobe when he had flirted with her, quite outrageously, through layers of diaphanous silks.

They were in Etta's bedchamber after a long day of dressmaking, when all those excuses not to become intimate were being obliterated by her desire for his arms once more and to know the conclusion to that suggestion for her to be clothed only in that transparent tissue. She was tired and her defences were no longer strong enough to hold him off. She had longed for him all day, wondering why her emptiness would only be assuaged by the sound of his arrival, wondering, too, if, against her will, she might possibly be falling in love with him. No. She must not allow that to happen.

Yet in the dim bedchamber where they had undressed, the deep sound of his voice overcame all former resistance. She felt the soft cobweb tissue being draped across her breasts. She felt him turn her towards him, lift her in his arms and lay her down on the bed in a pile of rumpled silks. She felt his hand resting upon her ribcage where the silk covered her skin, then the warmth of his smoothing hand through the fabric, the soft lapping of his lips over hers, meant to amplify further explorations.

She caught at his wrist as his caress moved upwards to her breasts, still unused to the surge of excitement it caused. His kiss stopped as he waited, feeling her grip slacken, letting him go, allowing him to hold her breast and to resume his kiss as her eyes darkened with approaching desire. Now the warmth of his naked body, the fresh male scent of his skin and the hardness of his muscular chest and arms added a more potent dimension to their contact. 'Lift your head,' he said. With one deft pull, he removed the gold mesh caul from her hair, burying his hand in the rich red tumbling mass of curls that spilled over the pillow and her shoulders, releasing the faint perfume of a rosewater rinse. 'This,' he said in wonder, 'is how you should be clothed. Just this. Nothing else. Better by far than silk tissue.'

'Show me what to do,' she said, wanting to hear it from him, not because she had forgotten. 'Will this be different?'

Tenderly, he pressed the tip of his finger to her lips. 'Shh,' he said. 'This is only the beginning. I rushed you through the first time. I cannot blame you if that was the real reason for your delays. This time, I shall not take you until you're ready for me. We'll do some exploring first.' He smiled at her in the dimness. 'And I need no compass for that. Each voyage we make together will be different, but if the first time is the most memorable, the second will be even more so.' As he spoke, his hand moved over her body, stemming her flow of concerns and diverting her senses towards the path of his teasing fingers. She heard his murmur of delight before his mouth covered hers, kindling a sudden rush of desire, flooding her thighs with a melting softness. Her mind rushed crazily from her lips to the sensations caused by his tenderly kneading hand, then to the startling warmth of his mouth upon the skin of her breast, the closeness of his dark head and body within her embrace, so different from that last fierce coupling.

Tentatively, her fingers absorbed the smoothness of his skin and the undulations of muscle and tendon, the thick silkiness of satin hair and the change of texture as she touched the back of his hand that still held her breast to his mouth. So much that was new to her, but none more so than that this powerful creature should have access to her body in so tender a manner, every secret place owning its own response. Slowly, as he discovered her, she found another existence that trembled and ached for more attention, greedily pushing back the hand that had moved on, arching herself into the newest crevices of his hard unyielding limbs, savouring their qualities and wondering at their steely strength and hardness. Now she began to understand that there was so much more to this process than her previous experience, exciting as it had been, and that perhaps being in love mattered less than she had supposed. Did love matter, if one could enjoy this so much with a man?

The question dissolved before she could dwell on it as his hands moved down her body, slowly, smoothing, caressing the small mound of her belly and the rounded hips while his mouth took her lips with his own, playing upon them so skilfully that her mind was taken to the very edge of awareness. Consumed by the sensation growing like a warm fire within her, she gasped at the urgency of a response that told her not to wait a moment longer. 'Now...please...do it!' she said, threading her fingers into his hair.

Broken sentences were healed by his nudging knees and for the first time she felt the unique experience of a man's weight on her before he lifted and entered with care that place made ready to receive him. Etta's long drawn-out 'ahhhh' came like an ecstatic sigh that he converted into a kiss, whispering words of endearment and admiration to accompany his careful movements, as if this were her first time. Now it seemed to Etta that nothing had prepared her for an experience like this where every rare sensation melded so seamlessly and with such accord. She now realised why no one ever spoke of it in anything like enough detail, for it was beyond description. If they had, they could not have conveyed the ecstasy of this giving and receiving, nor could they have described the all-consuming waves of pleasure that washed over her.

Time receded as their delight in each other took

over every other consideration, so he was delighted when she mewed softly and dug her fingers into his upper arms, turning her head from side to side into the sea of her hair in a frenzy of growing excitement. 'Sweetheart, am I hurting you?' he said, pausing in his rhythm.

'No...no! Faster! Quickly!' she cried.

Before the words faded, he was there with her, pulsating to a faster beat, his powerful body taking her with an energy that surprised even him. But now she was to experience that overwhelming surge when time itself is suspended in a rapturous void, when the cry of relief comes from another being, deep inside, contacted only at such times and no other. Hearing that cry from her again, he could be in no doubt of the bliss he had caused, or that it had coincided precisely with his own mind-numbing release that left him euphoric and sated.

Unable to speak, Etta cradled his head against her own, rising and falling to the deep panting of his chest, dampened by his perspiration. She pulled up the tangle of silks to cover him, stroking the back of his neck and following its valley down as far as she could reach, feeling her own emptiness as he withdrew from her.

Smoothing damp strands of hair away from her cheek, he placed kisses on her forehead and each of her closed eyelids while he mused on how different things might have been if she had chosen to carry her earlier resistance further. That she was volatile and unpredictable was no surprise to him any more, but not even he could have foreseen how far her passion would take her, this time. And while he harboured no

illusions about their future lovemaking and her thin
excuses, he fell asleep with a smile hovering over his
lips and a heavy tress of red hair splayed across his
chest.

Out of courtesy, Master Leon of Padua had put up
with three uncomfortable weeks of the Apothecaries'
hospitality before taking up residence with his friends
on Cheapside where a small but pleasant room was
prepared for him on the ground floor in which there
was space enough for him to study. As he left to attend the Apothecaries' Hall early each morning and
return at suppertime, he was never there long enough
for the two cousins to tire of his company, yet another
reason for Etta to feel that she had moved into a more
exciting phase of her life, for when the four of them
sat together at the supper table to discuss, and eat,
and exchange information so different from her parents' more domestic themes, she knew that no better
company existed. Which did not prevent her, even so,
from believing that yet more good company was still
to come, once she and Aphra were seen at court. So
many important names to remember. Such complex
etiquette. So many rules. And Whitehall Palace. What
a rabbit warren it was made out to be. Surely it could
not be as difficult as all that to find one's way around?

Their optimism in that respect was misplaced.
After walking the labyrinthine corridors, crossing
courtyards and enclosed gardens, the cousins came to
the conclusion that, if either of them had been alone,
they might still have been there a week later. Etta,
Aphra and Lord Somerville had dressed particularly

well that day with the intention of visiting Mrs Levina Teerlinc, his lordship's older sister, and to see what advice she could offer about the Queen's activities that week. Lord Somerville took them in his own barge from the Puddle Wharf jetty upriver to Whitehall Palace, a luxury of which the women were glad on that frosty March morning as the white sunlight bounced off the glassy water and made silver vee-shaped ribbons in the wake of the swans. A veil of mist hung low over the buildings along the riverside, thinning here and there to reveal gable ends and towers and then, at last, the sprawling white stone palace on the scale of a village.

Lord Somerville had dressed for the occasion in a suit of silver-grey brocade, the doublet and breeches slashed to show a creamy-white satin beneath, with a short matching cloak with wide embroidered guards along its edges. Gold aiglets dangled from every pair of laces. As they had dressed, Etta had been reticent about offering him any advice, for he had done admirably well without it, so far. But he had preened before her like a wooing lovebird, hoping for some comment, so she had adjusted the satin here and there through the slashes, checked the peacock feather in his flat bonnet and pulled the frill of his shirt closer beneath his chin. 'There,' she had whispered. 'I doubt the Queen will spare me a glance.'

'Will I do?' he'd said.

After that night of passionate loving, the memory of it was etched clearly in his eyes as they met hers, boldly. Etta's smile was dreamy as she replied, 'Very, my lord. As you well know.' He had smiled at the quirky answer without realising how much, at that moment, she feared he might look at some other woman that day as he was looking at her now. How many women did he know here? she wondered.

They walked up the steps through the impressive gatehouse directly into a series of gardens, covered walkways and more doors than they could count. Men and women passed them on morning business, becoming more and more numerous and better dressed as they entered ever more sumptuous rooms where footmen in the Queen's crimson livery stood to guard the doorways. Occasionally there would be a distant shout of recognition, to which his lordship would wave and call out his greeting, coming at last to a corridor of polished doors. Pausing outside one, he pointed to the small painted crest on the centre panel with the initials L.T. beneath.

Etta had not known what to expect, except that few of the ordinary rooms were spacious, not designed for anything more than sleeping and changing. Royalty did not encourage their courtiers to spend time anywhere but in their company. So when they entered, it became instantly clear that Mrs Levina Teerlinc was a favoured friend, an artist, who required rather more in the way of light and floor space in order to seat her subjects at a convenient distance from her. Having hoped to find her alone, they saw that she had the company of several white-clothed young ladies who sat on cushions on the floor to watch her paint their friend who was sitting with her back to the door.

Laying her brush down with great care, Levina was quite unruffled by the interruption, rising to greet her brother with a warm smile of happiness, her arms out wide to embrace him, then eagerly turning to Etta and Aphra with multiple kisses to both cheeks. She held their hands, apologising for receiving them in her apron. 'My work clothes,' she explained, smoothing delicate hands down the spotless white linen. 'No, my dear,' she said in reply to Etta's query, 'of course you're not intruding. You are my new sister-in-law. How could you be?' Levina Teerlinc showed all the signs of having been a very handsome woman in her youth and even now there was a sweet gentility that Etta instantly warmed to.

The sitter, however, felt differently about the interruption. Turning her head to look over her shoulder, she called to Levina, 'What is it, Mrs Terling? Tell them to come back later.' The voice was sharp and imperious, unused to being ignored. But it was probably due to the astonishment written on the faces of her friends that made her turn round completely to stare rudely at Levina's relatives, her own face then reflecting that same element of incredulity, recognising features so similar to her own. She and Etta might have been looking at their own images in a mirror: same slender build, same red hair parted in the centre under a jewelled French hood set well back on the head, same beautiful brows and mouth. Only the eyes were different, for Etta's were brown and dark-rimmed while the sitter's were pale blue and heavy-lidded. And angry. 'Who is this?' she demanded, rising to her feet.

Levina remained quite calm. 'I'll introduce you, my lady,' she said.

'Is it not *they* who should be introduced to *me*, as the Queen's cousin?' the lady insisted, drawing her fine brows together. The gold-edged ruff and lynx-fur collar appeared to be holding her head in place, not as wide as Etta's, but neither was her plain black gown as full or as sumptuous. Nor did Etta's triangular forepart of silver-grey brocade find any favour in the woman's eyes.

The Queen's *cousin*? This was most unexpected, and not at all welcome. Etta did her best to keep an expressionless face, but it was difficult when being confronted by an angry reflection. Was she…could she be…an unknown relative? Heaven forbid. In the circumstances, Etta decided on a certain coolness.

It was Lord Somerville who had more definite thoughts about this young woman who, of all people at court, he would rather his new wife had not met. He ought to have warned her about this trouble-making individual who was at court only because that was where her half-cousin Elizabeth could contain her mischief. He hoped no sparks would fly at this first meeting, particularly, for her presence could mean difficulties for Etta's future hopes.

'Henrietta, my dear,' said Levina, ignoring the lady's instructions, 'this is our new Queen's *half*-cousin, Lady Catherine Grey. Lady Catherine, this is my brother's wife, Lady Somerville. And I never tell him to come back later or he might well go off to the Indies between times.'

Unsure of the exact protocol in these circumstances, Etta decided not to curtsy but simply to bow her head in acknowledgement, for Lady Catherine was obviously the kind of woman of whom one must stay a step ahead in the ranking game. '*Half*-cousin?' she said. 'How interesting. It is always good to meet distant relatives.'

'And how distant is *your* relationship to Her Majesty?' said Lady Catherine.

'The Queen and I are half-sisters,' Etta said. 'We share the same father.'

The slight narrowing of Lady Catherine's water-blue eyes lasted only a moment before switching to Lord Somerville with a forced smile. 'Your brother, Mrs Terling? Lord Somerville?'

'*Baron* Somerville of Mortlake,' Levina said, proudly.

His lordship made a formal half-bow. 'I fear we have called at an inconvenient time,' he said, noting how his sister hurried to cover her paints and the tiny card portrait on which she'd been working. 'But we do not intend to stay long. Allow me to present to you Mistress Aphra Betterton, daughter of Sir George Betterton, Assistant to the Keeper of the Royal Wardrobe. He had the ordering of the gown you wore at the coronation, my lady.'

'*That!*' Lady Catherine snapped, looking away. 'Where I ought to have carried Elizabeth's train, at the very least. Things are not as they were in Queen Mary's time, I can tell you. *She* recognised my rank. My sister and I were her favourites.'

'And who was it commissioned your portrait, Lady Catherine?' said Etta. 'Is it to be for an admirer?'

None of them could have missed the hum of giggles from the ladies on the cushions at the mention of an admirer. But Lady Catherine was not about to give anything away on that subject. 'Family,' she said, briefly. 'Everyone has their likeness painted nowadays. You are new to court, Lady Somerville. Is it the Queen you've come to see?'

'I hoped to—' Etta began.

Lord Somerville broke into her conversation, knowing where it could lead. 'We came to see my sister. This is the first time she and my wife have met,' he said, for once careless of what such a woman could make of this information.

Lady Catherine was quick to take up the inference. 'Oh, didn't they meet at the wedding? Hurried, was it?'

'Not particularly,' said his lordship. 'How do you like being one of the Queen's maids? Obviously, you have more time on your hands now.'

Without admitting her humiliation at being demoted from Lady of the Bedchamber to mere Maid of Honour, there was little Lady Catherine could say to that, though she realised that in the matter of innuendo, she was no match for Lord Somerville. 'Well then,' she said, 'I shall take my leave. We do have duties to perform, believe it or not, and the Queen is not one to be kept waiting. Come, ladies. Make your courtesies.'

Behind Lady Catherine's back there was an exchange of sidelong glances and rolling of eyes. *As if they needed her instructions on etiquette.* They had also been newly chosen by Elizabeth, replacing all those who had served under Queen Mary, now only six instead of twenty-four. All of them were remarkably pretty. Lady Catherine turned to Etta as they passed. 'She doesn't see courtiers' wives, you know,' she said. 'You'll have to allow your husband to come here alone, even if she wishes to recognise you. Which she won't, even if she does.'

'Thank you for that advice, Lady Catherine,' said

Etta. 'I feel sure she will, even if she doesn't.' She saw
the last of the maids stifling her laugh with a hand,
twinkling her eyes at Etta as she dipped a curtsy. *She
will*, she mouthed, mischievously. The door closed,
leaving the rest of them shaking their heads at the
unconcealed malice of the woman.

'Take no notice of her, Henrietta,' said Levina,
leading her by the elbow to a window seat overlooking
the river. 'She lost her sister and her father, you know.
That's enough to make anyone bitter. She knows the
Queen dislikes her.'

Etta made the connection. 'So that's Lady Jane
Grey's *sister*. So why does the Queen have her at court
when they made her sister queen? Is she not a danger,
when her family are so closely related?'

'Better here at court where she can keep an eye
on her,' said Somerville, helping Aphra to sit on one
of the warmed cushions. 'Her mother, you see, is
the eldest daughter of your father's sister. Elizabeth
wouldn't completely exclude her from court when she
was once a Lady of the Bedchamber. That would be
a dangerous snub to the family. But neither does she
want Lady Catherine to be amongst her closest con-
fidantes, as Queen Mary did. Naturally, the two Grey
sisters, Catherine and Mary, are not too pleased to
have lost the influence they once had.'

'You'd do well to keep clear of them both,' said
Levina, who answered these days to the name of Mrs
Terling. Her quietly spoken manner perfectly matched
her amiable and honest face. Her hands were dainty,
too, now being drawn into fingerless mittens to keep
out the cold.

'Thank you for the warning,' Etta said. 'We do look

remarkably alike though, don't we? This is all going to be terribly confusing.'

'Not really,' said the artist. 'She lacks your loveliness, Henrietta. I can quite see why my brother chose you for his wife. And Catherine's eyes are not like yours, either, and her hair is a little paler, more like Elizabeth's. When you've studied them both, as I have, the differences are obvious, but of course people *will* compare you and so will the Queen. She doesn't like competition, you see.'

'Lady Catherine's dislike of the Queen is rather obvious, isn't it?'

Lord Somerville answered for his sister. 'Lady Catherine doesn't have the sense to hide her dislike,' he said. 'And the Queen is not obliged to hide hers.'

Etta was thoughtful. This was something she had not expected, neither the physical similarity to another of Elizabeth's relatives, nor that relative's animosity. But whether the Queen would acknowledge Etta, too, was a question she preferred to see as a certainty rather than a doubt, since she herself was no threat.

As she and Aphra examined the tiny examples of Levina's art, portraits of superb quality and the finest possible detail, their attention was wholly immersed in the skill of this talented lady. But the background hum of conversation between brother and sister had now taken on a slightly different tone until both Etta and Aphra realised they were listening to the Flemish tongue.

'Do you know any Flemish?' Etta whispered.

'No. I wish I did. I expect it's only sibling chatter, love.'

'Yes, I expect you're right.' Nevertheless, Etta had caught two names amongst the other words; Elion was one and Cecil was the other. Her uncle, Sir Elion D'Arvall worked for Sir William Cecil, the new Queen's Secretary of State. So why speak of them in hushed tones in Flemish? Could her Uncle Elion's visit to Mortlake have precipitated their move to Cheapside, for some reason? Had her husband already visited his sister here at Whitehall in the last few weeks without telling anyone? Levina had not been so very surprised to see him, had she?

'Come on!' Aphra said, nudging her. 'You're taking it too seriously, Ettie. Everybody speaks in their own language when they get half a chance, don't they?'

Etta smiled. 'Yes, of course they do.' All the same, she had been just a little dismayed by Lady Catherine Grey's hostility and that was before she had even opened her mouth to speak. And now her husband had things of a private nature to be shared only with his sister.

With some kindly advice from Levina about the Queen's movements that morning, they left her to follow another trail towards the Presence Chamber past fine rooms sparkling with candles and lined with colourful tapestries, over rush-strewn floors and past liveried servants with the red-and-white Tudor rose on their tunics. Here, well-dressed courtiers stood about in groups where others, less well known, wove in and out of the crowd, unsure where best to take their place when the Queen finally emerged from her Privy Chamber. At one end stood the Queen's throne covered with a rich figured brocade and a canopy over it, under which everyone was being careful not to stand.

The Lord Chamberlain recognised Lord Somerville at once. 'Ah, Somerville, at last you grace us with your presence,' he quipped, grasping him by the arm.

'My lord,' said Somerville, 'well met. Meet my wife, sir. Lord Howard of Effingham, Etta. The very man who can direct us where to stand.'

Etta curtsied to Lord Howard's bow and found herself being scrutinised by piercing eyes under shaggy eyebrows. She urged Aphra forward with a hand under her arm. 'My cousin, my lord. Mistress Aphra Betterton.'

'One of the Betterton clan, eh? I know your father well. But, Somerville,' he said, turning to his lordship, 'I can see why you might think it a good move to bring your lovely wife and her cousin here, but I must warn you that—'

'Forgive me for interrupting,' Somerville said, determined to portion the responsibility where it should be, 'but it is my wife herself who thinks it's a good move. You will need no explanation, I think.'

The piercing look continued. 'But surely you must have warned her?'

'I've done more than that, my lord, but the lady sees things differently.'

Before the conversation continued above her head, Etta intervened. 'My lord, we are half-sisters, the Queen and I. I have no other ambition than to see her.'

'A worthy ambition, my lady,' said Lord Howard, gravely. 'But don't expect Her Majesty to be overjoyed to meet *you*. She chooses who she wants to meet very carefully and those are mostly men. My two daughters, Douglas and Frances, are amongst her Maids of Honour. Be prepared for disappointment. Yes?'

'Of course, my lord. Thank you.'

'Well then, follow me, good people, and I'll show you where to stand.'

As they followed the black-robed Lord Chamberlain to stand near the doorway to the Privy Chamber, Etta noticed how the babble of voices had hushed, how richly dressed courtiers and petitioners had turned to stare, how most of them were men and how their eyes swept her and Aphra from top to toe with whispered comments. Men's appreciative looks were nothing new to her, nor to Aphra, but this was concentrated and overt, and anything but flattering. Both of them, however, had the satisfaction of knowing that their clothes were of the finest, their hair beautifully styled with jewelled billaments set back to show off the colour, Etta's ruff slightly more extravagant than usual, framing her face to perfection. Feeling the tension in the chamber, she slid her hand into her husband's, who pulled it through his bent arm and held it there for all to see while smiling across the room at a group of astonished acquaintances.

The double doors began to open, the two halberdiers pulled back their pikes with a snap of heels, the crowd fell silent and, with a gentle rustle of clothing, went down on one knee with heads bowed and eyes peeping.

'The Queen!' called the Lord Chamberlain, rather unnecessarily, as she began to move slowly into the corridor of kneeling admirers, pausing to look as he murmured into her ear and singling out those she might like to acknowledge. With the slightest crook of her jewelled finger, she signalled one or two to arise and to present her with small gifts which were passed on to her ladies with smiles of thanks, then allowing them to say whatever they had come for, to plead, petition, or to pledge their loyalty, in case it had been in doubt.

Stopping in front of Lord Somerville's group, she beckoned him to rise. 'So *there* you are,' she said. 'My one and only mercer baron. You were away across the North Sea this time last year, were you not?'

'Your Majesty's memory is phenomenal,' Somerville murmured.

'Yes, even as a princess, there's never been much wrong with my memory,' she replied, glancing towards Etta. 'You were not married then, were you? This lady is your wife, I take it?'

At close quarters, Etta was now able to see the similarities and the differences in their appearance, highlighted in their choice of black in all its silky opulence. She thought the Queen's gown was over-embellished and fussy. Her eyes, however, were sharp and wickedly perceptive, noting in one quick glance everything about Etta: the exaggerated ruff, the bright copper hair, the curvaceous figure within the confines of the boned bodice. But there was no gracious smile that Etta had hoped for, no delighted recognition, no warmth in the eyes as his lordship introduced her. 'The stepdaughter of Lord Jon Raemon of Risinglea, Your Majesty. Lady Somerville and I were married last month.'

Etta sank into another deep curtsy, then rose to present her with the gift wrapped in fine linen which one of the maids opened for her. Over the past weeks, Etta had embroidered a pair of gauntlets, the fingers of which were of soft white kid, the cuff richly garnished with gold thread, silk and pearls with the Tudor Rose in the centre of each one. It had taken Etta many hours of work. Elizabeth's hands were the source of her special pride and now she was impressed both by the value and the excellent workmanship. 'Your own work?' she asked, sniffing at them.

'Yes, Your Majesty.'

'Perfumed, too.'

Etta smiled, hoping that this could be the beginning of a conversation, but instead the Queen inclined her ear towards her Lord Chamberlain to hear his whispered explanation of Etta's parentage. Then, as everyone within hearing distance waited to see what would happen next, she deliberately spoke to Lord Somerville, ignoring the expectancy in Etta's eyes. 'Snared at last, then? Well, don't let that keep you from our court, will you? I need the advice of men like you. But whose idea was that monstrous ruffle? Don't tell me it was yours.'

'It was my idea, Your Majesty,' Etta said, speaking without invitation.

The Queen did not look at her directly but at her husband. 'Then perhaps you will explain to Lady Somerville, before she gets too wide for the doorways, that it is I who dictate the fashion here.'

As if to order, a buzz of laughter shook the air around them as the Queen moved on, leaving Etta still uncertain whether she had been recognised as a relative or simply as the face in the coronation crowd. Clearly, on this occasion, Elizabeth was keeping her cards close to her chest. 'It's all right,' she whispered to Aphra and his lordship. 'I suspect she was taken aback to see me. We must give her time to become accustomed to the idea. After all, it must have been quite a shock to her.'

'So you wish to try again?' Somerville said. 'I don't think she was as much shocked as annoyed.'

'Annoyed by what?' Etta said as they moved with the crowd. 'By the width of my ruffle? That was just a cover for her surprise. And she accepted my gift, didn't she? She liked it.'

Somerville kept hold of her arm. 'That's as maybe, but if we come here again, we shall have to make sure—'

'*If* I come here again?' Etta said, crossly. 'Of course I shall. She'll have to get used to seeing me here if she wants to see more of *you*. Which is what she said.'

'Etta, the Queen doesn't have to get used to any-thing, if she doesn't want to. If you want to come again to see her, you'll have to get used to her manner.'

'Oh, fiddlesticks!' Etta said. 'I can see through all that well enough. Those are Tudor manners. I'll win her over. Just give me time.'

'Well,' Somerville said in a low voice, 'if it's time you want, here comes one who might help you with that. Lord Robert,' he said, more loudly. 'Well met, sir. How do you?'

The tall, debonair young man who had been doing more than his fair share of eyeing Etta while the Queen was speaking to them now found his way to their side, taking full advantage of those who stood back in deference to let him through. The Queen's new Master of Horse, and high in her favour, was not the man to let anyone forget it. 'Somerville, what have you been up to since the Queen bestowed her favour on you? Blinding beauties with your new title, eh?' His blue eyes seemed to sweep over both women as if to discover what lay beneath the rich fabric and whalebone stays, his stance arrogant and graceful, his rich voice well modulated, his figure that of an athlete. The few women in the room were already plotting his whereabouts, especially the young Maids of Honour who ought to have been paying more attention to their royal mistress.

Somerville entered into the jest. 'So I have,' he said, 'but only one so far. Allow me to present Lady Somerville and Mistress Aphra Betterton to you.'

Lord Robert's eyes never left Etta's face as he bowed. They knew he was a man to beware of, for although his position as the Queen's most favoured male friend put him on a higher plane than most, this did not prevent other women from showing their desire for his attentions. His skin was tanned from his outdoor pursuits, earning him the nickname of 'The Gypsy' and, as a horseman, he had few rivals in England. 'Ladies,' Lord Robert said, graciously, 'what a delight it is to see two who put all others except one into the shade. You light up the room with your beauty. Shall we poor courtiers be seeing more of you? It would be a shame indeed if Somerville kept you from court.'

Etta pretended some unsureness, hoping he might insist on it. She glanced up at her husband, getting her reply in before he did. 'Her Majesty has left me in some doubt about whether I would be welcome to accompany Lord Somerville.'

Lord Robert bent a little to catch her eye. 'Of course she would welcome you,' he said. 'I can vouch for it personally. She liked your gift, my lady. It was an inspired choice for her beautiful hands.'

His confidence sent a thrill through her. It was exactly what she had hoped to hear after so many warnings not to expect too much and now she could hardly hide her triumph that the decision about a future appearance had been taken out of her hands by none other than the Queen's favourite, Lord Robert Dudley, younger son of an executed duke, no less, a man of great personal charm and outstanding good looks.

Lord Robert was about to move away when the Queen's sharp voice was heard from the end of the room. All heads turned in that direction, assuming that one of the petitioners had caused the royal displeasure. But a physical wave of shock sent the white-clad Maids of Honour swaying backwards as their irate mistress rounded on the nearest of them who had stepped upon the trailing fabric of the royal skirt as she moved forward. The maid swerved away to avoid the slap to her head and, as she came upright, red-faced, they saw that it was the Lady Catherine Grey who had literally put a foot wrong. Under the Queen's glare, she hid at the back of the group, catching Etta's eye as she did so. *There*, she seemed to be saying. *That's what she's like.*

In no time at all, Lord Robert was at the Queen's elbow, bending his head to hers, smoothing her temper with a whispered comment that made her smile. But the incident surprised Etta who had never in her life aimed a blow at a woman's head.

Several men recognised Baron Somerville on that eventful morning, stopping to speak to him as a friend and being introduced to Etta and Aphra. There was one, however, who recognised her when, if she had seen him beforehand, she would have done her best to avoid him. Surreptitiously, he manoeuvred his way to her side as Lord Somerville's attention was diverted. 'Etta, my dear,' he said. 'Things are looking up, I see. Will you introduce me to your lovely friend?'

She did not need to look to know who spoke to her, for only last year she and he had spent many a stolen hour talking together before he had been warned off. She had liked him well enough at the time and had felt sad that he had been attracted to her access to money rather than to her friendship. 'No, Master Hoby, I shall not. It would be best if you were to go.'

'Go, my lady? Go where? This is where I reside, is it not?'

'I know that you were not honest with me.'

'Then believe me when I say I've missed you. Unbearably.'

This was a conversation Etta did not intend to continue. Reaching out for Lord Somerville's arm, she grasped it hard enough to alert him. Instantly, he understood the situation and with one steely glance and a tip of his head sent Master Hoby off, catching the tail-end of his impudent leer at Aphra as he went. He kept hold of Etta's hand on his arm. 'Don't be concerned, sweetheart. There will be young bucks like that all over the court, pestering women. He'll not come back if he values his hide.'

'I hope you're right, my lord,' Etta said, seeing no reason to tell him that she and the young man were already acquainted.

Having survived Her Majesty's sarcasm, they waited for her to leave the Presence Chamber before moving slowly away, intending to say their farewells to Mrs Teerlinc. She had wanted to know how Etta fared. But a tap on his lordship's arm, too insistent to be one of the jostling crowd, made him turn to see a young page in the Queen's livery, intent on delivering a message. 'Her Gracious Majesty, my lord, wishes…' the page paused, then went on '…wishes Baron Somerville to attend her immediately. I am to conduct you to her, my lord.'

'And me?' said Etta. 'Does that mean me, too?'

'Only his lordship,' said the page, straight-faced. 'Please to follow me.'

The bewilderment in Etta's eyes could not be hidden. Laying a hand over hers, Somerville squeezed it, making her look at him. 'I shall not be long, sweetheart. You go straight to Levina and stay there until I return. Help her to find the way, Aphra, will you?'

'Of course, my lord. We'll wait for you there.'

Before Etta could protest again, he and the page were threading their way through courtiers to the double doors leading to the Queen's Privy Chamber where only she and invited friends were allowed to go. 'Smile,' Aphra said without looking at her. 'Keep smiling. Don't let your thoughts show here, of all places.' Linking her arm through Etta's, she urged her forward, smiling and nodding, being to her cousin the support and comfort they had expected her to be. Etta, on the other hand, would have hammered on those doors until her husband appeared, to insist that Elizabeth wanted her, too. Crossing the courtyards, Aphra could speak more openly. 'She'll want to ask him about you, love. That's what it'll be about. You wait and see. He'll not be there long. She'll have her work to do.'

'Yes, of course. Now, how do we get to Levina's room?'

Chapter Six

Several hours later, and with no sign of his lordship, Etta decided they must leave the comfort of Levina's room and return home alone. The dear lady had shared her food with them, as well as her precious time, and soon the light would be going.

As though their intentions had been anticipated by his lordship, a message came from him to say that they should take the barge back to Puddle Wharf and return home. Apparently, he was unable to say how much longer the Queen would keep him, but by then Etta could work out for herself that his wife's comfort was of no great concern to her. Nor was her safety for, as darkness fell, Aphra would be her only escort through the uphill streets from the jetty to Cheapside.

Fortunately, it was not as dangerous for them as they'd feared when two of Lord Somerville's barge-men walked with them right to the door. Etta gave full vent to her anger. 'If I'd known we'd be traipsing through the filthy streets in the dark,' she said, stamping her way upstairs, 'I'd have worn my street clothes instead of this. What can he be thinking of to stay there so long?'

'He would not have had much choice, Etta love,' Aphra soothed. 'Come on, now. Let Tilda help you to change, then we can eat.'

The Queen's court had not been what either of them had expected except, perhaps, for the richness, the luxurious halls and chambers, the display of wealth on the backs of everyone from pageboy to the Queen herself, scintillating with jewels. They had known something of that. But they had expected her to be interested in the appearance of a young relative, instead of which she had been more interested in the size of Etta's ruff. That had been a mistake. They had thought that the Maids of Honour would all be fast friends, but one young lady had shown them otherwise with her arrogant manner. The appearance of Master Stephen Hoby had been unexpected, too, and not at all welcome. Apart from the genuine interest of Lord Robert Dudley, whose influence with the Queen was very great, the day could not be called an outstanding success, especially when the man she was relying on most for support had still not made an appearance when the time came for bed.

It was Aphra who stayed up a little longer to talk with Master Leon of Padua who, if she were to admit it, was the one to whom she had most wanted to return to after this fiasco. Amongst all the leering richly clad courtiers she had seen that day, there was not one she would like to have spent time with. Those at court had talked incessantly about property and politics, while Master Leon's conversation was more about the properties of plants, about healing rather than conflict. 'Next time you go,' he said, quietly, 'I shall go with you.'

'But will your absence not affect your work?'

'Not at all. I think we might suggest taking Joseph, too. I don't like the sound of those leering courtiers.'

Aphra's violet-tinged eyelids drooped modestly as she smiled.

Reaching out a hand, Leon tenderly smoothed the pad of his thumb over the skin of her cheek. Just once. 'Joseph and I will wait up for his lordship,' he said. 'You go to bed. It's been a tiring day for you. Sleep well, mistress.'

'Aphra,' she said.

He smiled at that. 'Aphra...*bella donna*.'

'That's the name of a plant.'

'So it is,' he said. 'In Italy, ladies use an extract of the berries in their eyes to enlarge the pupil.'

'Do they? Why?'

'They believe it makes them more beautiful, but you would never need to do that. Your pupils are already enlarged.'

She gulped. 'It's the poor light,' she said, rising to go.

'Of course, *madonna*,' he said. 'Allow me to light you to the stairs.'

It was well past midnight when Lord Somerville arrived home to be greeted by the concerned faces of Leon and Joseph, having already learned from his barge master that his wife and her cousin were safe and sound. He was in no better temper than the women had been earlier. 'Don't ask me what that was all about,' he said, throwing his cloak in Joseph's direction, 'because I have no damned idea. I'm sure she could have waited for a more convenient occasion to ask me about Antwerp. You'd think she was about to go there.'

'Have you eaten, my lord?' said Joseph.

'After a fashion. In between answers. I'm starving.'

'Be seated, my lord. Food's all ready.'

Later, Etta sat up as he entered the bedchamber, squeaking the floorboards and casting a dim glow over the bed with the candle flame, a bed that showed every sign of being storm-tossed by sleeplessness. Her eyes were wide open and accusing, her lips compressed against her many grievances.

Placing his candle on the table, he came to sit on the bed with a sigh that sent the flame dancing sideways. 'That wasn't meant to happen, sweetheart. Was it?'

'What did she want you for?' Etta drew her knees up under her chin.

'I've been wondering that all the way home. We talked. She asked me about the shop. About the manor. About Antwerp. About me and Levina as children.'

'About me?'

He shook his head. 'Not…directly. No.'

'Well then, indirectly?'

'No. We ate a kind of supper, enough to feed a flea, then played primero and I lost twenty sovereigns to her. Yes, I know,' he said, defending himself, 'but everyone has to let her win, especially at first. Don't worry. I'll get it back.'

'That's more than our cook's annual wage, my lord,' she said, angrily. 'I suppose you danced, too?'

'Oh, a bit.'

'A bit!' she said sharply. 'Yes, I can imagine. You'll be high on her list of new admirers, then. Does she expect you to return to court?'

Another sigh. 'Yes, it looks like it.'

'When?'

'Tomorrow,' he said, untying the points on his doublet.

'Then I shall come, too. Will she see me tomorrow?'

He stood up, sloughing off the doublet, irritated by the inquisition. 'I don't know…well, yes, she's sure to. We'll take Leon and Joseph this time, so that…'

'So that if we're left to fend for ourselves again…'

'You didn't have to fend for yourselves. Didn't Levina look after you?'

'That's not why I went to court, my lord. I went…' Dropping her head on to her knees, she hid her face inside a heavy fall of red hair.

'Don't weep, Etta,' he said. 'It's only a small hitch. We'll find a way.'

Her head came up, her face showing no sign of tears, only a furious determination in her eyes that put a stop to his sympathy. 'I shall find my own way, my lord, since you'll be at her beck and call from now on. She may discourage wives all she likes, but I shall be an exception. If that Lady Catherine can get to see her, then so can I. And I'm more of a Tudor than she is. Has she forbidden me from attending, after accepting my gift?'

Hauling his shirt over his head, he threw it aside, stripped off his hose and came naked to the bed. 'Move over, woman. No, she has not forbidden you because she probably thinks you've got the message.

And I'm not going to forbid you, either, because I suspect you'd find a way of disobeying me. Wouldn't you?'

'Yes. I would.'

'Right. So we'll have another try tomorrow.'

'You'll take me with you?'

'Well, I'm certainly not going to leave you here to spend all my money at the goldsmith's.'

She slipped down the bed with her back to him, yawning loudly. 'Which is what I'd do, of course.'

'So what happened to our truce?' he said. But there was no reply and he could only suppose that the cold shoulder had returned.

Etta's decision to have little to do with Lady Catherine Grey was taken out of her hands on the following day by none other than Queen Elizabeth herself, when the royal command for Lord Somerville to attend her directly did not include his hopeful wife. Wearing a ruff of greater proportions than Etta's of the previous day, the Queen instructed the Maid of Honour she so much disliked, Lady Catherine, to escort Lady Somerville back to the water gate, where their barge was tied up, not knowing that, this time, Joseph and Leon were waiting in one of the sunny gardens with Aphra in the hope that Etta would re-join them with better news. The Queen had not deigned to speak to her directly and there had been nothing Somerville could do but squeeze Etta's hand, to smile, and to tell her he'd join her soon, which neither of them believed.

It had taken the Queen's favourite, Lord Robert, no time at all to see that his position was being challenged by Somerville, an equally attractive man whose recent title afforded him some clout in society. It was a game to Elizabeth, but a serious matter to himself, who immediately decided that the lovely Lady Somerville would make an excellent alternative companion, looking so much like the woman he loved. So as Lady Catherine unwillingly obeyed the Queen with a glare of hostility, he took a pace backwards, bowed to the hem of the royal skirts, then sidled away to take his position at Etta's side.

Robert Dudley's brother Guildford had married Lady Catherine's sister Jane. Both of them had been executed. But Etta's two escorts were in-laws with very different feelings towards their Queen and, as they set off towards the garden to collect Aphra and the two men, Etta could almost hear the cogitations clicking away inside their heads like clockwork until Lord Robert broke the ice. 'Lady Catherine, I think you may safely return to Her Majesty now. I will take Lady Somerville and her friends down to the water gate myself.'

Lady Catherine pursed her lips in doubt. 'I had hoped,' she said, 'to ask Lady Somerville about her wedding.'

'What can you possibly wish to know about that?' said Etta, sharply.

'You married without the Queen's permission, I understand.' When Etta made no reply, she continued to probe. 'Well, your husband didn't even invite his sister, did he? So I assume it must have been arranged rather quickly, without...'

Lord Robert frowned at his sister-in-law. 'What exactly are you implying, Lady Catherine? And what does it have to do with you? Are you thinking of marrying again? Because if so, you'd better be more than careful how you go about it.'

'Again?' Etta said. 'You are widowed, Lady Catherine?'

'I am not widowed, no,' she replied, clearly unsettled by the way the questions had been turned on her. 'I was married at fifteen, when my beloved sister married Lord Robert's brother, but we were obliged to divorce. That's all.'

'I'm sorry to hear it,' Etta said. 'My own marriage to Lord Somerville was not a grand affair because we both preferred a simple ceremony. My lord bought a special licence.'

'So no calling of the banns?'

'No, but one has to swear that there were no previous agreements, just the same.'

'A simple ceremony indeed. What a shame.'

Etta's eyebrows lifted in surprise, suspecting that she had said too much to this unlikeable woman. 'Why is it a shame? We saw no shame in it.'

Turning away, Lady Catherine shrugged her shoulders. 'No friends or relatives there? No feasting? No dressing up? With all your husband's wealth, too. I *am* surprised.' Walking away, she gave Etta no chance to respond, even though what she had said found a sensitive chord deep inside that hurt Etta because she knew it was the truth. All those wonderful things that help to celebrate a marriage had been wilfully left out, just to make the point that her hand had been forced. And now she had passed this private information to a woman whose dislike was almost tangible.

'That was not very clever of me, was it?' she murmured to Lord Robert. 'What happened to her husband after the divorce? Is he glad to be free?'

He held out a hand for her to place hers there. 'No, they pleaded non-consummation so that the marriage could simply be annulled instead, but they were not successful. They see each other regularly here at court. If she has it in mind to remarry, though, she'll have to tread carefully, because Her Majesty is very unlikely to allow it.'

'Could that be why she's asking me about banns and special licences?'

'Either that, or she hopes to make some kind of mischief, my lady. If you take my advice, you'll not give her any more ammunition.'

'I would be most grateful for your advice, my lord.'

'On how to handle my waspish sister-in-law?'

'No, I don't care a fig about that. You see, as the Queen's half-sister, I came to court hoping to observe her and I cannot make any headway unless she allows me to be in her company. So far, she has hardly spoken to me and now she sends me home, and I'm not sure enough of royal protocol to know whether that is a banishment or simply her way of saying not today thank you. I wish she had not gone off with my husband,' Etta added, plaintively. 'He knows more about these things than I do.'

Lord Robert stopped, looking round for a bench where they might sit together. 'Come over here with me, my lady. We need to clear this up.'

'I wish somebody would,' she said, sitting beside him.

He angled his body towards her, bending his head close to hers, feeling a thrill of masculine pleasure in her vulnerability. 'Well now, for one thing, if our dear lady had banished you, you would not be asking me for confirmation. So far, she has never left anyone in doubt about whether to return to court or not, even though she has been Queen for so short a time. She would not have cared how you departed, much less sent a woman to escort you, and she would not be openly vindictive towards the new wife of a man she has just honoured with a title.' He placed a hand over hers, purposely not elaborating on the subject of the Queen's male friends. 'Oh, don't worry, my lady. It won't last. She's being inundated with suitors from all parts at the moment and this is simply her way of showing them how desirable she is.'

'Yes, I see. But how may I get to speak with her if she won't even look at me?'

'She has looked at you, but perhaps she finds it too difficult to accept another of her father's daughters at the moment. There are others, you know, though I don't suppose any of them are as lovely as yourself. But you must have noticed how few men bring their wives here?'

'Yours too, my lord? Is she obliged to stay at home?'

His cheeks tightened as he looked away, disturbed by the truth, but wondering how to soften it with a half-truth. 'Amy? Yes, she is not welcomed by the Queen, but she'd not last two days in this hive of…I mean, in this place.'

'I shall,' Etta said. 'I shall not give up unless she forbids me to show my face.'

'Then I shall give you that advice you asked me for. Come to court each day with your husband and look for me when he must attend the Queen. I shall be your companion whenever I can, in between duties, and when I cannot, I shall delegate that pleasure to a young man in my employ. You will not be left alone at any time. In this way I shall bring you to her attention and I shall convince her that your only wish is to be in her company. That's all.'

'Yes…yes, and tell her, if you please, that I am no threat to her.'

'Depend on me, my lady. It may take a little time, but if I cannot convince her of your loyalty, then no one can. Tomorrow, she intends to hold an archery contest over in the gardens. Come suitably dressed. You and I will be in the same team, while your husband will be obliged to team up with the Queen. She has a very winning way with men. None of us can say no to her.'

A tight ball of pain pressed on her throat, unlike anything she had experienced before. Lord Robert's words, idly spoken, hinted strongly that any man would fall in love with the Queen whether they wished to or not and that Somerville would be no different in that respect. Even now he would be laughing with her, striving to please, admiring, courteous and respectful, competing for her approval. Etta knew how women looked at her husband, but never had she thought the Queen would be one of them, or that she would so blatantly use her authority to keep him beside her when he ought to have been with his wife. Was this really what she herself would have to endure to be here at court? Was it going to be worth it? And why, suddenly, did she feel such pain at the thought of sharing her husband? 'I ought to go and find my three companions, my lord,' she said. 'Shall we…?'

Picking up the hand he'd been holding, he raised her to her feet, waiting for the closer approach of two courtiers before lifting it to his lips for a longer-than-usual kiss accompanied by a look of deep admiration that would have melted the knees of most women. It was clear he wished the courtiers to see them together. 'Now, my lady,' he said. 'Which garden was it?'

But only Joseph was there to explain how Lady Catherine Grey had arrived half an hour earlier to tell them that, on the Queen's orders, they were to take the barge back to the jetty at Puddle Wharf. She had said that Lady Somerville would be returning later with her husband. 'I refused to go,' Joseph said, 'so Master Leon and Mistress Betterton have returned home. I'm glad I waited, my lady.'

'The scheming little *bitch*,' Lord Robert muttered under his breath.

So Etta returned with Joseph, taking a wherry from Whitehall where boats waited two-deep for customers from the palace buildings. Fortunately, Joseph had the fare, but the usually pleasant river trip was marred, this time, by yet another failure to achieve anything significant except the promise of help from the Queen's favourite. As Master of Horse, Robert Dudley's duties were time-consuming, so Etta did not expect too much from that offer. More sobering, however, was the picture in her mind of Lord Somerville smiling into another woman's eyes. That night, the candle had burnt itself out long before he returned. She heard the click of the bedchamber door, but pretended to be asleep, and when he came to the bed and laid his warm hand upon her hip, she made no response.

* * *

As soon as Lord Robert Dudley had bowed himself discreetly out of the Queen's presence to follow Etta that day, Somerville had guessed what was uppermost in the man's mind and that he himself was in no position to prevent it. It was no comfort to him, either, to know that some of his predictions were being played out at court, that the Queen was reacting to the perceived threat of a beautiful rival in her hive, that Etta was digging her heels in, in defiance, and that Dudley would be sure to hit back at the one woman whose patronage was so essential to him. Etta, he was sure, did not understand how dangerous the man was, how he could make women fall in love with him and how this was certainly not the way for her to win the Queen over. Nor would she have the slightest notion how hurt she would be when Dudley returned to his mistress's favour. Court games were a complete mystery to her and Dudley had no qualms about using women to bolster his ambition. He was already doing that with the Queen herself.

Etta's disappointment at the lack of progress only made her more determined to take whatever course was offered though, as a newly wedded woman, she had not yet acquired the knack of letting her husband into her confidence. In the privacy of their chamber next morning, he had wanted to know what transpired between her and Robert Dudley and, because she was still piqued by his enforced absence just when she had needed it most, she resented his questions. 'Lord Robert offered me his help,' she said, drawing a fine linen stocking up to her knee, 'and I accepted it. Thank you, Tilda. You can leave me now.'

Somerville waited until the door closed before persisting. 'What kind of help?'

'Help at court. What else?' She took the other stocking and held it up to the light. 'Well,' she said, 'you were not there to be of much use, were you? I have to accept it wherever I can and he said he'd do all he could. He will partner me in the archery contest, since you are to be in the Queen's team.' Sitting on the edge of the bed, she drew up her skirts and attempted to reach her foot over the widest hoop of her farthingale.

Taking the stocking from her, Somerville held it away. 'And you think, do you, that by making the Queen jealous, she will be delighted to have you around? Is that what you believe?'

Etta made a grab at the stocking, but he held it away. 'Why should she be jealous?' she retorted. 'Surely she allows him to speak to other women from time to time? Give me my stocking.' Again, she grabbed, but missed.

'Dudley's offer of help, Etta, will come at a price,' he said, pushing her shoulders until she fell backwards on to the bed. The bendy hoops of the farthingale collapsed on top of her, covering her face with a mound of fabric from which she could not escape, while Somerville grabbed her bare foot and held it between his thighs. 'And if he so much as lays a finger on you, woman, he'll have me to reckon with. Keep still while I put this on you.' Taking hold of her foot, he slipped the stocking over her toes.

'Don't be ridiculous!' she shouted at him through

the barrier of skirts. 'What do you care what I get up to with him while you're dallying with *her* all day and night? Let me up!'

'Be still. I care, since you ask, because you're *mine*. And I do not *dally* with the Queen, either.' He wrestled the stocking over her heel and ankle, then began a slow journey upwards towards her knee.

'Don't tell me you talk about the price of kersey with her.'

Behind the barrier, he grinned. 'I doubt she wears any kersey. Shall I ask her?'

The foot gave a violent plunge before he caught it again, rolling the stocking as high as it would go, but letting his hands stray even further. 'Get off!' she cried, wresting her foot out of his grasp. 'Ask her what you like. Let me up. My gown will be a mass of creases before we start.' Struggling against the skirt and hoops, she managed to catch at his hand and haul herself upright, though his firm grasp retained her, holding her close to him.

'Just the same, woman, remember what I've said about Dudley. He'll use anyone in any way to get what he wants and, believe me, he wants the Queen. She flirts with men because she thrives on their adoration and flattery, that's all. So when she finds another man to feed her vanity, Dudley retaliates. It's a game they play. He's had more women than almost any man at court. Everyone knows it. Don't rely on his help, that's all I'm saying.'

'Is it really? I thought you were saying something about him laying a finger on me.' She found herself wanting him to say it again, to tell her that she was his alone, that it was about more than ownership but about raw jealousy and his deep desire for her.

'Don't be alone with him,' he said, pulling her hard into his arms. 'Keep Aphra and Leon with you, and Joseph, too. Do you hear me?'

'Yes,' she said, before his mouth covered hers. His kiss was anything but gentle and she realised that, mixed with the teasing of stockings and legs and far-thingales was a serious warning that matters could so easily spiral out of control in a place where every movement was watched, every word overheard. She had already been hugely inconvenienced by a spiteful woman to whom she had foolishly given information out of misplaced sympathy. She would have to learn to tread more carefully. Pushing herself away, she hurried down the stairs to break her fast in the warm dining parlour, feeling a sense of disappointment that, instead of suggesting what she might do to further her cause, he had dwelt upon what she should not do.

Dressed for a chilly morning out of doors, Etta and Aphra wore sleeveless fur-lined over-gowns, jaunty feathered felt hats, leather shoes and gloves, Etta in jade-green velvet and Aphra in apricot. Accompanied by Leon and Joseph, the river trip to Whitehall was bright with reflected sunlight shattered by swans and their new families. This time, they made straight for the jetty at the garden stairs that led them past raised beds of red brick where early plants showed inside wooden rails of green and white. At every corner, tall red-and-white striped posts were topped with gilded heraldic beasts, unicorns, griffins, stags and dragons holding shields before them as if to guard each plot.

Groups of noblemen were already drifting towards the grassy area where straw archery butts had been set, tended by pages who would keep the contestants supplied with arrows. Couples dallied, kissed, and giggled round every bush until a hush told them of the Queen's arrival.

From the direction of the Queen's Privy Garden, the royal entourage flowed like a shining ribbon of colour along the gravel pathways, their feathers, jewels and furs catching the sun, bright against the shadowy walls. The Queen wore black, although her sable furs did not hide the sheen of pearls on the bodice beneath, or the slender figure, but the brief nod in Etta's direction seemed to indicate that, this time, her choice of a very small ruff had been approved. Etta and Aphra sunk into deep curtsies as she approached, but her smile was for Lord Somerville.

'You shall be in my team,' she said to him, taking her bow from Lord Robert. 'And you, my lord, shall choose another. Now, who's going to put money on my team? Somebody take the wagers. High stakes, everyone.'

'I'll pay your dues,' Somerville whispered to Etta. 'Leave it to me.'

'But I don't intend to lose,' Etta said. 'I'm as good as anyone here.'

'That may be,' he said in a low voice, 'but you must allow Her Majesty to be the winner. I told you, she doesn't like to lose.'

'Nor do I,' she said. 'Ah, Lord Robert, thank you.' She accepted the bow with a smile. 'Aphie, love. Will you hold my gloves?' As she turned to her cousin, she caught sight of a well-dressed young man moving to

Lord Robert's side and realised with displeasure that it was the same one for whom her eyes had searched on the morning of the coronation parade, the same who had spoken to her two days ago. Master Stephen Hoby, whose tailor's and gambling bills had risen beyond his means. She whispered into Aphra's ear as she gave her the gloves, 'Stay close to Master Leon and Joseph, Aphie.'

It soon became apparent to Etta that the Queen's eyesight was nowhere near as good as her own, or indeed most of the others. None of her arrows went anywhere near the bullseye, yet all the contestants deferred to her in what Etta felt was a most ridiculous charade. Even her husband was obeying the Queen's unwritten rules. Etta, however, decided the game should be played fairly, aiming her arrows at the centre of the butt and scoring the first bullseye. Then the second, and the third.

The contestants fell silent as the Queen turned stiffly towards Etta and then, to everyone's amazement, addressed her in fluent Italian as if to catch her out at *something*, if not in archery. 'Your diplomacy is far from perfect, my lady, is it not? I hope you will soon learn that your Queen sets the standard here, not the wives of her courtiers.'

Fortunately, it was well within Etta's capabilities to understand what had been said and to reply just as fluently, though she noticed the looks of horror and bewilderment on the faces of the crowd. Curtsying low, she rose to look into those short-sighted brown eyes. 'I beg Your Majesty to forgive me, but I understood that you were purposely holding back in order to allow your poor subjects a chance to shine. Had you not in your charity done so, I know you would have won and there would have been no contest, would there?'

She knew by the slight parting of the Queen's lips that she was completely unprepared for that answer, though her expression gave nothing else away. But nor was Etta prepared for the Queen's loud peal of laughter at the cleverly flattering reply and, when the sycophantic applause of the courtiers died down, the Queen simply nodded at her. *'Brava,'* she said and turned away to speak to Etta's husband. Etta found that she was trembling, but whether from fright or elation she was not sure. All she knew at that moment was that she would like to have felt Somerville's arms around her and his deep voice murmuring in her ear. At Mortlake, she knew where his fooling around with her stocking would have ended, but that morning his lecturing had annoyed her and the harsh lacing and boning of the court dress was not conducive to a romp on the bed. Which, in retrospect, was perhaps just as well.

Behind her, Lord Robert's voice was a substitute of sorts. 'Well said, my lady. Beauty and wit together. Somerville is a fortunate man.'

His flattery grated on her, but she managed not to let it show. 'Thank you, my lord. My husband warned me. I should have listened to him.'

'Then think, my lady. If you'd taken his advice, Her Majesty would probably not have spoken to you, would she?' He moved away to take his turn at the butts, giving Etta time to appreciate his grace and to recall what Somerville had said about Lord Dudley's danger to women. He was indeed a fine figure, dark-haired, neatly bearded, eyes of deep blue; no wonder the Queen was enamoured of him. But what kind of physical need urged her, Etta wondered, to so publicly encourage the attentions of a married man?

She was not given long to ponder the question before realising that someone had come to stand beside her, expensively suited in tawny brown, black and gold, his flat velvet bonnet set at an angle on thick sand-coloured hair. This time, it was she who spoke first. 'Go away,' she whispered. 'We do not know each other.'

'Hah!' He smiled. 'That will not do, Lady Somerville, and you know it. Lord Robert Dudley has commanded me to escort you whenever he cannot. And since your very wealthy new husband cannot, either, I am happy to oblige.'

'I have my escorts, Master Hoby. You are freed of your obligation.'

'Is that so?' He turned to look over his shoulder. 'Where, exactly?'

Etta turned to look, too. In a corner of the garden beside one of the heraldic posts stood Aphra with Leon talking animatedly to Dr John Dee, the two black gowns in stark contrast to the colour around them. With hands gesticulating and white beard flapping, the dear man was obviously delighted to meet another scholar, while Aphra was engrossed in their conversation and doing exactly what Etta had said by staying close to Leon. But where was Joseph?

Etta and Stephen Hoby had once been good friends, enjoying their time together all the more for being hidden from Etta's parents. Young men with neither title nor obvious means of support made unsuitable partners for a lord's only daughter and Etta, aware that she was flouting their wishes, had been careful that their contact remained innocently verbal. She had been sorry to hear, when her father discovered it, that Hoby was known to her Uncle George as a young man who had once worked at the Royal Wardrobe. She had never felt him to be any kind of threat, nor did she now; more like an inconvenience and a disappointment. He had told her he was a courtier, and had recommended himself to her with his sunny disposition and self-assurance. They had laughed and been carefree together then, but now she was the wife of a baron and everything had changed.

Her eyes searched for Joseph. 'Have you told your master of our acquaintance?' she said to Hoby.

'He knows nothing of our friendship, my lady. And, yes, since you are too polite to ask, Lord Robert pays me well. As you can see,' he said, laughing down at her.

'We cannot be friends, Master Hoby. My husband would not approve. But tell me something before you go, if you please.'

'I was not about to leave. But carry on, my lady.'

From his lips, her new title sounded strange. 'What exactly does his lordship intend you to do in this role that my friends cannot do just as well?'

'Your friends are as new to the court as you are, Etta.'

'You must not call me that any more.'

As if she had not interrupted, he continued. 'So they do not know who to be wary of, who will seek to find you alone. Even now, as we speak, there are at least two such men who have noticed your likeness to the Queen and who would have come to your side as soon as Lord Robert walked away. You would not care for them, I think.'

She turned to look. One of the men was her uncle, Sir Elion D'Arvall. 'That's…' She stopped herself just in time. 'That's true,' she said. She would like to have assured him that Lord Somerville would never allow any harm to befall her, but the words dried in her mouth as she saw how he was otherwise engaged, surrounded by the white-dressed Maids of Honour, the Ladies-in-Waiting, and the paraphernalia of betting and scores. She could not rely on him to come between her and any unwanted male, but neither could she allow her former friend to step into the breach and assume the role of protector, no matter what Lord Robert had told him to do. Only a few weeks ago, she might have tried to anger her new husband by reviving her friendship with Stephen Hoby, but things had changed, and now she felt uncomfortable with him. If she wished to anger Somerville, it would not be with a man like this.

'All the same, Master Hoby, I would rather take my chances on my own. My friends are here and so is Lord Somerville, and I am quite able to look out for myself in company. I shall tell Master Dudley so. Let us say an amicable farewell, if you please.'

'Etta,' he said, 'you cannot do this. Can you not see how it is with me? All this time I've longed to be with you again and, now I've been given the chance, I find that you spurn me. Is this your way of getting your revenge on fate?'

'Master Hoby,' Etta said, crossly frowning as she searched again for Joseph, 'this has nothing to do with revenge. I am now a married woman and I will not jeopardise my marriage by being seen with you. That's all.'

'But I adore you,' he insisted in a low voice. 'And now I see how it is. All that talk of not wanting a title. You soon changed your mind on that, didn't you? Wealth and titles take the place of love, after all.'

'Stop this talk at once!' she whispered, angrily. 'There was never any talk of love between us and you know that as well as I do. If your true motives were discovered, you have only yourself to blame for that. It was my uncle...'

'Betterton. Yes, I know Sir George well enough. And that's his daughter over there, isn't it? Your lovely cousin, eh?' He turned to look at the group with an expression in his eyes that Etta had never seen before until yesterday, when Master Hoby had revealed only too clearly what was on his mind after being refused an introduction to Aphra.

She felt the hairs on her arms stand up in alarm. 'You had better go. *Now*. You've said more than enough.' As she spoke, she caught sight of Joseph's tall figure making his way towards her with his master's fur-lined cloak over his arm.

Reaching her, he shook it out and placed it round her shoulders, pulling it together under her chin where its warmth soothed her. 'His lordship sent me to get it off the barge,' he said. 'He feared you might take cold out here, my lady. Who was that?'

Her Uncle Elion had disappeared and Master Hoby was already deep into the crowd as Etta turned to look. 'Nobody,' she said. 'A man I thought I knew. Take me to the others, Joseph.' A chill stole over her as she pulled the cloak tighter across her body, absorbing the masculine aroma of the fur along with her husband's concern for her comfort. The bitter aftertaste of her conversation with Stephen Hoby lingered through her meeting with Dr Dee and his obvious delight at being introduced to the assistant of his friend, Dr Ben Spenney. It was only to be expected that he and Leon would have much in common, but they might as well have been alone for all the notice they took of the Queen's movements and, as an escort, Etta rated Leon as less than efficient. At the same time, she wondered if Aphra might be safer at home for as long as Stephen Hoby harboured a grudge against her father, Sir George Betterton. The thought of gentle Aphra being in danger from such a man was not easily dismissed.

To her relief, they were soon joined by Lord Somerville who, after greeting Etta and the others, led her away to sit with him alone on a stone bench. She intended to thank him for his thoughtfulness in sending for her cloak, but before she could speak she found herself being questioned with some gravity about why the Queen's fool, a certain Jack Grene, should know so much about their wedding ceremony.

Etta looked blank. 'I've never heard of Jack Grene,' she said, 'much less spoken to him.'

'That's him over there,' said his lordship, indicating a smallish man wearing the Queen's livery generously sprinkled with Tudor roses over his breeches and hose. He was lying on the cold ground beside where the Queen stood, gazing up at her with a miserable expression on his face. 'Somebody has told him that I was too miserly to give you a respectable wedding, so who *have* you been talking to?'

Her heart sank as she remembered. 'Oh, no,' she said. 'Surely not.'

'Surely not who?'

'Lady Catherine Grey.'

'Oh, well done. That's all we needed. What on earth possessed you to tell *her*, after what I said to you? After what Levina said?'

'Yesterday. Truly, I spoke of our wedding out of compassion, that's all, because she'd been made to divorce her husband and I hoped to give her some comfort by telling her that ours was not a lavish affair. I said nothing about you being miserly. Nothing even *remotely* like that.'

'Well, thanks to your compassion, my lady, it's now all round the court that you were not allowed the wedding you wanted because I was too mean to spend on it.'

Covering her face with her hands, she wondered what else she would have to contend with that day. 'I said nothing like that,' she muttered through her fingers. 'Nothing, *nothing* like that. Why would she tell the Queen's fool such a tale?'

'Because she knows he has a wide audience and that there's nothing the court likes more than juicy titbits of that nature. You can no doubt guess how he's embroidering it with some salacious personal details, just for laughs.'

'Surely Her Majesty would not allow that?'

'She allows anything so long as the jests are not about her.'

'Forgive me, my lord. It was my wish to have a simple wedding, not yours. What can I do? Shall I go and speak to this Jack Grene fellow?'

She would have liked nothing more than for him to take her hand and smile, and reassure her that they would face the ridicule together. But he neither smiled nor took her hand. 'I must stay. You shall go home,' he said.

'Please,' she whispered. 'Don't send me home because of this. The Queen actually spoke to me, didn't she? That's a start.'

'I can take the crude jests, but I don't intend for you to stand and listen to them. You go back to the Sign of the Bridge with the others and take Dr Dee with you. Prepare a dinner for everyone and I'll join you later. It's time we all ate together, for a change.'

'And you'll come, too? Really?'

'You look pleased,' he said.

'Of course I am. Will the Queen release you?'

'She won't need me. She has a French deputation coming to woo her.'

'Then I shall prepare a feast, my lord, and we'll have a merry evening.'

Still he did not smile and Etta suspected that this latest annoyance had made him more angry than he had admitted to her. She had been generously provided for in every way and meanness was the last thing anyone could accuse him of. Perhaps, she thought, those friends who knew him well would put a stop to such ridiculous jibes. She would have made some kind of gesture to show her regret at their last night of celibacy, a kiss, or a squeeze of her hand on his, but his grasp of her elbow closed the conversation with some abruptness, steering her back to the group where, after inviting Dr Dee to sup with them that evening, he walked off without another word to Etta.

It was a detail that did not escape Aphra's notice. 'He's preoccupied,' she said. 'I don't suppose for one moment that he intended to attract her attention like this. He cannot refuse her command, Etta love.'

Even as they watched, Aphra's words lost their comfort when two of the younger Ladies-in-Waiting came forward to meet him with smiles of welcome, their arms linking with his to take him to the Queen. Etta would have gone to warn them off, but Aphra stopped her. 'No, don't. It's nothing. It will embarrass him. Let him go.'

I don't want to let him go. I want him here by my side.

His lordship did not look back, leaving Etta with the empty feeling that those two could, between them, make sure he forgot to return home in time for dinner, that the life of pleasure at the royal court could easily change a man's mind and make him forget his duties at home. It had already happened to Robert Dudley. 'You go with the others,' Etta said to Aphra. 'Here, take my lord's cloak and wait for me at the garden stairs where we came in. I must find a house of ease.'

The Queen's entourage had moved off towards the palace, giving Etta a fair indication of her direction in relation to the river and its many jetties, so she ignored Aphra's reservations and offers of company and set off alone to find one of those nooks built into the thickness of the wall for the relief of ladies. The pungent smell of waste matter usually led one to their location, though men usually relieved themselves in the bushes or a deserted corner of the outer wall marked for such purposes. As convoluted as a rabbit warren, the narrow whitewashed passages divided and subdivided into a maze where Etta soon began to doubt her orientation until, hearing the high squeak of a woman's laughing protest, she moved unsurely towards the sound. A man's indistinct voice joined in, causing Etta to hesitate for fear of disturbing a private moment.

But the urgent needs of her body combined with her curiosity, moving her on round the corner where, at eye level in the dim light, she saw two velvet-slippered feet and bare legs jerking madly from the depths of an alcove where a man was bent over a woman, his arms holding her against the cold stone sill of a window. His white shirt hung half out of his breeches, and the back of his sandy-haired head obscured the woman's face, their panting and laughing making them oblivious to Etta's presence.

Shocked by the brazenness of the act, she stifled her cry with one hand, swivelling round to run back the way she had come, taking turn after turn towards whatever light was showing. With a thud that hurt her shoulder, she collided with a man's body and swerved to escape as his arms caught and held her, pushing her hard against the wall. 'Hold it!' he said. 'Who's this, then? Well, if it isn't Somerville's woman. What are you doing here, my lady? Eh? Looking for a bit of light relief from your skinflint husband? Is he so mean with his attentions, too? Well, I can show you some little tricks.'

'Let me go! You are impertinent, sir. I am looking for...' she knew not to give him this private information when his disrespect showed him to be no gentleman '...the garden stairs to the jetty,' she said, squirming inside his embrace. 'Let go of me!' Rather than let her go, he placed himself in her way as she beat frantically at his chest with her fists.

During those weeks of preparation, Lord Somerville had taught her how to use a dagger, but she had not brought it with her and now she blamed herself for being foolishly optimistic about the intentions of well-dressed men who appeared to turn into lunatics as soon as the Queen's back was turned. One other thing he had taught her, however, was how to disable an attacker, so now, without a second thought, she brought her knee up high through all the layers of petticoat, farthingale and overskirt, jabbing hard into her assailant's groin and using all her strength to make a connection with his codpiece. She heard his screech of pain, then felt the sudden release of his grasp upon her arms, dropping away to clutch at himself as he doubled up, gasping obscenities.

Fired up by that success and by the outrageous events, she recalled her husband's next instructions to catch her assailant's ears tightly in her fists and to swing his head hard into the nearest object. The stone wall was at her elbow, so she slammed him into it as she'd been told, realising for the first time how much harder it was to perform such unladylike defences than to have them described to her in a more dispassionate moment. His head, with shoulders attached, seemed to weigh a ton, but the crack as it hit the wall brought a wave of nausea to her throat.

Leaving him crouching on the floor and moaning in agony, Etta stepped over his legs and ran like a hare along the passageway, half-blinded by the fear that she might once again be running into danger. A noise ahead made her swerve and flatten herself against the wall as a hand-linked chain of people ran towards her, feeling the uncomfortable bounce and pull of her wide farthingale as they knocked it askew. Two burly young courtiers in velvets and silks held a young white-aproned woman by each wrist, her linen coif hanging round her neck to reveal brown hair tumbling around her shoulders. She threw a laughing glance of helplessness towards Etta who could only stare and watch, horrified, as they disappeared round a corner.

For a moment longer, Etta wondered how she was to extricate herself from this nightmare and how she was to avoid meeting that man again, who would certainly seek some revenge for his hurts. She leaned against the wall to stop the trembling, then froze again as a long shadow slid round the corner ahead. Another man. *'Joseph!* Joseph…oh, for pity's sake get me out of here!' Her voice was hoarse with fright.

Concern was written deeply in the young man's face as he took the last few yards at a trot. 'I was worried, my lady. What's happened? Are you all right?'

'No…yes…I'm lost, Joseph, and I still haven't found what I'm looking for.'

'I've just passed it, my lady. Down here. Come this way. Are you sure you're all right? You're upset.' He took her hand, too familiar, but comforting.

She could not tell him what had happened or what she had witnessed, for Joseph would be obliged to tell his master and that would almost certainly be the end of her visits to Whitehall Palace. To add to the problem, the man who had earlier declared his love for her, who had taken on the role of her protector against what he believed were predatory males, was

the same man she had just seen with the woman in
the alcove, apparently wearing his disappointment too
lightly for it to matter.

On the journey back to the jetty at Puddle Wharf,
Etta was silent and thoughtful, her head reeling with
the events of the morning, so unlike anything she
had expected. On the one hand, the Queen had spoken to her at last and, although not exactly friendly,
had not forbidden her to return. She ought, she supposed, to be thankful for that, yet she had hoped for
a less frosty reception. Now it looked as if the Queen
found Lord Somerville to be of more interest than
herself, and that, by insisting on appearing at court,
she herself had put him in the difficult position of
having to spend time there without her. And by the
look of things, it was not only the Queen who wished
for his company, either. The women in the Queen's
retinue were all, without exception, beautiful, witty,
magnificently dressed and young enough to be flattered by the attention of the wealthy, handsome and
titled mercer. Who could blame them for taking advantage of his wife's absence? But was it really her
likeness to the Queen that was having the opposite
effect from the one she had intended? Etta had been
warned, but surely the royal confidence could not be
so shaken by the appearance of another Tudor woman?
The idea was ludicrous.

So far, Lord Robert had done little to help except
by including her in his archery team. Tomorrow, she
would explain to him that the assistance of the man
she had misjudged so badly, Stephen Hoby, would not
be needed, for had she known what kind of a man he

was, she would never have called him her friend. The scene came back to her in full detail, but then begged for comparison to her own passionate encounter with his lordship in the banqueting house by the river, in daylight, differing only by being legal and on their own property. Now, watching the oars make silver ripples on the water, she began to experience again that terrible emptiness as her lord had left to go with the two alluring women and to realise, perhaps for the first time, that what she felt was the pain of being in love. That ache. That need. The longing. Why did it hurt her so to compare that scene of her husband's departure with the one in the passageway where two laughing men pulled a pretty girl with them?

Only moments before, Stephen Hoby had expressed love for her and, instead of laughing it off as ridiculous, she had been angry without realising that her anger had been because it came from the wrong man. Admiration, pleasure in her body, desire, and every other expression of satisfaction, but never love. What if he did not return when he'd said? How could she pretend not to care that he preferred the company of other women to hers? How could she convince him that she could become a suitable courtier, after all the embarrassments of the day? And how would she bear the wait till he came home to her?

Chapter Seven

At the Sign of the Bridge there was less opportunity for thoughts of love's pain, for they had a guest and meals to organise, and a household to run after their absences at court. Because it was Lent, the menu contained his lordship's favourite fish, crabs and lobster, plaice and trout, and as many fruits as Etta could find at this time of the year to supplement those dried over winter. Cheeses, sauces, pasties and platters of salmon covered the white linen cloth laid with the best silver and glass tableware in Dr Dee's honour and, as darkness fell, Etta's expectations rose in anticipation of his lordship's arrival.

Dr Dee and Master Leon would not have noticed if the supper had been delayed for hours, but Etta and Aphra could not allow the food to spoil so were obliged to interrupt the talk about the controversial role of rue and to promote instead the uses of dill and fennel with fish. Laughing about the fine line between medicinal and culinary, the men clattered into place at the table just as Etta was handed a note by Joseph, arrived by royal messenger, he said. Etta knew before she read it what it would contain.

'Oh, dear,' she said, keeping her voice light. 'My lord will be delayed. He asks that we start without him. How disappointing. Come then, we must make the best of it and leave enough for him to eat later.' Trying hard to give him the benefit of the doubt, to believe that it was not his fault but the Queen's, Etta nevertheless found it hard to forget the manner of their parting.

Aphra understood the effort her cousin was making to be the perfect hostess, being to her the support she needed with both the duties and the conversation, but her heart ached for Etta, after all the effort she had made. When the men's talk showed no sign of waning, Aphra suggested leaving them to it. 'Do we have a chamber for Dr Dee?' she said to Etta. 'It looks as if they're going to stay and wait for his lordship. We can't send him home at this time of night, can we?'

'No, indeed we cannot. I'll have the little chamber next to the counting house prepared. Shall you tell him?'

Etta's despondent expression tugged at Aphra's warm heart. She put her arms round Etta's shoulders, hugging her like a mother. 'I know,' she said. 'I know, dearest. You go on up. He'll be back before you're asleep. You'll see.'

There were tears in Etta's eyes as she croaked her thanks, wishing her cousin a goodnight. Once within her bedchamber and with only Tilda to see, she sobbed quietly as, layer by layer, her finery was undone and shaken free of the salt tears that dripped off the spangles. Between the soft linen sheets, her pent-up fears turned to desperate weeping as now all the frightening events of the day crowded in, forcing her to ask herself whether her ambition to be in the Queen's company was ever going to be realised when the only positive thing to come out of it so far had been to reveal her love for the man she had married. Which, of course, was no bad thing except that her insistence on being at court had resulted in their being held apart for reasons of which she could no longer be certain. Judging by what she had witnessed that day, her former view of a disciplined and perfectly mannered court was sadly out of date, and how was she to know in what way that might rub off on her husband, a man of the world with a far greater experience of life than she? Yes, experienced in all departments.

For hours she lay awake, listening for the click of the latch through the muffled street sounds below, the cry of the night watch, the chiming of bells, the spasmodic bellowing of drunks, the slamming of doors and windows, the yapping of dogs. She thought she must have slept before something within the house woke her. Was it a door? Voices? She waited, but all was quiet again. Surely he must be home by now? The candle had long since died.

On bare feet she padded along the passageway, feeling the panels until she saw the dim light of a candle filtering through the partly open door of Lord Somerville's counting house, the one to which she had been shown on her first visit here. Holding herself back against the panelling, she heard the low voices, then saw shadows move and dance across the opening. That would be Joseph talking to Somerville. He was home. At last. *Home with her.*

She wanted to cry out, to rush in through the open door, to throw herself at him and to hold his beautiful black-haired head against her breast, to cover him with kisses, to scold and weep and plead with him not to leave her again, to feel his arms and the strength of his body. So it was with every ounce of restraint that she stood there to watch his face and hands as he lifted packages off the floor to check and count them, obviously concerned that none had been opened. Then, overwhelmed with relief, she tiptoed back to her bed, too tired to wonder what her husband was doing at this time of night that could not be done in daylight. Then she slept.

She thought she must be dreaming when the bed tipped, the covers moved over her, and warm arms came to enclose her, more determined than the hesitant hand on her hip of last time. A remnant of the last sob rose into her throat as she melded herself into his contours and felt the deep rumble of words vibrate in his chest. 'Ah, lass,' he said. 'You've been weeping?'

Her voice was hoarse. 'It's all right,' she said. 'You're here.'

Gently, his hand moved over her face to touch the swollen eyelids and lips, following each touch with his mouth, kissing away the recent signs of distress. He would have attempted an explanation, but that was not what she needed most while only half-awake and clinging to him like a child. Few words passed between them as wave after wave of pleasure washed over her, his hands sweeping over her body, convincing her as nothing else could that his desire was as keen as ever, no matter who or what had kept him from reaching her that night.

His wooing was briefer than usual for, still on the edge of sleep, she was already in her mind at the point where her dreaming senses were ready for him, her body tingling with a sudden awareness that fulfilment was only one move of his hand away. With a cry of desire, she took him inside her and urged him on with the soft rake of her fingertips along his back, responding like wildfire to his hunger, as eager as he to revisit the deep well of their passion. Joined, complete and in harmony at last as they had not been by day, they gave each other that pleasure they had both missed while attempting, not entirely successfully, to make it last, to make up for lost opportunities. Too soon, the moment rushed towards them with a ferocious speed neither of them could control, taking them beyond awareness, holding them suspended before the mindless lethargy of completion tipped them into sleep.

Wrapped closely in each other's arms, they came awake as sounds from below warned them of approaching dawn, letting drowsy memories sift through their consciousness. 'Lie still,' Somerville whispered as Etta reached for the bell to summon Tilda. 'We're staying at home today.' He placed a finger gently upon her lips to stop the protest. 'Hush, woman. I have business I must attend to and you're not going there without me.'

'But surely,' Etta said, loath to let him off so lightly without some kind of explanation, 'you being there won't make much difference to the business, will it?'

He sighed, aware that she deserved a reason for last night's absence. Heaving himself up on to one elbow, he pushed a swathe of red hair off her face, smiling into the two drowsy brown eyes. 'Yes, it will,' he said, 'whatever you think.'

'How do you know what I think?' she whispered.

The smile faded. 'You think I was kept at the palace because I preferred to be with others rather than with my wife. That's not so. Just as I was about to leave the palace to come here, I received a message from my man at the Steelyard to tell me that the Stationers' wardens had been there, asking to take a look at my imports from Antwerp. He told them to return today when I would be there.'

'The Steelyard? That's where the northern merchants have their warehouses, isn't it?'

'Yes, just further along the Thames from the Puddle Wharf jetty. My ships load and unload there, then the merchandise is carried up here to Cheapside.'

'So you went there straight from the palace.'

'Yes, I had to. I don't want the Stationers poking about in my warehouse whether I'm there or not, so I had to move the Antwerp imports quickly.'

'In the dark?'

'That's the best time, when the streets are quiet. Then Dr Dee and I had to go through them last night…'

'Wait a minute… Dr Dee was with you, in your office? They were not fabrics, then?'

'No, not fabrics. The Stationers' wardens must have been tipped off about what was wrapped inside the bales.'

'Dr Dee's books,' she said. *Packets of them.*

'That's right. And today we have to get some of them out of here to his private clients. He believes Master Leon will want to take some to the Apothecaries.'

'My lord, this is dangerous.'

'It's a risk, but we're not in any personal danger, if that's what you mean. Plenty of almanac pamphlets are sold for a penny or two at the stationers' stalls along St Paul's, but these are bound books of prognostications. We both know it's an offence, but it's not treasonous material. Don't worry, we know what we're doing.'

Etta was silent, recalling that awful moment yesterday when one man had been quite prepared to insult the wife of Lord Somerville without a second thought. Which did not suggest to her that the dreadful man had anything to fear by way of revenge from his lordship. Were there men at court who bore him a grudge, perhaps? 'So who could have tipped the Stationers off?' she said.

'Oh, anyone with a grudge against Dr Dee, I suppose.'

'Or against you?'

'Or me,' he agreed, kissing the tip of her nose.

In some respects, the decision not to visit Whitehall that day came as a relief to Etta's cousin. Aphra had felt the trembling hand in hers as they had sat on the barge together, felt the tense silence, too, and the barely controlled distress that Lord Somerville's message had caused, later. A new marriage was bound to bring problems, especially one as controversial as Etta's, but Aphra had also seen occasions when something akin to love had been very close to the surface. Knowing her cousin for longer than Somerville, however, gave Aphra a greater insight into her volatile temperament and she would like to have warned him that two swallows do not make a summer, as the English say.

After receiving early morning messages for them to call at the Sign of the Bridge that same day, dozens of Dr Dee's devotees brought their wives to the mercer's shop ostensibly to choose from the new consignment of fabrics that had recently arrived via Antwerp on one of Somerville's ships. Business was brisk that day, with Etta and Aphra on hand to welcome them upstairs for a warming drink and a rest before leaving with parcels weighing rather heavier than the fine fabrics inside would suggest. Even Dr Dee himself was there, staying to talk with friends, signing books and discussing the contents, considerably lessening the print run which, by late afternoon, had dwindled to only a few dozen. These, Master Leon assured him, would be taken to the Apothecaries' Hall from where they would quickly be distributed.

That evening, the supper table had nine guests happily crammed along its sides, all of whom helped Lord Somerville and Dr Dee to celebrate the fact that the Stationers' wardens had found nothing to interest them in the warehouse. The danger appeared to be over, though no one was any nearer suggesting who might have been responsible for alerting the Stationers in the first place.

Praising Etta for what had been a hugely successful day, Somerville outlined plans that made no mention of a return to Whitehall Palace and, while she was pleased to receive his admiration as a competent hostess, she could not suppress the disturbing feeling that her own personal quest was being bypassed.

He was, of course, a successful businessman whose varied concerns demanded that he must be where he was needed and, having already spent several days at Whitehall, Etta was in no position to grumble. But, unable to go there without him, and still having made no progress, she found it hard to show the same contentment as he did at bedtime when he mentioned the day's successes.

Assuming that her lack of conversation was due to natural tiredness, he expected a lukewarm response as he drew her gently into his arms, having seen no indication of the irritation rankling inside her at the thought of more days of lost time. Words were of no use to her and her scheme, such as it was, was slipping out of her control. There was only one way she knew to release her anger without causing damage. So when his tender kissing over her face reached her lips, she grasped a fistful of hair at the back of his head to slew his mouth across hers in a kiss that took him completely by surprise by its almost savage urgency. And when he would have slowed down, she forbade it by rearing above him to keep his head imprisoned upon the pillow, venting her frustration with fierce kisses instead of words.

It did not take him long to realise that the wild side of his wife had been unleashed and that Etta intended him to be on the receiving end of it and so, for a while, he allowed himself to be used, resisting the temptation to laugh at the nips to his earlobes, chin and throat. Then, suspecting that his passivity was not what she wanted, he put up a mild resistance, rolling with her across the great bed and taking turns to be mastered and master in a battle that was, at times, less than gentle. Far from complaining, Etta retaliated with her nails until her wrists were caught and held away while his mouth sought her beautiful breasts, keeping her still with the movement of his lips and teeth, teasing, pulling and suckling until she cried out that this was unfair, unchivalrous, disallowed. Pleasure for its own sake had not been intended.

'No it isn't,' he growled, freeing her arms. 'You started it.'

Until then, she had not realised how tired she was after the efforts of the day. But having used up what remained of her energy in this unequal tussle with a man whose strength was formidable, even in its gentlest form, she could summon up no more. Resting her lips on the hard bulge of his shoulder, she signalled her submission with a softly biting kiss. 'Don't go thinking I want you,' she whispered, 'because I don't.'

'Of course you don't,' he replied, looking into eyes dark with desire. 'How could I ever have thought it? Shall I persuade you, then?'

'No,' she said. 'I don't need your persuasions.'

But his hand was already there, persuading her thighs to melt and open for him, making her groan with aching readiness, arching her body to meet him and to welcome him inside her with a sigh. 'I know what this is all about,' he said.

She let him have the last word as, with his first masterly possession of her, she felt her anger dissipate in the exquisite pleasure that grew and grew until the shattering climax, emptying both their minds of all except the harmony of their beings. It was the one thing, Etta mused, that had the power to heal a rift between them, even to making her forget what it had all been about.

* * *

Somerville's suggestion that she and Aphra might pay a visit to see Sir George at the Royal Wardrobe the next morning coincided perfectly with Etta's wish to ask her uncle one or two pertinent questions about Master Stephen Hoby. It was some time since she had seen her two brothers and cousin, and while not wishing to divert them from their duties, she knew they were often the recipients of the kind of gossip women needed to know about such as, for instance, whose wife had been given new fabrics and what the Queen's silk woman was making for the royal use.

The claustrophobic rooms lined with shelves of materials, chests and coffers, baskets and bales, order books and record books by the hundred, linen bags to hold clothing and boxes of braids, ribbons, wires and threads, brought back strong memories of when Etta and Lord Somerville had first met, when he had introduced himself as plain Master Nicolaus. She had used his first name rarely since then, for she knew that to do so regularly would be signalling a return to that easy and affectionate relationship when matters had been within her control. Now, however, she was learning to forgive him and her parents for that deceit and, as the weeks passed, the sting was becoming less painful as her love for him grew stronger.

Aphra's good-natured father was happy to see them, though he was as busy as ever with the Queen's orders. As a new monarch, he told them, there was so much needed for the occasions denied her by her half-sister, Queen Mary. Sir George thought it would take months, if not years, to supply all her needs by which time, he said, they'd have to start again as fashions changed. Already the Queen was adopting a wider ruff. Had Etta noticed?

Etta said nothing, exchanging glances with Aphra. Her twin brothers at the Royal Wardrobe appeared to have grown since their last meeting, and seeing them again brought a certain guilty sadness that they had been denied a share in their sister's wedding day. Michael and Andrew harboured no grudge, but their hugs and looks of concern for her happiness suggested to Etta that they sympathised with her for the way things had turned out. It was her cousin Edwin, Aphra's younger brother, who supplied her with the information about which she had intended to ask Sir George concerning Stephen Hoby. It was Edwin himself who had brought that young man's offences to the attention of his father, resulting in dismissal from the Royal Wardrobe and the end to Etta's friendship with him, which Sir George had not known about until then. He had been obliged to pass on this information to Etta's father, Lord Jon Raemon, with the inevitable result.

The five young cousins huddled together in the spring sunshine that blazed through a large window on to a palette of jewel colours piled on top of an enormous cutting table. Sir George was going through a list with his master tailor, allowing the young people time together. Edwin was still apologetic, after all this time. 'I couldn't pretend I hadn't seen what he was getting up to, Etta,' he said. 'He was friends with all three of us, too, and I think he thought he was safe enough, that we'd turn a blind eye. Especially as you took a liking to him.'

'What *was* he up to?' Etta asked. The five of them were close and Etta knew that Edwin would have done nothing to hurt her intentionally, but he had his loyalty to his father to consider.

'Pilfering,' said Edwin.

'Yeah, it's called *theft*,' said Andrew, less charitably. 'He was always having some new suit made. We wondered how he did it on our kind of pay.'

'Well, he gambled, remember,' said Michael. 'He must have won…'

'Hundreds, yes,' said his twin. 'He did and lost it again. That's probably…'

'Why he took stuff from here. Yards of it missing. Braids…'

'Aiglets, guards. Did you not wonder…?'

'Why he was so fine and prinked out, Etta?'

She could not resist a smile at their shared thoughts and sentences. 'No, I don't think I did,' she said. 'Men always owe money to their tailors, don't they?'

'Hoby owed money to everybody, even though he supplied his tailors with the cloth,' Edwin said. 'All three of us saw what he was doing, Etta, but it was me who told my father. I'm sorry. I know you liked him, but he was not honest.'

'Don't be sorry, Ed,' she said. 'I like him a lot less now. He's not what I thought. He lied. He told me he was a courtier.'

Edwin frowned at her, suspecting there was more to be said. 'You mean, you've seen him since?'

'He's at court now,' she said. 'Yes, I've spoken to him, too.'

Michael's whisper was vehement. 'For pity's sake, Etta. You shouldn't have done. The man's a scoundrel.'

'Shh!' she said, laying a hand on his arm. 'It's not

what you think. We are not in the least friends. He's in the employ of Lord Robert Dudley, no less.'

'The creeping little *worm*!' Exclamations came from all three men.

Aphra stared in disbelief. 'We should tell Father,' she said.

'Tell me what?' Sir George said, coming over to them. 'What ought I to know about?'

'Stephen Hoby, sir,' said Edwin. 'At court, in the employ of Lord Robert Dudley. How did he manage that?'

'By forging a reference from me and being well dressed, I suppose,' Sir George said, laconically. 'He certainly doesn't lack ambition, does he? You've seen him there, Etta?'

'Yes, Uncle. But I'd rather my husband didn't hear of it, if you please.'

'If I can be sure you're safe from Hoby, then I shall make sure Somerville doesn't. Now, you three, you've idled long enough. Back to your duties. Etta, Aphra, come over here and take a look at this pair of sleeves and tell me if you've ever seen finer embroidery.'

Etta would like to have found a way to speak to her uncle about Aphra's safety, about the way Stephen Hoby had looked at her, about what she herself had seen of his activities in the passageways of Whitehall Palace, and about the possible grudge he might bear Sir George himself. But Aphra was there and Sir George appeared to have enough to do without concerning himself further, so no more was said. Nevertheless, the first thing Sir George did when Etta and Aphra had left was to pen a letter to Lord Robert Dudley, which he dispatched that same day by personal messenger. Dudley was not the kind of man to take kindly to being deceived by a young wastrel like Hoby.

The contact between sisters and brothers was a welcome, though brief, diversion that morning at the Royal Wardrobe, picking up the gently teasing manner of their childhood when they had spent much of their time together. Being the natural offspring of Lord and Lady Raemon, the twins shared none of Etta's volatile characteristics. But Aphra and her brother Edwin were alike in many ways, which had allowed him to ask her without fear of offence whether their parents had suggested a marriage partner for her yet.

'Oh, they made noises about it before I left to stay with Etta, but they know how I feel. Perhaps it's as well I'm not at home.'

'Why, love?' he whispered. 'You're not…is it Ben…do you still…?'

Aphra shook her head. 'No, course not. Dr Ben will find himself a clever wife of his own age. And I, well…who knows?'

'So who's this Master Leon who lives at the shop? Ben's assistant. What's he doing in London? Making eyes at you?'

'Silly!' Aphra said. All the same, she blushed as she turned away. 'He's with the apothecaries and getting a reputation. He knows Dr Dee and he's…'

'Ho-ho! I see how it is,' Edwin laughed. 'Say no more.'

'Hush. It's not like that.'

'No?'

'No. Give my love to Mother.'

'Give it to her yourself.'

'When?'

'Tomorrow. Take the amazingly reputable Master Leon with you. I'll tell her to expect you.'

'If he's free.'

'He'll be free. He'll probably fall over himself to meet the parents.' He strode past her, laughing, pretending to stumble as she gave his back a gentle shove.

As a very private person, especially concerning her emotions, Aphra was bound to wonder how much she had unintentionally revealed to Etta and her husband about her growing friendship with Master Leon. She had always known that her affection for her uncle, Dr Ben Spenney, was rather more than the usual warmth between close relatives. In his wisdom, Dr Ben had done nothing to encourage this except to share some of his knowledge with her. He had studied in Italy and London, and had returned to his home at Sandrock Priory just as Aphra had reached those impressionable adolescent years, tanned, self-assured, handsome and recognised as a leader in his field. And now, his assistant had followed on his heels with similar attributes and the additional attraction of being free and open to all Aphra's many qualities: her quiet intelligence, her gentle beauty and compassion.

The stillroom was situated at the back of the premises away from the noise and smells of Cheapside where the air was cooler, sweetened by bunches of herbs drying upside-down from racks above Aphra's head. When Leon passed the open door on the way to his room, she was standing in one corner with her hands cupping her face as she looked up in some anxiety. Leon stopped. 'What is it? Can you not lower the rack?'

Aphra pointed. 'A thrush,' she said. 'Up there. It can't find the way out.'

Leon stepped inside. 'Open the window wider,' he said.

'I have done. It won't go. It's frightened.'

The softly speckled thrush tried again, hurling itself against the window with a clatter before coming to rest on the bent curve of a basket, its eyes round like beads. 'There,' Aphra said. 'Now it might allow me to catch it.' She cupped her hands in readiness, but Leon stopped her.

'No,' he said, quietly. 'Let me.' Moving very slowly towards it, he stretched out his forefinger and placed it just in front of the thrush's feet until he touched the claws. Aphra could scarcely believe it, for the bird was quite calm, hopping on to the finger and sitting there as Leon carried it to the open door, lifted it and let it fly away.

They faced each other, smiling. 'That was wonderful,' Aphra said in admiration. 'Does it always work?'

For an answer, he held out the finger to her, sideways, as if inviting her to hop on to it. 'I've never tried it on a human bird,' he said. 'Will *la bella donna* come to me, do you think?'

Aphra hesitated, looking from the finger to his eyes to see if he jested. But the expression was one she had noticed before when he had not thought she was looking, when she had wondered if he would ever take the next step and speak to her. She hooked her hand around his finger and gave in to its pull until she was close enough for him to raise her hand to his lips.

From there, it was only a short distance to her mouth for a kiss as light as the wing of a moth, lingering over the lovely fullness, exploring the contours and tasting the fresh sweetness of a first love. The prolonged touch of his skin upon her face was a new experience for her, one she thought she could get used to with its woody aroma of rosemary and rose water. And when his arm stole softly around her shoulders she sighed, laying her head upon him for a deeper kiss that sent all thoughts skittering away into the folds of her body. His warmth, his firm physique and strong embrace were things about which she had recently allowed herself to think before sleep, when she summoned to memory all their contacts during the mornings and evenings. Would they now begin to take on a more substantial meaning?

'Aphra,' he said. 'You've come to me, have you? At last?'

'I don't know what this means. Tell me what it means, Master Leon.'

'It means, my lovely bird, that I need to speak to your parents. I shall ask their permission to woo you. Is that how it's said in England? To woo? It sounds rather like the noise an owl makes.'

'To woo, yes. Or to court me? But they will want to know what you have in mind. What *do* you have in mind?'

He threw back his head, showing his white teeth in a soft laugh laced with masculine mischief that made Aphra blush for the second time that day. 'Really?' he said. 'You want to know what I have in mind? I don't think I dare go into that kind of detail. But, no, I shall tell them that I want you for my wife and that I cannot live without you. Do you think they will allow it?'

'Perhaps, sir. But then they will want to know what I think of the idea.'

'Ah, yes. What do you think of the idea, my bird?'

'I think, sir, that you have not yet asked me for my hand.'

'Have I not? I thought…'

'No, not yet.'

His hard kiss was not entirely unexpected, intended to persuade her. 'There,' he said. 'Now you must say you'll have me as a husband, if you please.' Then, for good measure, he kissed her again until she was breathless and laughing. 'Say it,' he demanded.

'Yes…yes, I will…now please stop…I need to breathe.'

'*Brava!* Then I shall speak to your parents, yes?'

'My brother suggests we should go tomorrow.'

Holding her at arm's length, he studied her face. 'How so?' he said.

'He seems to think…'

'Your brother has not seen me.'

'No, but he's seen me. Apparently, it shows.'

Shaking his head, he laughed down at her. 'We shall get on well together, your brother and I,' he said. 'So it shows, does it? Well, I like that very much. We shall go and see them tomorrow, together. What were you doing in here?'

'Mixing a love potion,' she said in mock seriousness.

'You need a love potion?'

'It was not for me.'

'Then throw it away. I don't need it either.'

'I'll give it to the washerwoman for her hands. It will do just as well.'

'Shameless woman! What kind of apothecary's wife will you make?' Kissing her again, he thought she possessed every attribute an apothecary's wife would ever need, and more. Dr Ben had certainly not exaggerated. 'I love you,' he whispered. 'From the moment I first met you, little bird, I loved everything about you. Marry me, dearest Aphra? Be an apothecary's wife?' He could tell, from the way she returned his kisses, that she was by no means averse to the idea.

For Etta, the day had held nothing like the joy of her cousin's, this being the second day away from the royal court and nothing to show for all her efforts. The sumptuous gowns and accessories remained in her chests except for the few she had worn, and her husband had not been able to do much, so far, to further her cause. It was true that he'd made no promises, but her own expectations had not seemed unrealistic, nor could she see any valid reason for the Queen not to recognise her own half-sister when she had a half-cousin in her household. That was all she wanted. Recognition, for she was not as sure as she had once been about living there for part of the time. The things she had witnessed had shocked her and left her feeling unsafe. Worse than that was the way the Queen was monopolising her husband, unashamedly flirting with him and keeping him at court as if there were not enough men, like Lord Robert for instance, to flatter her. That had come as a shock, too. Nor had she ever experienced such pain after discovering that it was love she felt. Love, that all-consuming emotion with neither rhyme nor reason that came without invitation and made one bleed with helpless longing, making one say the wrong things, behave irrationally, pretend a pride that had long since disappeared and feign hate as she had last night. She would not demean herself by asking him what the Queen's attentions meant to him, nor did she think she wanted to hear it. It might be more than she could bear.

So it was a combination of the new and painful love with the more familiar Tudor caprice that prevented her from welcoming her husband as a wife ought on his return home after a busy day at the warehouse dealing with hard-bargaining merchants. He let the strained manner pass without comment, the monosyllabic replies to his queries about her day, the failure to ask him about his and the compressed lips instead of a smile when he related an amusing incident. Aphra and Leon supplied the innocuous conversation, but failed to draw Etta into it, except to say that nothing of interest had happened to her, nor was it likely to.

She excused herself from their company using tiredness as an excuse, hoping and yet fearing that Somerville would follow to disclose the real cause, which she did not know how to explain with courtesy. He did, goading her into a response with an unhelpful, 'All right, let's have it. What's the problem this time?'

Removing her French hood and throwing it aside, she found that the net caul holding her hair had snagged into a tangle that tightened as she wrestled with it. 'This time?' she said. 'I would have thought you'd know by now. Oh, *damn* this thing. Where are my scissors?'

He strode over to her, prising her wrists away.

'Leave it to me. Merciful heavens, woman, you cannot take your temper out on your hair, surely?'

'There's nothing the matter with my temper, my lord. It's my patience that's coming to an end. How much longer must I wait, I wonder?'

'Wait? Wait for what?'

'You *know* for what. What must I do to make her see me? She sees enough of you, heaven knows, so why not me? I shall be old and grey before...'

'Etta, you're being unreasonable. There's nothing you can do about it.'

'There *must* be.' Taking the gold net from him, she threw it aside, rounding on him in a flare-up of frustration that had simmered for days. 'There *has* to be. I won't accept that there's nothing to be done.'

'Listen to me,' he said, angrily. Taking her wrist, he drew her to the end of the bed where the wooden panelling was solid enough to sit on. Roughly, he sat her down, keeping hold of her to make her attend to him. 'Listen. It might take some people months to get as much as a nod from her, so if you're finding a few days too long, I suggest you stop thinking about your close relationship and occupy your time with something more interesting. So far, this business has dominated every waking moment of your life. To what avail? I'll tell you. It's making you into a shrew. We're all supposed to organise our lives around you and this pointless obsession of yours, and *that's* what's so unreasonable. Now, you either learn some patience or forget it. Not even you can make the Queen do what she doesn't want to do.'

Despite the mutinous expression, her eyes brimmed with angry tears, her voice husky with emotion. Forget it? What could he mean? 'It's all very well for you to say that,' she said as tears overflowed on to her cheeks. 'It cannot possibly mean the same to you as it does to me. You knew it before you married me, my lord. And now you're asking me to forget it when you must know how impossible that is. Elizabeth is my flesh and blood. She is half of me. I need her to recognise me. Can't you see that?' She felt the dull thud of the words between them. *She is half of me.* His hand loosed its grip on her and she knew by his silence that he had been hurt. Impetuous words spoken in haste. It was he, not the Queen, who was half of her, yet she would not unsay it.

'What I can see,' he said at last, 'is that your parents did you no favours when they told you of your parentage, for everything you've done since then has been working towards that connection, hasn't it? Everything. Even the marriage you didn't want, unless it was on your terms. It's not an attractive trait, Henrietta. It's making you manipulative. Self-obsessed. And it's a waste of precious time when you could have been putting your mind to more profitable things.'

'What profitable things? How could this connection not profit you, too?'

'That's not why you're pursuing it, is it? You would go ahead anyway, whether it was for our mutual good or not. I never wanted to spend time at court. I could not have made that plainer to you, my lady. It's a den of vice, and greed, and malice. I wanted to spare you that.' He stood up and walked over to the window, withdrawing his comfort so that she felt the coolness along her side.

Tears poured freely down her face while the conflict inside raged out of control, fanned by his rebukes which she knew were not without foundation. She longed to tell him of her love, how her romantic ideals of court life were already becoming sullied and shabby, how she needed him to be near her and how, while she wanted to please him, she found it impossible to let go of this all-consuming ambition, fostered for too long to abandon now.

'There's no need to spare me,' she retorted, pushing the tears away. 'I am a Tudor and I can hold my own in any company. If you cannot protect me, there are others who will. All I need is another day or two at court. I've not come all this way to give up now.'

'"*Pride goeth before a fall*",' he quoted under his breath.

'I shall not fall. When do you return to Whitehall?'

'Tomorrow,' he said.

'Then you'll take me with you?'

For some moments he looked at her without answering, the tearstained cheeks, the pleading eyes, the proud tilt of her head and the cascade of hair rippling over her shoulders. 'On my terms,' he said. 'I have a reputation to maintain.'

It was the first time he had ever mentioned his reputation to her, seeming to emphasise her selfishness. Self-obsessed, he'd called her. 'Yes,' she said. 'I understand that. I'm sorry, but I need another chance. What terms?'

'That you remain with my sister and wait for me there. I believe she wishes to paint your likeness.'

It was better than nothing. 'I will wait for you with Levina,' she said.

'Then I bid you goodnight, my lady. An early start tomorrow.'

'You're not coming to bed?'

He walked to the door without looking back. 'I have work to do,' he said.

The candle flame had burnt down to the last inch before Etta summoned Tilda to help her undress and prepare a rich gown for the next day.

'Mistress Aphra?'

Aphra turned at the sound of her name. She had thought she was the last one to retire. The cat rubbed itself against her skirts, waiting for its last milk of the day. 'My lord? I thought you had gone up.'

'A few words, if I may? Just a concern. A rather delicate matter.' He indicated the bench, inviting her to sit while he placed himself on the opposite side of the table. Pewter dishes had been laid out for the morning's porridge and a single candle burned low.

'I think I know what it is you wish to say, my lord,' Aphra said, seeing an unusual hesitation in Somerville's manner. 'If it's about Master Leon…?'

He raised a hand to stop her, smiling at her concern. 'No, my dear. It has nothing to do with that. Master Leon will always be welcome here as long as you wish it. No, this is about Etta.' He glanced at the door to the stairway. 'I need to know…well…things that I am apparently failing dismally to understand.'

'About Etta?'

'Yes. You've known her all your life, haven't you?'

'Indeed, yes, my lord. We've always been close.'

Now she began to see what this was about. Poor man. It had not been a good start, though anyone could see how he loved her. 'This need of hers to attend court is not helpful, is it?' she said.

The look he gave her was so loaded with relief and gratitude that she wanted to hug him like a mother. His eyes closed as a sigh escaped him, as his hand hovered like a bird's wing over the table. 'I don't want you to think…'

'No, my lord. I don't. But Etta started life with a disadvantage the rest of us don't have, and although she received every loving care from her step-parents, that could never completely replace the emotional tie of her natural ones.' She paused, wondering if she was going too fast, or in the wrong direction.

He nodded. 'Go on,' he said.

'To many…most…people, this would mean very little. She has step-parents, comfort, safety, what else could she possibly need? And now you're wondering why she should be so obsessed with getting to know Elizabeth. What is it all about?'

'Yes,' he whispered. 'That is exactly what I'm wondering, mistress. I'd be grateful if you could shed some light on it for me. I can understand her being curious about court life, especially when Lord and Lady Raemon have always refused to take her there because of the gossip there always is about royal relatives. They have not given her that reason, of course. Her mother is no more than a name to her.'

'And that, my lord, is exactly the problem. Her parents, both of them, are no more than names and the only other relative she knows of for certain is also just a name and always will be unless she can learn more. Do you see?' His nod prompted her to continue. 'She needs to connect with someone of her own flesh and blood, to find out more about herself. She wants to know who she really is. Oh, dear…' she sighed '…this is so difficult to explain. I have my parents and brother to confirm my place in the family and I can compare myself with them on all levels because I am part of them and they of me. You can do the same with your sister and family. Levina has inherited your father's talent as an artist and you have your father's business sense and love of beauty. But Etta will never know what she has inherited unless she can get to know, or simply observe, her only relative. Elizabeth. No one will talk to her about her mother, which has done her no favours because now she believes they can find nothing good to say. So what if she has inherited something of her mother that she doesn't care for? How will she ever know? It's a risk, but she desperately needs to find out, my lord. Now I wonder if the risk might be too great if it means putting in jeopardy what she's just begun to experience.'

'Experience, mistress? What is this experience?'

Aphra paused, looking into his eyes to test the ground before she trespassed. 'I mean *love*, my lord. Her behaviour is often difficult to interpret, but I know her well enough to recognise that she's deeply in love. Yes, with *you*,' she added, noting the incredulity flicker across his comely face. 'Had you doubted it? Oh, do forgive me. I have no right to ask you this, but it's a new experience for her, you see, and, being Etta, there's sure to be some conflict between that and the other business.'

'She's a strong character, Aphra. It's obviously not convenient for her to tell me, yet.'

'Etta may be strong, my lord, but she's vulnerable,

too, and not at all as sure of herself as she appears to be. She wishes to please you above all things and to make you proud of her, but she has not yet found a way to reconcile her body's needs with those of her heart. The problem is hers as well as yours. Have I helped?'

'You have, Aphra. You've answered my questions before I asked them. I cannot begin to thank you.' He stood up, taking her hand and touching the knuckles lightly with his lips. 'Etta must never...'

Placing a finger to her lips, Aphra smiled and shook her head.

Chapter Eight

Had Somerville known of Aphra's plans to visit her mother with Master Leon the next day, he might not have given in to Etta's pleading. Nor could he spare Joseph from the urgent duties for which he was needed in the counting house, for ships could not be held up for lack of paperwork. So he and Etta went to White-hall on the private barge with few hopes of pleasing either of them, his lordship grumbling that he didn't have time for this kind of business when he had more important matters on hand and Etta quietly wondering how she could make better use of this opportunity than sitting still for a portrait. It would, however, provide her with a reason to make several return visits.

Leaving her with his sister Levina, Somerville went off to obey the Queen's command to attend her and, Etta thought, to praise her looks, her skills, her unselfish, un-shrewish, unmanipulative character. A rose without a thorn. Unlike herself whom he found too thorny to make love to. Full of resentment and feigned affability, she sat still for Levina's preliminary sketches until the need arose to relieve herself.

Unfortunately, Levina's close stool had just been removed for emptying so, assuring Levina that her directions were perfectly clear, she reached the foetid
gardrobe without incident. On her way back, the directions seemed not to work in reverse order as well
as they ought, until a window set deep into the wall
suggested that she might find her direction from there.

Outside, down below her, the garden was laid with
plots of spring hellebores and daffodils, hedges, lawns
and pathways along which groups of courtiers strolled,
conversing and laughing. This was obviously one of
the Queen's private gardens where only her most intimate friends were allowed, for there was Lord Robert
Dudley some way behind Elizabeth's unmistakable
figure, her pale red hair and magnificent gown of sil-
ver-threaded grey silk shimmering with gemstones.
A long white veil floated behind her and by her side
walked the tall athletic frame of Lord Somerville, his
head inclined to one side to hear what she was saying. As Etta watched, her husband bent to pick up a
tiny flower from the plot and present it to Elizabeth
with some soft-spoken tribute. Elizabeth threw back
her head and laughed, peeping up at him coquettishly,
like a young lass.

Knowing she ought to stop looking and return to
Levina before more damage was done, Etta found
herself unable to avert her eyes or move away from
the painful scene. Trembling with the insecurity of a
one-sided love, she watched Somerville's tenderness
and chivalry manifest itself in the way it had rarely
done with her, though it did not occur to her that this
might be because she had rarely given him the opportunity, except in bed. Only during those first meetings

with him had she shown him the personal interest the Queen now demonstrated, giving him the time and encouragement to behave as lovers do. Though he had made love to her on several occasions now, there had been no exchanges of loving talk, for the only subject of any importance to Etta so far had been her personal quest and Somerville knew it. Now it was too late, for he had begun to look elsewhere for those tender signs. After last night's harsh words, she had lost him to the one woman who had it in her power to exclude her. Was this what he had tried to warn her of last night when he'd suggested she abandon her quest? Was this what he'd wanted to spare her from? The humiliation of losing him after only a few weeks of marriage?

The Queen half-turned to someone behind her, two women, one of whom bulged in front with the heavy weight of an unborn child. She staggered against her friend while speaking to the Queen, clearly asking permission to withdraw, turning again into her friend's arms as her mistress shook her head in irritation, waving her away and resuming her walk with Lord Somerville. Behind them on the path, the poor woman slumped through the supporting arms to the ground and was quickly surrounded by a group who lifted and carried her away, leaving a pool of water to spread like a dark stain into the gravel. Somerville halted and looked back, but the Queen slipped a hand through his arm and walked on, insisting on his company, oblivious to the tragedy.

With a sob, Etta turned from the window to run down the passageway, her distress compressing her lungs and hurting her throat. Doors lined the next section, all with small crests painted on, like Levina's.

Which one was hers? Half-blinded by prickling tears, she flung open one of the doors, realising too late that this was not Levina's room, that the two naked figures on the tangled bedding were not on Levina's bed, either. Pale red hair streamed like silk over the side nearest the door and, as the young man raised his head to look at the intruder, the woman saw her upside-down, her pale eyes prominent with fright.

By coincidence, Etta had dressed that day in a pale grey silk threaded with silver in a style so like the Queen's that, at first glance—and an upside-down one at that—she could easily have been mistaken for Elizabeth. Her French hood was also of the same silk with a crescent-shaped billament studded with gems that she had sewn herself, with a softly transparent silk veil to drape over her shoulders. So when the unknown young man leapt up with a yelp and scrambled to his knees, gabbling words that included 'Your Majesty', the redhead beneath him rolled over to see if he was correct and, finding that he was very much mistaken, screamed a volley of abuse at the fast-closing door.

Etta could hardly believe that such words could be a part of Lady Catherine Grey's vocabulary but, she thought, perhaps that was what living in this dreadful place did for one.

Shaking and bewildered, Etta hastened to turn yet another corner where more crests on doors revealed initials, too. Then, to her great relief, one of the doors opened, the occupant looking up and down the passageway, searching for her guest. 'Etta, my dear, there you are. Come, I was getting worried about you. Why, what on earth is the matter?'

'Lost,' Etta gasped. 'Again.'

Her distress had to be explained but, since there were now multiple reasons for it, Etta chose the last one although it was in fact the least of them to matter. It came as no great surprise to Levina, however. 'That would be young Hertford,' she said, handing Etta a beaker of ale. She adjusted a cushion behind her. 'There now, my dear, don't let it bother you. That kind of thing goes on all the time at court.'

'Who is Hertford?' Etta said. 'I thought Lady Catherine was still in love with her former husband.' The beaker shook.

'No, dear. The Earl of Hertford is the late Jane Seymour's brother. His father had hoped to marry him to Lady Catherine's sister, the one who was executed, but he'd better not be seeking to ally himself with the Grey family. Elizabeth would never allow that. Too many royal connections, you see. They'd be seen as a threat to the throne. She's a foolish child to risk pregnancy. Very foolish.'

And too many names, Etta thought, that I shall never remember. Of all people she would rather not have encountered in that way, Lady Catherine was probably the most dangerous, and only time would tell what their next meeting would be like. But of far more importance was what she had seen of the intimacy between Elizabeth and Lord Somerville that had not only shocked her, but had also made her see more clearly than ever how her recognition of love had come too late. Elizabeth was young and feminine, attractive, intelligent, and she could summon any man to her side to idolise her, as they did. She was the glorious one, never to be scolded as she herself had been, never to be told that she was manipulative or self-obsessed. Nor would anyone ever tell her that her lack of compassion was an unattractive trait. If that was an example of the Tudor magnetism then she, Etta, had better start to disclaim it rather than boast of it, for never would she have ignored a woman in that terrible plight as Elizabeth had done. Never. And imagine what might have happened if she too had found herself in that poor woman's situation with Elizabeth ignoring her distress. What an awful coldness. Her heart must be made of steel.

The events of the morning, and those of the previous days too, had begun to shake the foundations of Etta's determination to be a part of the Queen's court or to know any more about her. How could she respect and love a woman whose heart was impervious to kindness, who stole women's husbands and drove a wedge between them? Had Somerville been right? Should she leave now and go home? Or should she stay and fight, and play the woman at her own game?

In one way, the question was answered for her when Somerville arrived to say that the Queen had told him he must stay. It was well after dark and Levina had gone down to the great hall for supper but, since no provision was made for the wives of courtiers, Etta had been obliged to stay in the room and dine on a few biscuits and an apple. Alone.

'Alone?' Somerville said, frowning.

'As you see,' said Etta. 'You dined with the Queen, I take it?'

'No. She eats in the Privy Chamber when she feels like it. I came to…'

'To tell me that you have to stay with her. Yes, no surprise there, then.'

He sighed, squatting on his sister's drawing stool and flipping back the loose panels at the base of his doublet. 'Etta, the choice is not mine, I can assure you. If she wants to keep me here, there's little I can do about it. But I won't have you staying in here alone all evening while Levina is away and I'm not sending you home on your own, either. I shall take you with me. Can you dance in that gown?'

She thought how handsome he looked in his tawny brocade suit, the gold edgings and aiglets, the creamy-white frill around his neck just catching his hair at the back. The thought that she might have lost him was like a dagger twisting in her heart, but she would not be cowed. She would fight on and she would never behave as the Queen had done. She thought of the dances she and Aphra had learnt, thinking that by now they would surely have been in the Queen's favour, dancing every night and sharing her days. She thought of the gowns they'd had made for evenings of dancing, crusted with embroidery and gemstones, slippers of satin and velvet, the fans and headdresses. 'Yes,' she said, 'I can dance in anything. But don't let me spoil your evening, my lord. I shall find companions, I'm sure, and if you can flirt with Elizabeth, then you'll surely not object to me following suit. Discreetly, of course.'

His look held none of the warmth she craved. 'Don't play this silly game with me, Etta. You know the circumstances. You wanted to be here, not me. You promised me, once, that you would do nothing to embarrass me. I expect you to keep that promise.'

'What a pity you didn't make a similar promise to me, my lord.' She stood up, smoothing down the creases in the silvery silk, adjusting her French hood and tucking away a strand of red hair. 'There, that's the best I can do at such short notice. Shall we go and sing for our suppers? Have you played the lute to her yet, as you once did with me?' He did not answer her at once, but wrote something hastily on a scrap of paper that lay on Levina's work table, pushing it between the handles of her paintbrushes.

'What's the note about?' Etta said. 'Information, is it?'

'Yes,' he said, knowing she would not believe him. 'And the situation is bad enough without your sarcasm, Etta. Come, let's go.'

His warm fingers enclosed hers, leading her out of the stuffy room and, for the time it took them to walk in silence towards the sound of music, Etta could almost pretend that nothing had come between them to cause her such unbelievable heartache. She didn't know how she would get through the next few hours of seeing him smile at Elizabeth, the Queen, the way she wanted him to smile at her.

The sounds of music and laughter grew louder as they passed through a series of anterooms towards the magnificent hall where a blaze of light and colour engulfed them. Every surface sang with a cacophony of rich pattern, silks shot through with metal threads, lace, gems flashing against tapestried walls, feathered fans, satins and rich brocades, making Etta blink with an overload of beauty. The Queen's ladies sailed through the crowded hall like rich galleons festooned with floating scarves and decked out in a riot of brilliance while the men, no less gaudy, cavorted round them, posing and posturing for their attention. Etta felt the lure of the glamour through the soles of her feet as they fidgeted to the rhythm of tabors and reedy pipes, her skirts already swaying to the tripping dance steps, although her eyes were now more critical than they had been before, wary and watchful, ready to be disappointed again by some behaviour of the Queen's.

Somerville's arm tightened on her hand, preventing her escape. She looked up at him impatiently and saw him mouthing words intended only for her to hear. But the noise was too great and, instead of asking him to repeat it, she assumed it would be a warning of some kind, reminding her how he had consistently thrown doubts in her way. He wanted a family. He did not want a life at court. The Queen's favour could not be relied on, and so on. Now, due to her persistence, it could happen and she was no longer certain she wanted it.

The crowd was thick and the two of them were caught up in the surge of bodies to the end of the hall where Elizabeth was enthroned on a huge velvet chair surrounded by her maids, while Etta felt the restraint of her husband's arm acting like a brake on her progress. 'Not yet, Etta!' he said into her ear. 'We must wait for the Queen's invitation.' But it was too late. The musicians and dancers finished on a long note and the bending bodies parted to make a space around Etta and her husband. It was then that she wished she'd had a chance to change. The Queen's day gown had been exchanged for an extravagant creation of shining white satin embroidered with coloured silks and gold thread, with pearls and a forepart encrusted with shimmering spangles. In her hair were more pearls and feathers in an arc that framed her face, emphasising her affinity with Diana, goddess of the moon. Unfortunately, the magnificence also emphasised the ordinariness of Etta's silver-grey silk, creased after a day's wear, her shoes no longer clean, her hanging purse and fan unsuitable for evening wear.

Her curtsy to the Queen was graceful, her head bowed in deep reverence, her ears straining to catch any words of greeting. But the Queen's words of greeting were directed at Somerville, not Etta, and it was his hand that raised her up while he repeated the words she had missed, in her impatience. 'You are to stay in the hall until I come for you,' he whispered. 'Walk backwards three steps and curtsy.'

Unable to believe that she was being overlooked yet again, she sought the Queen's face for confirmation and saw the steely dark gaze boring through her as if Etta's every intention was being understood and put in its place. *I will accept you when I am ready,* the Queen was saying through her eyes, *and not a moment before. Do not presume.*

A slight tug on her arm reminded her what she must do and there, before the glittering court, she was forced to accept the royal rejection, modified only by Somerville's light kiss upon her knuckles. She would not allow her disappointment to show, smiling at those nearest her and feeling some relief when her hand was taken by Lord Robert Dudley, drawing her away to one side as though he could sense her humiliation at the Queen's public dismissal. She watched her husband's departure in response to the Queen's imperious summons, forcing her face not to betray her distress. In a moment, taking hold of herself, she decided to make the best of what was on offer, the company, the admiring faces, the music and dance, entertainments, and so far none of the questionable behaviour she had witnessed in other parts of the palace. And if Lord Robert wished her to stay by his side, then so much the better. Somerville could hardly complain that she was being taken care of by the Queen's favourite, surely?

He needed no encouragement. Leading her into the next dance, Lord Robert drew all eyes towards him and his newest partner who resembled the Queen so closely that, at times, it was difficult to tell that it was not her. Well aware that she was attracting so much attention, Etta danced like a goddess, concentrating on every movement with her brilliant partner, smiling into his eyes and recognising the unmistakable desire. He appeared not to conceal his admiration and she saw no reason not to take full advantage of this warm regard after the recent husbandly disapproval. But while she smiled and appeared to bask in this attention, in the strong hold of his hands and the assuredness of his directions, she knew in her heart, rebellious as it was, that she would never want this man as a lover, that the only man to make her heart skip a beat was the one now sitting close to Elizabeth, with eyes only for his Queen. It took all her efforts to steel herself against the painful scene, talking merrily to those ladies who came to make her acquaintance and to those men who remarked on her likeness to the Queen and to ask how this came about. One of those men was the bold ill-mannered courtier who had grabbed at her in the passageway only days before. Now, he was all false smiles, leaving her with the bitter taste of duplicity about which both Hoby and Somerville had warned her. And to her relief, Stephen Hoby was nowhere to be seen. There would be no need for her to mention him to Lord Robert.

At the sound of her name, she turned to find that Lady Catherine Grey was about to show everyone in the group how well she was acquainted with Etta. 'Yes, do tell us, Lady Somerville, the reason for your resemblance to Her Majesty? Everyone knows of my own relationship, but we're all dying to know about your beloved lady mother, aren't we, ladies? Was she one of many? Or don't you know?'

Etta's heart gave a lurch, for the woman's tone implied more trouble. But before Etta could reiterate what she had already said on the subject, Lady Catherine took her by the shoulders as if to kiss both cheeks, taking the opportunity to whisper a warning in her ear. 'Don't you dare speak about what you saw.' Her smile at such close quarters was acid-sweet, her pale eyes threatening.

Never having been one to accept intimidation without a fight, Etta turned her full attention to Lady Catherine, turning defence into a challenge. 'First, my lady,' she said, 'perhaps you can tell me who it was informed the Queen's fool that my wedding was a shabby affair, due to my lord's stinginess? Since I cannot remember speaking about my wedding day to anyone except yourself and Lord Robert, perhaps you can suggest the origin of such wicked lies?'

To those who watched, it looked like twin sisters sparring, one of them stronger, bolder and lovelier than the other. Obviously not expecting this, Lady Catherine braved it out as best she could. 'I remember nothing of any talk about your wedding,' she said. 'Your memory is at fault, my lady.'

'And so is yours, dear sister-in-law,' said Lord Robert. 'I was there.'

'I don't remember. Anyway,' she said, looking round for support, 'what does it matter? Who knows how Jack Grene gets to know things?'

'I do so agree with you, Lady Catherine,' Etta said, keeping her smile fixed in position, 'who knows how Jack Grene gets to know *anything*? He thrives on scandal, doesn't he, and if it's not scandalous, he'll make it so, for laughs. Better be careful what we tell him then, hadn't we?' She saw how accurately she had scored by the expression of fear in the woman's eyes, yet it was too soon for Etta to lower her guard when Lady Catherine came back for another attack, like a dog with a favourite bone.

'So are you going to tell us about your mother, Lady Somerville? There must be some ladies here who remember her well, not to mention the men. Who was she, exactly? Did she keep the King's attention for long, or was it one of those brief affairs he had while his dear wife was expecting the heir to the throne?'

In all her years, it had never been a pressing concern of Etta's to know the details of her mother's relationship with King Henry VIII whose need to take mistresses during his wives' pregnancies was both well known and accepted, with varying degrees of patience from the wives in question. It was more important to Etta to know what kind of woman her mother was, rather than the King's demands on her. That was something she might not have had much choice about. Nor could she see any reason to discuss the subject with this troublemaking woman. As if by divine intervention, she caught the eye of a man threading his way through the crowded room to be at her side, saving her from a difficult situation which she now realised she was ill equipped to manage. 'Uncle Elion! What a delight. Have you come to ask me to dance?' she called.

'Indeed I have, my niece. My lord. My lady.' Sir Elion D'Arvall bowed to Lord Robert and Lady Catherine, the epitome of a diplomat. Working with Lord William Cecil provided him with every contact and his dislike of the malicious Catherine Grey was unconcealed when he linked arms with Lord Robert and Etta and walked away from her. 'That one would get her own mother into trouble, if she could,' he said. 'Is that not so, my lord?' he said.

'Indeed it is, Sir Elion. My advice would be to keep well clear of her.'

They found a space beside a tapestry showing Daniel in the lions' den and, although its images were too large for Etta to see, the subject seemed appropriate. At that moment, she felt as if things were sliding out of her control. 'So why would she bring up the subject of my mother, Uncle Elion? Is she implying some kind of trouble there?'

Standing between the two men, she could not avoid seeing the glance that passed between them. 'No,' Sir Elion replied, 'but that won't prevent her inventing some. I'm afraid the royal court is like that, Etta my dear. Heaven knows, if there's no scandal to report, people will exercise their imaginations. Resembling the Queen as you do, I think you may have to expect it.'

Lord Robert nodded in agreement but stayed beside her as, one after another, soloists kept them entertained with love songs to the accompaniment of the lute. Their messages of unrequited love were always aimed at Elizabeth while she lapped up the sentiments like a cat with cream. All who watched and listened knew it to be a convention that she herself encouraged, but that did not make it easier for Etta when Somerville took the lute and sang a haunting melody about one who would not speak her love for him. His powerfully sweet baritone won the loudest applause of the evening, but there were tears in Etta's eyes, for it seemed to her like yet another sign that she had lost him.

Sir Elion noticed her distress. 'Don't take it seriously, Etta,' he said, placing an arm around her shoulders. 'I don't think you'll last long in this place if you take these things at face value. Is it time you went home?'

Etta nodded. She would not be the Queen's friend tonight, or indeed any other.

'Then leave it to me.' Giving her a quick squeeze, he left her in the care of Lord Robert who, although more hardened than she to the ways of the royal court, still felt keenly the temporary loss of the woman to whom his life was dedicated. Having few scruples about using others for his own ends, his close attentions to Etta, whose resemblance to that woman was so convenient, began to overstep the mark when he manoeuvred her into a shadowy alcove, laid a hand on her throat and tipped her chin up towards his face. For her, the day had been disastrous from the start and, even when she had thought to salvage her scheme by joining in the Queen's entertainments, unkindness had followed her, adding to the rejection she had suffered.

Never had she felt so in need of some small show of comfort after Uncle Elion's kindly meant warning that this place was not what she had thought. But Lord Robert was not the man she wanted. 'So beautiful,' he was whispering. 'If you were mine, lady, I would not bring you here.'

Placing a hand on his cheek, she turned him away from her, ducking her head out of range. 'And I ought not to have come,' she said. 'But thank you for your concern, my lord.' Just in time, they pulled apart to see past the backs of the sparkling crowd to where the Queen had risen from her chair. Courtiers sank to one knee until she and her ladies had disappeared, then rose like a huge sea of bright colour, the tall figures of Somerville and Sir Elion fording their way through it to reach the back of the room. 'My lord,' said Sir Elion to Lord Robert, 'Her Majesty commands your presence.'

The looks exchanged between Lord Robert and Somerville spoke volumes for anyone understanding the code. Aware of each other's helplessness under the Queen's manipulating thumb, the rivalry between them was tempered by some sympathy, each acknowledging the other's bow with a relief that they were now able to resume their rightful roles. Even so, as the Queen's favourite kissed Etta's knuckles, Somerville could detect the remains of a tear upon her lashes. 'What's he been up to?' he said as soon as he was able.

Etta would have retorted in the same tone, something critical and unhelpful, but Sir Elion saw it coming and interrupted them both. 'Keeping your wife from the wolves, lad. Now, take her home. She needs a hide thicker than an elephant to spend any more time here. I'll walk with you to the jetty.'

Calling at Levina's room to pick up their cloaks and say their farewells, Levina handed her brother a slip of paper which he quickly pushed into the front of his doublet, then the three of them went in silence to the water stairs where the barge waited, bobbing gently on a dark incoming tide. Etta and her uncle hugged, sympathy and darkness enclosing them, but she did not see her husband pass the slip of paper to Sir Elion. In the barge, Somerville tucked a rug around her knees as they pulled into the middle of the river where a stiff March breeze made Etta gasp, but as he peered more closely, he saw that her shoulders were shaking with sobs. Saying nothing, he drew her close to him and held her in his arms, rocking to the gentle sway of the barge as the men pulled hard against the current.

For many reasons, this was not the time for an inquest into what went wrong. Again. Etta was too exhausted to eat and the others had long since taken to their beds so, like two weary pilgrims, they went straight to bed without any expectations of physical contact when so much rancour lay unspoken between them. But all it took was for Somerville to reach out a hand towards her, touching her fingers as she lay rigidly on her back and whispering her name, 'Etta', for her to turn to him, seeking the bliss of his embrace. There was too much to say, so they said nothing, finding all they needed in the warmth of naked flesh and gentling kisses, and in the wonderment of their bodies' needs.

Lethargically, they lay on their sides to entwine and seek each other in a manner they'd not tried before, thinking it might be uncomfortable. But it was not. It was the tenderest act that seemed to console and reassure them, after a day of terrible doubts, that they still had need of each other. Even when the climax surged like a breaker along the shores of their sleepy bodies, they clung and nestled into each other like lost children, satisfying their hunger before all else. And with her lips on the rhythmic pulse at the base of his throat, Etta was almost asleep before he had withdrawn from her.

After all her husband's reservations, warnings and precautions, and after last night's total failure to make any dent in the Queen's armour, Etta had to acknowledge that it was never going to happen under her direction, only under the Queen's. Everything that could have been done had been and now even discussion about future tactics seemed pointless in light of the royal rebuff. Somerville himself had come to the same conclusion by leaving for the Steelyard before Etta was dressed, apparently seeing nothing to be gained by going over the same ground again or enquiring too closely into what had gone wrong. The Queen had kept him by her side, exercising her rights as his sovereign, but ignoring any womanly feelings of compassion. She was young, unmarried and powerful. She had waited twenty-five long and sometimes frightening years to come so far and the taste of power and success was still with her. She would choose her friends very carefully, none of whom would be allowed to outshine her. Not even a half-sister. Especially not a half-sister of such beauty. Somerville knew this, but so far had been unable to convince Etta, whose Tudor blood had imbued her with a rare determination.

In some ways, Etta was relieved to avoid Somerville's questions, for she did not want to tell him how she had seen him with the Queen. Her emotions were too painful to describe and she was not sure she could bear to hear him make light of it, as he surely would. Nor did she want to admit that, by following her dream, she had opened Pandora's Box, the latest affliction being the insinuating questions about her mother. Now she had to know. She could only think it was the self-obsession Somerville had accused her of which had prevented her finding out before.

Breaking her fast with Aphra and Leon over a plate of ham, cheese and warm bread, Etta heard the latest gossip to come from Aunt Maeve, Aphra's mother, particularly that their old grandmother, who had been unwell, had recovered enough to return to her own cosy dower house at D'Arvall Hall. Leon was well aware that he had been vetted and approved, and could now tell his good friends at the Sign of the Bridge that he and Aphra would eventually marry when he had been home to Italy to ask for his parents' blessing. In the midst of her own sadness, Etta managed to summon up a smile of genuine happiness for them.

'The other news,' Aphra said, 'is that your parents are back in London.'

Of all things, that was exactly what Etta needed to hear. 'When?' she squeaked, hugging her cousin.

'Yesterday, I believe. Why, love? What is it? Have you missed them?'

Etta nodded and wiped her eyes. 'I need to see them,' she said.

'So let's go. We can go today, unless you're going…'

'No, I doubt if I'll be going to Whitehall again, Aphie.'

'Not ever? What's happened? Oh, dear, I ought to have been with you. Tell me, love.'

Including the Queen's apparent conquest of her husband, Etta told her how the day had gone from bad to worse, ending with the unpleasantness of Lady Catherine Grey and the disturbing questions about her own mother, which must be explained. 'My mother and father will know,' Etta said. 'Father was married to her once, remember.'

'Yes, so that you would take your stepfather's name. That's not unusual,' Aphra said. 'Queen Anne Boleyn's sister did the same when she was the King's mistress and she was a well-loved lady. Her daughter is one of the Queen's ladies. So if *your* mother had been related to Elizabeth, you might have had more success. Never mind. We can find out a bit more than we know already.'

They were not to know, when they set off that morning to visit Tyburn House, that the 'bit more' was hardly enough to raise Etta's hopes of being in possession of all the facts, for Lady Virginia had never met the lady, and Lord Jon was infuriatingly hazy about Etta's mother except to say why he married her.

They sat together by an open window overlooking the knot garden with the orchard beyond, where daffodils danced in the bright sunshine and white doves sat in rows on the mossy wall. Lord Jon laid a hand over his wife's as he raked up old history that he had tried, during his happy marriage to Lady Virginia, to forget. 'For money,' he said, looking out at the colourful scene. 'That's the top and bottom of it. I needed money to keep my estate going when my father died in France. Magdalen had plenty of it and she needed a titled husband. So that was it, really. Mutual benefits.'

Sensing that no more details were forthcoming, Lady Virginia filled in some of the missing bits. 'Magdalen Osborn was one of Queen Jane Seymour's ladies,' she said.

'So is that when the King fell in love with her?' said Etta, thinking more of the romance than the lust.

'Probably,' said her mother. 'I think it was likely he took her as his mistress when Queen Jane was pregnant, because Magdalen died in childbirth three months after Jane.'

'How very sad,' said Aphra. 'So the King lost both his beloved wife and his mistress within months of each other.'

'But just think,' said Etta, not in the least abashed by such a tragedy, 'if my mother had lived, she might have become the next queen. Now there's a thought.'

Lord Jon shifted his position, clearly uncomfortable with the idea. 'Yes,' he said, slowly, 'but she was married to me, you see. The King's natural inclination to make use of people never failed him. Anyway, your mother would not have made a good queen, love.'

'Why, Father?'

Having discovered that he could not answer her, Lord Jon turned to his wife for help. 'She was a very beautiful woman, Etta,' said Lady Virginia, 'but perhaps a little too self-centred to make the best queen. I'm sure she would have adored you, but I'm glad we were given the chance to make you ours.'

'Didn't her parents offer to adopt me?' said Etta.

'No,' Lord Jon said. 'Sadly, they refused to have anything to do with their daughter when she became the King's mistress. They didn't approve of that kind of arrangement, although fortunately for me that didn't affect her wealth inherited from her grandparents. So I decided to keep you with me at Lea Magna and hire a staff to care for you while I set about finding a lady to marry who would love you as her own.' His smile at his wife was filled with adoration.

'And he did,' said her mother. 'You were two years old when I became your stepmother.' Almost without realising it, Lady Virginia steered the questions and answers more towards Etta and themselves than Magdalen Osborn, which might have been difficult for them to answer truthfully other than to say that she was very beautiful, wealthy, and sought after, the King's mistress and full of life. 'Now,' said Lady Virginia, 'tell us about your expeditions to Whitehall. Have you spoken with the Queen yet?' She saw how her stepdaughter reached for Aphra's hand as if for comfort and guessed immediately by the pain in Etta's eyes that all was not as well as they'd hoped.

Frankly, Etta told them about what had happened, with no more result than that the Queen was driving a wedge between her and her new husband and that the once rosy picture of the royal court had become distinctly tarnished.

'But surely, Etta,' said Lady Virginia, 'you cannot believe Lord Somerville is paying her any more attention than he's obliged to? All men have to pay her compliments. It's what she thrives on. You cannot take this kind of flirting too seriously?'

Usually, Etta kept her tears well under control, but now they rose to the surface like a hot spring, shaking her frame with sobs that interrupted every attempt to explain. It was not only that she had failed in her quest for recognition but that, even after only a few weeks, she had not managed to hold on to her husband's allegiance. That, for a beautiful and intelligent woman, was more humiliating than any other factor, brought home to her fully now as she spoke it out loud to her parents. She saw no reason to mention the physical side, for she had naively believed from the beginning of her relationship with Somerville that love was not an essential ingredient for lovemaking to be pleasurable. Last night, half-asleep, they had made love again, deriving from the act the physical commitment they had been deprived of during the day, Etta supposing that this was what any man would do with any woman who lay naked in his arms, while she wanted him and no other.

'So you love him, then?' said her father, leaning on his knees to look at her. From him, the question came as a shock, although the weeping had begun to free thoughts suppressed for too long.

'Yes,' she croaked. 'Yes…I do…I do.'

'Does he know, dear?' her mother said.

'I don't…don't suppose so. We started off on the wrong foot, you see.'

'That may be,' said Lord Jon, 'but you risk staying on the wrong foot unless you tell him what he needs to know. It's up to you, Etta, to put things right between you. You were the one to insist on following up your Tudor relationship. You were the one to make a fuss about marrying him because he was our choice and now you make use of him to get you to court. So your plan has miscarried. So who's to blame for that?'

'Jon, dear,' said his wife. 'That's a little unfair, isn't it? Etta's not to blame.'

'Then who is? Elizabeth fancies every personable male she sees, just as her father fancied every personable female. It's up to the wives to keep them out of her clutches, in my view, by every means they know. It's too late for Dudley's poor wife. She lost her husband years ago. But you don't have to, Etta. Somerville was determined to have you.'

'Yes, Father,' Etta replied, hotly. 'So much so that he deceived me, taking away any choice I might have had.'

'For pity's sake, lass! Open your eyes. When a man will go so far to get the woman he wants, doesn't that say something to you? But listen to me, Etta,' he said more gently, 'a man like Somerville has his pride, too. You don't imagine he wasn't affected by all that fuss you made, do you, especially when he thought you were keen on him? So do you really expect him to speak of his love for you before *you* tell him how you love *him* and how much you want to make up for not allowing him the kind of wedding he wanted?'

'He's never said he wanted…'

'No, nor will he unless he hears it from you first. What means most to you, your marriage, or Elizabeth? You're going to have to choose before it's too late.'

'Jon, I think you're being a little harsh. I'm sure it's not too late. Is it, Etta?'

'He said he didn't care about having a big wedding,' she said, sadly.

'Well, he would, wouldn't he?' said her father. 'But

think about it. He's probably London's most successful mercer, an alderman in his Company, well respected and honest. Think of all his friends who'd like to have celebrated with him. Not to mention our own family. He's too proud to show you his disappointment, but believe me, he'd enjoy showing off on his wedding day just as much as we all do.'

'I only said it out of pique. I thought he was trying to please me.'

Lord Jon leaned back, groaning softly as he glanced up at the raftered ceiling. 'You've a lot to learn about men, my lass. Only a Tudor could have come to that conclusion.'

The comment, although hitting the target, was funny enough to bring huffs of laughter to their lips and for Lady Virginia to place an arm around her step-daughter's shoulders. 'Reading a man's mind is an art,' she said, smiling. 'You'll get the hang of it, eventually. Have you given up entirely on your royal ambition?'

Etta shrugged. 'I don't fancy returning to White-hall,' she said.

'Well, I think you might be having your mind made up for you, Etta,' said her father. 'It would be best for you and Somerville if the Queen and her court packed up and left.'

'Oh?' said Lady Virginia. 'Do you know some-thing I don't know?'

Straight-faced, Lord Jon looked gravely at his lovely wife. 'Oh, I doubt that, dear heart. But I heard yesterday from your brother George at the Wardrobe that the court moves to Richmond Palace within the next three days. There now, that might help to solve the problem, don't you think?'

Fortunately, they did not ask Etta what she thought about the royal move for, if they had, she would have been too confused to give a sensible answer. Richmond Palace was only a short horse ride away from Mortlake Manor, and it therefore remained to be seen which of them, she or her husband, would suggest returning to Mortlake first.

Chapter Nine

There was much for Etta to ponder on the way home to busy Cheapside, her parents having unwittingly pointed out failings in her dealings with her lord that she knew to be true and impossible to excuse. She had not mentioned his desire for a family, for there she did not have a leg to stand on, knowing how they would agree that her self-centredness was getting in the way of her duty. The same trait in her mother had, apparently, stood in the way of her duty to her husband, too. And that was the second time she'd heard the fault mentioned recently. As for the Tudor trait of making use of people, that had struck an ill-sounding chord that she resented, for why would not any man or woman make use of a spouse's connections? Everyone did that, surely? But there was more than that in her father's uncompromising words about it being up to her to put matters right between them and the more she thought on it, the more she believed he did not understand how difficult that would be. A simple declaration of her love might already be too late. Although Somerville could make love to her and not to the Queen, the very fact that she looked like Elizabeth might, for all she knew, be one of the reasons why he still wanted her in his bed. The thought was not an attractive one and yet, if that was what it took to keep him close to her, then so be it. As her stepfather had said, who was to blame for that?

She and Aphra had stayed at Tyburn House for a light midday meal and had taken a wherry home, stopping for some shopping on the way through Cheapside, then going upstairs to change before supper. Etta was still in her chemise as her husband came into the bedchamber with all the dust of a day's work on him, taking in the scene with one glance. 'Ask Tilda to leave us,' he said, holding the door open. The maid slipped out.

'What is it?' said Etta. 'Is something wrong?' She held her hands over her breasts to prevent the chemise slipping off her shoulders. A thrill of excitement passed through her as she saw the look of desire in his eyes, his urgent need for her.

'No,' he whispered, reaching her in one stride. 'Nothing's wrong.' He took her hands away and watched as the chemise slid over her curves to make a pool around her feet, lazily inspecting the exquisite fullness tipped with rose-pink that firmed under his gaze, invitingly. For a few moments, his inspection continued over her belly and breasts and then, as if he was unable to bear the suspense, he let go of her hands and pulled her towards him in an embrace that crushed her skin against the metal fastenings of his doublet.

If Etta suspected that he might be imagining himself making love to Elizabeth, she gave no sign of it for her need was as great as his and no amount of pride would stand in the way. Not this time. Not ever. So she gave in to the demands of his hands and mouth as they took their fill of every contact, helping him to untie the points of his hose without taking her lips away from his. She felt the surge of white-hot desire drive them on, closer and closer until, somehow, she knew the weightlessness of being carried, then the thrilling softness of his bulk pressing her into their bed, opening her to him like a flower in the sun. Suddenly, they were striving, rhythmically, to reach further with each thrust, to know again the all-consuming passion of owning and being owned, of giving and taking. Etta felt his hand in the wild red tangle of her hair, heard him whisper endearments that she took for herself, refusing to share them with the woman who threatened her happiness. 'Ah, beautiful, red-haired, wild creature. What spell have you cast on me that I can think of nothing but you all day?' His lips took over from the words, scattering kisses into her hair, on her neck, and on the hand that came to touch his face. The scent of him in her nostrils was his alone. Like a potent drug.

Unlike last night's gentle coupling, this was the expression of a day-long desire held tightly in check by a vigorous man in the prime of his life, now released in a blinding fervour of passion. Predictably, the pinnacle was reached too soon as they came together for the final explosion, crying out with the intensity of sensation, his magnificent body, still clothed, straining with the effort of making it last for one more second.

They lay together, recovering, reeling from a surfeit of excitement while his hand played over the soft undulations of her body. He saw the marks on her breast caused by the sharp aiglets fastening his doublet and was instantly apologetic. 'Forgive me, sweetheart. I could not wait. Are you hurt much?'

Inside, she wanted to say, *we are hurting each other.* 'It's nothing,' she said.

Later, as they dressed for supper, she told him about her visit. 'My parents suggested it was time for me to stop,' she said, watching Tilda's fingers nimbly pin up her hair.

He came to sit on the chest at the end of the bed from where he could see her face in the mirror. 'Stop what?' he said.

'Going to Whitehall. Seeking the Queen's approval. They don't see it happening. Do you?'

'I never have, Etta. But the choice is for you to make.'

'I've made it. I'm wasting my time there.'

Through the mirror their eyes met, querying, searching for another meaning. 'You're sure? After all the preparations? The costumes, the dancing lessons…'

'Were a waste of money, weren't they?'

'No, that kind of thing is never a waste of money, but your expectations of their value were high, weren't they? Perhaps a little too high. Do you want to return to Mortlake?'

As the last pin went into her hair, she turned to face him, yearning for him to tell her that all her fears were groundless, even before she spoke of them. 'So you know the Queen and court are to move to Richmond, my lord?' she said, attempting to keep any hint of accusation out of the tone. *Please say you didn't know.*

'Yes, I knew that. I've known it for a few weeks. They'll be back in London again by Easter.'

'So is that why you suggested we move back to Mortlake? To be near her?'

She saw the cloud of pain pass over his eyes. 'No, Etta,' he said, gently. 'I didn't suggest we both move back there. It's you who ought to go. I have business here in London that I must attend to, personally. I could return to Mortlake on the tide each evening and be home in time for supper, but I'd be quite happy for you and Aphra to be there. You could ride and tend the gardens, and do all the things you can't do here. Summer's on the way. Things are starting to grow.'

There was something in the way he said that which seemed to match his detailed scrutiny of her breasts and belly before they made love, making Etta wonder if the idea of 'growing things' was the reason behind it. Now, it didn't seem to matter to her any more that she might become pregnant. In fact, the thought of bearing Nic's child was a deeply attractive one. 'So it would not be inconvenient for you?' she said.

'I'm quite used to it. I've been doing it for years. That's why I have my own barge.'

'Why does the Queen want to be at Richmond, suddenly?'

'It's not sudden. She wants to do some hawking, I believe. She might even invite you to join her if she knows you're at Mortlake. Would you like that? Shall I buy you a gerfalcon of your own? I keep my falcons there already, but I've not had much chance to use them. There's plenty of heron there.'

It sounded all so reasonable, so sensible for her to distance herself from a place that, so far, had not given her a single day either of enjoyment or satisfaction. On the contrary, she had come away from Whitehall frustrated, humiliated, unfed and harassed, ignored by the one for whom she'd made all the effort and, even worse, looked like losing her husband to her. More recently had come those unkind hints from Lady Catherine Grey about her mother who, as mistress of her royal father, would inevitably have been the target for slander and innuendo, even in her lifetime. If Lady Catherine had mud to sling in her direction, then she, Etta, did not want to hear it. Her parents were right. While she was still desirable in his eyes, for whatever reason, she had better try to repair the damage which had been, she admitted, of her own making. The Tudors were not, it seemed, the easiest people to live with. 'Yes,' she said, looking down at her hands, 'I would like a gerfalcon of my own. Could we buy one for Aphra, too?'

He leaned towards her, taking her face between his hands and kissing her on the lips more gently than half an hour ago. 'Of course. That's the least we can do if we're to take her away from her Master Leon so soon.'

Her eyes lifted to his in surprise. 'You've noticed?'

'Oh, yes,' he said. 'There's not much that escapes my notice, sweetheart. They make a perfect couple, don't they?'

She nodded, envying her cousin and her pleasant uncomplicated young man the kind of easygoing relationship without the storms that had beset her and this noble intelligent creature, for whom her love was growing day by day. This would be, she knew, a good time to tell him so, while he was doing his utmost to soothe her fears about the Queen's romantic intentions. There were, however, certain things she found it hard to dismiss from her mind, of which the decision to spend his days in London while she was at Mortlake was one. What about the furtive messages passing between him and his sister? Why could he not have shared this with her? Did it have something to do with him staying in London, or was she making something out of nothing?

He kept her face between his hands, watching her eyes. 'I've seen that look before,' he whispered. 'Come on, let's have it. Complications, are there?'

Etta took his wrists, freeing her face from his scrutiny. 'No, I'm probably imagining things,' she replied. 'I must not pry into your business, my lord.'

'Pry? What's this about? What's troubling you, sweetheart?'

'It sounds trivial when I say it. Normal, even. Those notes.' She turned his hands, palms up, then curled his fingers in and held them there.

'Notes? Oh, the notes. Yes. To Levina. What about them?'

'I asked you if it was information and you said yes. But was it?'

'Yes. I told you.'

'But *she* gave *you* one, later. Was that information, too? Are you an informer? Is that why you decided we must attend the court, after all?'

'I inform in a very minor way, yes, but nothing for you to be concerned about. It coincided with our plans. If it hadn't, I would still have taken you there.'

'Would you? But isn't it rather dangerous? That *does* concern me.'

'Listen. It's the information that's dangerous, but

these things have to be known about by those responsible for the Queen's safety and that means her throne as much as her person. So Cecil, as chief minister, needs all the information he can get from wherever he can get it. Levina has access to many people at court who are happy to chat to her while they're sitting still. She learns quite a lot that she can pass on to me, in case it's useful and, as her brother, I can visit her freely at Whitehall Palace with my wife without arousing any suspicion.'

'Ah, I see. So you tell Sir William Cecil what she tells you.'

'No, I pass on any information to your uncle, Sir Elion D'Arvall.'

'Who would not want to be seen chatting to Levina, personally.'

'Exactly. As Cecil's man, that *would* arouse suspicion. But there's a certain person well known to Levina who is being closely watched at the moment, since it's known she is very friendly with Señor Feria, the Spanish Ambassador. It's because of this and her relationship to the Queen that leads Cecil to suspect that Spain would support her, if anything should happen to Elizabeth.'

'You're talking about Lady Catherine Grey, aren't you? Do you mean Spain would help to make her Queen if…? Heaven forbid! That's what happened to her sister, Lady Jane Grey, the Nine-Day Queen. And she was beheaded.'

'Yes, that's who I mean. So anything she gets up to, who she sees, who she talks to, is passed on to Cecil. Levina is very helpful there.'

Etta's hands left his and flew to her mouth, covering it, her eyes wide, remembering that dreadful day when Aphra had not been with her. 'Who she sees? Oh, my goodness! I saw her. With that man… what's his name…the Earl of something…on the bed. I rushed into her room instead of Levina's. It was so embarrassing. I told Levina about it, Nic.'

'That would be the Earl of Hertford. Well, well. Cecil has suspected something like that for some time. He was only waiting for some proof and for them to do something seriously stupid before he tells the Queen.'

'They *were* doing something seriously stupid,' Etta said.

'Then that's probably what Levina wrote in the note she gave me. I didn't get chance to read it, but passed it straight on to your uncle. Cecil will have it by now. Well done, sweetheart.'

'But I feel dreadful, Nic. She spoke to me about it that night, warned me not to say a word. But I already had.'

'She would. She knows that if the Queen gets to hear of it, there'll be deep trouble for them both. Her as the Nine-Day Queen's sister and him as the brother of Elizabeth's former stepmother, Jane Seymour. The Seymours are still eager to get close to the throne, but that kind of connection is not allowed by the reigning monarch. It's too close and far too dangerous. She's digging a deep hole for herself, that one.'

Etta brought his hands up to her face to lay her cheek upon them. 'Then I hope she doesn't discover my part in her downfall, when it comes. I didn't know there were people like her at court. I'm glad not to be returning. I've already found out more about the place than I really want to know. I don't fit in there, do I?'

'No, love. And apart from looks, you are nothing like your half-sister, thank heaven. I've seen quite a lot of her in the last few days, at close quarters, too, and I know who I'd rather be married to and take to bed. My sensitive, compassionate and adorable wife. You have little in common with her, sweetheart.'

'Do you mean that, Nic?'

His answer came in the form of a kiss that took her mind away from those troubles of the past few days, a kiss that, had she allowed it at the Royal Wardrobe on that memorable day, might have avoided all the resistance of the past weeks that had caused so much personal heartache.

The first week of their return to Mortlake Manor kept Etta and her cousin busy from morn till night both inside the house, where some alterations had been made, and outside where the gardens had begun to change into a medley of greens. The weather was kind, allowing them the chance to take their new gerfalcons out into the surrounding parkland, with the falconer, and to use the other gift Somerville had bought them, two beautiful white greyhounds.

For the first few days, Master Leon stayed with them before returning to Sandrock Priory and his tutor, Dr Ben Spenney, to whom the news of his success with Aphra would come as no great surprise since it was he who had suggested it to his pupil. But as one guest left another arrived in the form of Dr Dee, Royal Astrologer, who found Somerville's invitation to stay for as long as he wished highly convenient when the Queen still 'forgot' to pay him for his services. He was wise enough, however, not to trespass on his hostess's generosity or to monopolise Somerville when he returned home each evening from London and Etta had no cause for complaint that she was not receiving her due share of attention from the husband to whom she had irretrievably lost her heart. For a few days, at least, it began to look as if the tribulations of the Whitehall episode were being replaced by a more normal way of life in which Etta had occupations enough to keep her mind off her failures. Not once did she hear *I told you so* from Somerville, and if he knew any details of the Queen's move to Richmond Palace just round a bend in the river, he was careful to keep it to himself.

But Etta was not to remain in ignorance for long when the next person to seek asylum was her diplomat uncle, Sir Elion D'Arvall, whose lodgings at the palace were not at all to his taste. 'All very well having gilded domes and fountains if there's nowhere for folk to lay their heads,' he grumbled. 'Mind if I borrow one of your rooms for a few weeks, Etta? I won't get under your feet.'

'You're more than welcome to get under our feet,' Etta told him. 'There's room for your man, too. Stable your horses with ours.'

'Thank you. Beautiful place, this. So comfortable. And you look happier.'

Etta looked rather less than content on the next day when Uncle Elion arrived with a message from Lord Robert Dudley inviting them to join the Queen's hawking party on the following day. He had seen Etta and Aphra in the park with their falconer where the Queen and her court had flocked like brightly glittering flowers on the other side, indulging in one of the

Queen's favourite pastimes. Neither Etta nor Somerville rushed to accept the invitation, but could see no way out of it without causing offence. Sir Elion was quick to reassure them. 'I know you've decided not to get involved again,' he said, 'but this is out of doors and very informal. And I shall be there, too, on horseback. You can stay on the fringes, if you prefer. And home is only a field away, isn't it?'

'I think we might have to accept, Etta,' Somerville said.

'Will you come, too?'

'Of course I will, sweetheart. I want to see how the birds and hounds behave.'

'But what if…?'

'Don't anticipate problems. We'll be Lord Robert's guests, not hers.'

Despite her reservations, there was a certain appeal to an invitation to show off her skills with the new rather heavy gerfalcon, whose speed was phenomenal. The greyhounds had been trained to take the heron off the falcon and, in the last few days, the larder had benefitted from several kills. Etta's and Aphra's mounts were also beautiful creatures with pure Arabian blood in them and Somerville had had saddles of Cordovan leather made, tooled and silvered with matching bridles. After Etta's unfortunate lack of proper dress on the last occasion, he was keen for her to be seen at her best, if only to put to rest the belittling gossip that Jack Grene had put about. He was also aware of Etta's damaged pride as she saw her well-laid plans come unstuck, so it was by his and Sir Elion's persuasions that the invitation was accepted for the following day, with just enough time for the cousins to fix long curling plumes to the tall crowns of their black velvet hats, like the one the Queen had worn for the archery.

That same evening after supper, Dr Dee brought in his crystal scrying glass to show them something. 'Rather disturbing, my dears,' he said, placing it carefully on the table. 'See what you make of it. There, take a look, my lady. See anything?'

'Only a distorted image of myself,' she said. 'Do I really look like that?'

They took turns to look into the crystal globe by which the astrologer set much store, but saw nothing remarkable. 'What did you see, John?' said Somerville.

'Perhaps I ought not to say, if you couldn't see it. But what I detected was a tall crowned hat like the one the Queen wears for hunting,' said Dr Dee.

'A hat? So what's strange about that?' they said.

'It was strange because it had an arrow passing right through it.' Pointing with his long well-shaped finger, he jabbed at Etta's hat. 'Like that.'

No one laughed or contradicted, or ridiculed. No one spoke.

Etta poured glasses of wine and handed them round while wondering if the arrow was in the Queen's hat or hers. She decided not to ask, but when Dr Dee returned to his room to study, she asked her husband and Uncle Elion if they should warn the Queen.

'We're hawking, not hunting,' Uncle Elion said. 'We shall not be using any arrows.'

Usually so confident and determined, Etta admitted to Somerville that she could not, on this occasion, summon up any positive expectations that the Queen would show any pleasure at her presence. At best, she believed she would be ignored. Sitting up in bed, watching him cast aside one garment after another to reveal a back rippling with muscle, wide shoulders, narrow waist and neat buttocks, she rested her chin on her knees, her eyes skimming over his body as he turned to her. 'This experience has really deflated you, hasn't it, sweetheart?' he said, standing with hands on hips, magnificently naked. 'I wish it had been otherwise.'

'Oh, I'll recover. But this last week has been *so* enjoyable and now it's being interrupted and I didn't want it to be. Yes, I know we get to dress up and be sociable, but those people are not my friends, except for one or two, and our being there is not going to serve any purpose, is it?' She realised at once how clumsy her words sounded and how selfish her thoughts. 'On dear, that came out wrong,' she said. 'Of course it will serve some purpose, my lord. It will show them how generous my husband is to me and my cousin. We shall outshine them all and I shall make sure they all know what a splendid house we have on the banks of the Thames. And Uncle Elion will agree with me.'

As she spoke, the look of pain in his eyes was replaced by a smile that creased his face. 'I think you're getting to like Mortlake Manor, are you not?' he said, approaching the bed. 'But one day of being sociable now and then is no bad thing. There will be times this summer when we shall have to entertain and be entertained.'

'Yes, of course, my lord. And I shall not mind that

at all. Your friends and fellow merchants will be made
welcome and I shall make you proud of me.'

Sitting on the bed, he gently raked his fingers
through her hair to feel the silky texture over his
hands. 'I am already immensely proud of you, my
Lady Somerville. And don't concern yourself about
Elizabeth. Tomorrow, as I said, we are Lord Robert's
guests.'

She moved her face closer to his, placing her arms
across his shoulders. 'So will she concern herself with
you again?' she whispered. 'In the way she does?
Flirting with you? Accepting your flowers? Taking
you from me?'

Looking deeply into her eyes, he searched for the
green serpent of jealousy and, to his satisfaction,
found it. 'She will never take me from you,' he said.
'All that girlish flirting is what she enjoys most because it does no harm, not even to her reputation. It's
the nearest she'll ever get to having a husband, Etta.
Her father got women pregnant with that kind of behaviour, but she knows to go so far and no further.
She cannot afford to do otherwise.'

'Not even with Lord Robert?'

'Especially not with him. He already has a wife.'

'As you do.' Tears of love and relief prickled behind her eyelids.

'Exactly. Which is why she'll never steal my heart
or my body. They belong only to my wife.'

Etta's eyes glistened with tears. 'Your heart, my
darling? Really?'

Slowly, he swung her sideways to lie beneath him
on the crumpled sheets, her hair flowing around them
like a pool of water at sunset. 'You've doubted it, I

know. But there was no need, beloved. My heart has always belonged to you. *Always.'*

The time for more explanations was past, for now their bodies had begun to respond to the nearness of soft warmth and caressing hands, of searching mouths and the urgent pressure of limbs. Each time this happened, Etta found something new to excite her, for he was a wonderfully sensitive lover who could gauge her mood to perfection and make every loving a joy, teasing her into a deeper awareness of the responses her body was capable of, moulding her innocence into womanliness, albeit an unpredictable Tudor woman. His soft reassuring declaration lit her fires as nothing else could, easing her away from those doubts that threatened to damage her first hesitant feelings of love.

She sensed a change in him, too, as if her jealousy had inspired him to prolong every intimate caress as he had the second time, making up for those spontaneous and often frenzied occasions that were almost over before they'd begun. So he spun his loving into a web of desire that snared her, moaning with rapture, until she could wait no longer for his tender invasion, urging him to soothe that aching place, to fuse his body to hers. Without her bidding, words filtered through her deepest sighs, speaking of thoughts for so long kept back, now released into sounds of love for him alone. 'I love you,' she whispered. 'I don't know when I knew it, Nic. I should have told you before that I want you…love you…love you.'

'The sweetest words you could ever say, my wild tempestuous Tudor woman. I did not think you could have given yourself to me without feeling a little love for me. Am I right?'

'I thought I could, my dear lord,' she gasped, laughing as he stopped for her to answer. 'Don't stop. But, yes, I loved you even then. Heart and soul I am yours. I want to bear your children. We've delayed for too long.'

'Have we?' he said. 'I don't remember any delay.' His banter brought a smile into her kisses and joy into her heart as the talking stopped, for now it seemed as if he had heard everything that was important to him in the space of two or three heartbeats. Taking the cue from her, he delayed no longer in bringing her to the peak of rapture that released them simultaneously into a maelstrom where they clung, whirling in space, crying out with the intensity.

Gladly, Etta bore his full weight until, having covered her face with breathless kisses, he fell to one side, gathering her to him with murmurs of admiration. Easing her up, he held a glass of wine to her lips. 'Sip this,' he said. 'I think we may have made a new little Benninck. Lie still, beloved.'

Her hand smoothed his cheek and slid downwards, but by the time it reached his ribs, she was unable to take part in any further discussion on the subject, though the angelic smile playing about her lips suggested that, as sleep found her, she might have agreed with him.

Despite Etta's initial reluctance to accept Lord Robert's invitation, she felt the importance of being seen with her husband on her beautiful white mare with its new expensive harness and wearing her most fashionable riding dress meant to flaunt his generosity to both herself and Aphra. Her blue-green velvet gown with embroidered cuffs, fastenings and collar set off the bright copper of her hair, bundled into a pearl-covered gold mesh caul under the high-crowned hat, her green-dyed leather gloves matching her soft boots and the green tassels hanging from the mare's bridle. In dusky pink, known to the trade as Maiden's Blush, Aphra was equally as lovely, and even as they rode across the fields to join the royal party, they were watched with close attention and some envy.

Lord Robert was the first to greet them with Sir Elion D'Arvall, both men heaping them with compliments and making them glad they'd made the effort when, after this, no one would ever doubt Lord Somerville's liberality. It did not please the Queen, however, for both her current favourites to be elsewhere than by her side and Etta was able to demonstrate only once how obedient the hounds were before Somerville was summoned to attend her. But now it seemed to matter less to them, having found at last the assurances they had both longed to hear. One more day with the court, and they could resume their new-found happiness.

The Queen, resplendent in chestnut-brown and gold, wore a white plume in her high-crowned hat, although on this occasion her magnificence was only a little more remarkable than Etta's. Carrying a handsome peregrine falcon, she rode side-saddle as, time after time, the greyhounds raced across to the flapping herons under the falcon's claws before they could cause more damage with their struggles. Etta's hounds soon drew the attention of the Queen and, by a gradual process of successes, Etta and Aphra found themselves nearer to the royal party than they had intended to be. When the food hampers were undone and spread upon makeshift tables, however, both Etta and Aphra kept to the fringes of the group where the Queen sat, having decided to bring food of their own in the falconer's saddlebags.

In the weak spring sunshine, there was no need for them to seek the shade of willows, hawthorns or alders that clustered along the banks of the river, yet as Etta glanced across at the pale green fronds where herons often lurked knee-deep in the water, she saw a movement that puzzled her. There it was again, sliding behind the trunk of a tree, half-hidden by the long sweeping branches that almost touched the ground, a man who held one arm out in front of him, taking aim with a bow and arrow at the royal party.

There was no time to shout a warning for it would not have been heard against all the chatter so, without a second thought about how to prevent the catastrophe, Etta pushed past her cousin, knocking her sideways. Then, lifting her skirts and yelling at the top of her voice, she raced across tablecloths and plates of food, between swaying bodies and hands clutching at hats, drinks, and each other, her feet treading down skirts until she reached the Queen. Launching herself at the gem-studded royal body, she fell on top of her with a shocking thud, bringing her down flat on to the grass with a shriek of warning that came just as another scream sounded from Aphra who stood some way behind her. Nose to nose with Elizabeth and with her arms around her, Etta found it difficult to extricate herself and could only prise herself upwards to turn and look at the scene of devastation, muttering,

'Your Majesty, forgive me…a man…look…running… *quick, somebody!*'

Familiar with danger of all kinds, the Queen recognised that Etta was not attacking her, although the method of salvation might have been more dignified. Heaving Etta aside, she accepted the helping hands of her ladies, but was stopped short by the sight of Mistress Aphra Betterton holding a black velvet hat in her hands with a strange expression of disbelief on her face. It had an arrow stuck through the crown with its point just appearing through the white plume.

'Is that my hat, or yours, mistress?' said the Queen, adjusting her sleeves and skirts.

'It's mine, Your Majesty,' Aphra said, putting a hand to her bare head. 'I think.'

The Queen touched her own hat to feel it still in place. 'So it is,' she said. 'That arrow, I suppose, was meant for me.'

Helped to her feet by Somerville and Sir Elion, Etta was inclined to keep on apologising, but the circumstances were so bizarre and the Queen so much in command of the situation that she could only watch as a crowd of men hauled a very tousled but well-dressed young man towards them while someone carried the bow he had been using. The absence of a quiver to hold more arrows suggested that there had been no intention to try a second shot. Blood streamed down the lower part of the man's face as he was dragged before the Queen, his eyes defiant in spite of his first punishment.

Etta's cry of recognition was stifled by her hand before it could escape and she was relieved to hear Lord Robert identify him. 'Hoby,' he said. 'Is this how you repay those who once employed you? Ungrateful wretch! You'll hang for this.'

But Stephen Hoby was not inclined to answer any questions. Instead, his once-merry eyes slid past the Queen, past Etta too, to rest upon Aphra's white face and then on the hat she held, to all who watched indicating his disappointment that his arrow had missed its mark. It was only Etta who understood, from this malicious glare, that it was Aphra who had been the target, not the Queen. Revenge. Sir George Betterton's only daughter. The man who had dismissed him.

The cry of distress that Etta had held back now escaped. 'Affie!' she cried. 'Oh, Affie! It might have… oh, the wicked…*wicked* man!' Leaving Somerville's supporting arm, she rushed to her cousin's side, holding her close, hardly able to believe that the young man who had once been her friend could harbour so much evil. 'Affie, he nearly *killed* you.'

'No,' Aphra whispered, holding Etta away, 'he didn't, love. It was meant for the Queen. You must believe it. The Queen herself believes it. Everyone does.'

It was true. Although the main aim was to restore the Queen's dignity and some order to the trampled scene, everyone was convinced that Etta's quick thinking had saved the Queen's life, in disregard of the golden rule that no one might touch the Queen without her permission.

Still refusing to speak, Hoby was marched away by the Queen's personal bodyguard to an unmerciful fate, a tragic end to a life that Etta could never have imagined only a few short months ago. It could not fail to affect her. Trembling with shock, she clung to her cousin for mutual consolation, but it was Lord Somerville and Sir Elion who provided them both with the support of their strong arms as the Queen, still regal after her rough handling, thanked Etta. 'That was well done, Lady Somerville,' she said. 'That arrow was meant for either me or my hat.' She glanced at Etta's, now restored to its position. 'So perhaps that ruffian does not approve of the fashion. Nevertheless, we cannot have malcontents using us as target practice, can we? You have my thanks, my lady. You have courage, too.'

On wobbly legs, Etta made a deep curtsy. As she rose, she saw that the Queen was already turning away as if nothing of particular importance had happened. For Etta, however, the afternoon was spent in her husband's company and that of her cousin and uncle while accepting the compliments of those who had seen her amazing act of heroism. There were kind words for Aphra, too, whose serene beauty and gentle manners had come so close to being extinguished by a man known to have been, until only recently, in Lord Robert's employment. Yet to those who saw what had happened, it looked like the insane act of a desperate man who stood no chance of escaping, even if he'd been successful. It was a conclusion not lost upon Etta, who could not help wondering whether she could have done something to prevent it.

To have her husband's company that afternoon was a bonus neither of them had expected, yet a cloud came to put a damper on their plans for the evening when Lord Robert came riding up to them with an invitation from Her Majesty. 'To attend the entertainments this evening at the palace. Yes, all of you. There, my lady,' he said to Etta with a smile that clearly expected one in return, 'an invitation at last, eh?'

'Please thank Her Majesty for us, will you, my lord?' said Somerville. 'We are honoured indeed.' As Lord Robert rode away, Somerville placed a hand over Etta's. 'A refusal is not possible, sweetheart,' he said. 'Just one more evening, that's all. She obviously wants you to know how grateful she is. You can share the heroism with Aphra.'

Contradictory thoughts clashed in Etta's mind, tugging her in two directions, for only a few weeks ago she had been hell-bent on obtaining the Queen's favour, and now she had it, she had found another kind of favour a thousand times more precious to her. An evening spent in the lioness's den held no appeal for her, even though she had gained the admiration and respect of so many courtiers to carry her through it. 'You'll have to be with her, I suppose,' she said, 'and I wanted you with me.'

His hand squeezed hers. 'And I want it too, my love, believe me. Wait until we get home, and I'll show you, shall I?'

That made her smile at last, enough to discuss with Aphra what gowns they would wear for a first and last evening at Richmond Palace. With her cousin, she shared her concern that, now it was too late to matter to her, Elizabeth might command her, after all, to attend her in some capacity and so upset Etta's new plans to make a home and a family for the man she adored. How ironic would that be? 'Tell me it won't happen, Affie?' she said.

'It won't happen, love,' Aphra said, obligingly. 'If she offers you a position, tell her you're with child.'

Etta stared at her, remembering the scene she had witnessed in the Queen's garden when one of her ladies had passed out, her request to leave ignored. That image had done nothing to enhance her perception of a loving and compassionate Queen, and the thought of being in a similar position herself hung like a dark shadow over her hours of careful preparation.

Chapter Ten

Etta's last evening appearance in the Queen's company had been a sartorial disaster, but on this occasion she had time at home to choose her most dazzling gown of the popinjay shot-silk she had seen on that momentous visit to the Royal Wardrobe. The rich blue-green, worn with a cream stomacher, dazzled and sparkled with gold embroidery and jewels and, rather than cover her hair, she agreed with Aphra to wear it piled with gold mesh twined between plaits, feathers and ropes of pearls, presenting a vision of vivid colour against Aphra's virginal creamy-white with the merest hint of rose embroidery over the full sleeves. Now they had the experience to know that they would cause a sensation. They travelled by horse litter across the park to the courtyard of the palace, while Lord Somerville and Sir Elion rode alongside them.

Although familiar with Richmond Palace from the outside, neither of them had seen the interior which, they had been told, rivalled even Whitehall in its magnificence. Chambers, corridors, galleries and state rooms glittered with every kind of decoration in a blaze of light and colour, richness from floor to ceiling, every surface patterned with gold leaf and gemstones, polished wood and silk drapes and countless honey-scented beeswax candles.

The buzz of voices and music met them long before they reached the magnificent hall on a wave of guests in gorgeous gowns and plumed hats, velvet and gold braid, rustling silks, pearls and pendants as big as bricks and as gaudy as a flower garden. Immediately, and with only time for a whispered farewell and a touch of hands, Lord Somerville was summoned by the Queen and Etta knew then that nothing had changed in that direction. 'Just a few hours, sweetheart,' he whispered as he left her with Aphra and Sir Elion. There was no time for repining, for Lord Robert soon came to the group already augmented by those who had heard of the Queen's dramatic deliverance from death that afternoon. Etta and Aphra were surrounded, drawn into the dance and surrounded again, telling what happened with as much modesty as they could, but subjected to a deluge of praise, thanks and admiration, along with the unavoidable observations about the Queen's own half-sister being the one to save her life. Neither of them had expected or wanted such adulation, especially not in the Queen's presence, but this was better, Etta told herself, than having to suffer the malice of Lady Catherine Grey.

Had it not been Lent, they might have expected a masque devised by the Master of Revels, but the Queen was not one to give up her dancing for forty days. Not even for one day. 'Play *la volte*!' she called to her musicians. 'Come, let us see who still has a spring in his step. Three couples.'

Etta's eyes were upon Somerville, sure that he would be obliged to invite the Queen to partner him, all the company waiting to see if she herself would lead the way. A scattering of delighted applause rattled round the hall as Somerville removed his short cape, then his rapier, setting the example for two others to do the same before leading their ladies on to the floor, hands held high, toes pointing. Playing to a fast hopping beat of three-four time, the musicians set the pace for each couple to entwine arms and turn, with eyes linked in a kind of stylised disdain while Etta's heart beat to a rhythm of envy hidden behind her smile and clapping hands. How she wished she had been his partner instead of Elizabeth, or that Lord Robert had invited her to be his.

The watching courtiers crowded round the edges of the hall, as close as farthingales would allow, whispering comments and whooping as the men performed high kicks and twists in the air, which their partners could not do. A man's voice in Etta's ear made her turn to see who spoke, then to frown with annoyance as she saw that it was the man she had disabled in the passageway, now plying her with information she did not want. 'Your lady mother was the best at this, you know. My father told me how she liked it when he put his hand there…see?'

It was impossible for her not to understand what he meant when the nearest dancing couple were performing the high lift with the man's left hand on one of his partner's hips and his right hand holding the whalebone stomacher, the pointed base of which was level with the tops of her legs. It was a perfect lever, managed correctly, by which the man could hoist his partner high up against him, but one could see how it might have been open to abuse by predatory men and promiscuous women. Was this dreadful man suggesting to Etta that her mother was one of these?

She tried to move away but the press of people around her was too great and, trying to catch a glimpse of Aphra or Uncle Elion, she found only Lady Catherine Grey close behind her, ready with her malicious tongue to add more insinuations. 'It was not only *your* father,' she said, her voice covered by the fast music, 'it was *anybody's* father. She was known as Mount Magdalen, you know. Did you not know that, Lady Somerville?'

'I shall not listen to this,' Etta said, swinging round, but being forced to turn back when bodies blocked her way, pressing forward as Somerville and the Queen reached their part of the floor, high-clapping, swirling, jumping and twisting in perfect unison, each engrossed in the precision of the dance. The audience clapped in delight, for now it appeared to be a contest between Elizabeth and Lord Robert as to which of the two could be more exciting.

A feeling of sheer panic rose in Etta's breast as the man behind bent again to her ear. 'She's right, my lady. Magdalen Osborn would go to bed with any man. She was insatiable, they say. There's old Lady Portingale over there. She lost her husband to her. So did others. They're none too pleased to see *you* in the Queen's favour, I can tell you.'

'So did you throw yourself at Her Majesty as a last attempt, Lady Somerville?' said Lady Catherine. 'Very clever. You have the same brazen streak as your mother had, by all accounts. Henry's Whore, some called her, and see where it's got you, then. Your husband is infatuated with the Queen, isn't he?'

'Stop it!' Etta cried, her voice clashing with the music and the whoops of delight. The Queen was being lifted high above Somerville's head as if she were a doll, sliding down the length of him, smiling into his eyes as she passed, unaware of how this made Etta crumple with jealousy. Again, Etta turned to escape, but the man's leg was deliberately in her way and she could not step over it. 'I shall not listen to this. You are lying, both of you,' she cried.

'Ah, but it's true, Lady Somerville,' said Lady Catherine. 'You may have got yourself a title, but you're a bastard, aren't you? I'll wager even the whore herself didn't know who your father was when she'd open her legs for...'

The rage that had been building inside Etta suddenly exploded into a howl of anguish as she stuck her elbows out, jabbing at those who would have kept her there and forcing herself between them in a furious whirlwind of rage. 'You lie...you *lie!*' she panted, her lungs hurting as tears filled her eyes. 'Lies...*lies*! Let me through...the door...where...?' No one was allowed to leave the room before the Queen, but the look of utter wretchedness on Etta's lovely face, her waving arms and running feet drew the two guards to attention and, without question, they allowed her to pass through into another hall where a scattering of servants turned in alarm to watch as she flew past in a flood of tears.

Blindly, she ran across rooms and along panelled passageways lit by the flicker of wall torches, having no idea where she was going, wishing only to escape

the sounds and sights of that dreadful place. Sobs
racked her as the taunting, damaging words echoed
in her head, closing her ears to the sound of her name
being called behind her. 'Etta... Etta, please...stop!'
It was Aphra who caught her just as she turned into a
covered walkway surrounding the large open expanse
of the Queen's Garden, where low clipped hedges
made patterns of new spring growth. Out there, darkness hid every detail, nearly bringing Etta to her knees
with a cry when she crashed into a stone bench and
fell heavily on to it.

'Etta, darling...oh, dear one! What's happened?
Tell me, love.' Aphra's arms went round her cousin,
rocking her, hoping to hear what had gone so terribly
wrong. But Etta's frenzied despair would not allow
words to form. Instead, the night air absorbed the
sounds of her uncontrollable weeping that came with
the heartbreak of newly discovered truths, delivered
with deliberate cruelty. Now she knew exactly to what
lengths people would go to prevent an outsider from
gaining the Queen's favour, even when they had no
future there, either. And now she knew the reason why
none of her relatives, nor her husband, had wanted her
to pursue her dream. They must all have known of her
mother's reputation and wanted to spare her the un-
savoury details that would surely be offered by those
who wished her ill. Soaking Aphra's shoulder with her
tears, she howled her misery, sharing her deep humiliation with the mental picture of her husband holding
Elizabeth above him and letting her slide slowly down
his body to the floor, to the delight of the onlookers.
It was called for, in *la volte*, but they had taken it to a
different erotic level in full view of the court.

Through her strenuous weeping, Etta heard Aphra speak, then felt her arms loosen their hold on her. 'Don't go, Aphie,' she sobbed.

'Your Majesty...forgive me...if I loose her, she'll fall.'

'Here, let me,' said the Queen. 'She's a Tudor. She won't fall.'

Skirts rustled around her and another pair of arms held her like a child against a mother's breast, still warm from recent exertions, encrusted with gold and gems. For some moments, Elizabeth allowed the weeping to continue until the first few half-words began to emerge. 'Your...pardon... Your Majesty... I could...not stay...any...longer.' The shoulders shook, smoothed and patted by royal hands.

'Tell me,' Elizabeth said, 'what it is those two wanted you to know?'

'You saw?'

'I see what goes on in my court, yes, Henrietta. What was it?'

'About my...my mother. Oh, the things...they said...so unkind.' Fresh sobs broke out again as the insults bored into her like red-hot irons.

'Then listen to me, Henrietta. Are you listening?'

Etta nodded, accepting the Queen's handkerchief.

'You can choose whether to believe what you heard about your mother, or not. It's up to you. But just remember you're not alone in this. I, too, had to hear what the royal court said about *my* mother. They called her a whore and concubine, amongst other vile names. My own father, your father, called me and my sister bastards. Yes, my own father had us both declared illegitimate. I was a child of three, but old enough to understand the meaning of those words and the disrespect that went with them. I was too young to attend court when…when my father married Jane Seymour, but I remember the beautiful lady called Magdalen Osborn who became the first Lady Raemon. She came to see me at Greenwich Palace and she was always so kind to me, treating me with respect and bringing me clothes when I had very few. She would tell me stories, too, about dragons and beautiful princesses. One never forgets that kind of thing, Henrietta. That's why I rewarded Nicolaus Benninck, your husband, who showed me kindness later when I most needed it. Some did it to feather their own nests for the future, but not him. He has not come begging favours, as some do, nor is he the kind of man to be unfaithful, my dear—neither in word nor in deed. So think kindly of him and of your lady mother, too. Speak only of her with love, as I do mine, as one who was kind to small frightened children. Those who do otherwise are sad creatures, are they not, Baron?'

Etta looked up and saw him standing a little way off, listening. 'I should have protected her, Your Majesty,' he said. 'She ought not to have had to listen to such filth. I shall never forgive myself for allowing it to happen.'

'But I wanted…wanted to come…here,' Etta said, still weeping. 'I insisted.'

'Insisted?' Elizabeth said, sternly. 'Queens and husbands insist. Wives obey. That's all there is to it, Henrietta. Now hear me. You saved my life this afternoon and for that I shall ever be grateful. But the role you hoped for can never be. We can never be closer than we are at this moment, sister to sister, and you will have to take the word of a queen that there are very sound reasons why you cannot be officially acknowledged as a relative. That would be dangerous for both of us. You tried, I know, and I tried to make it difficult for you without subjecting you to a public repudiation. We Tudors are determined, tenacious, self-willed creatures.'

'Yes,' said Etta, recognising something of herself, after all.

'So now you must go home with your good husband and obey him in all things, as I shall never have to do. Think only on the things you have and not on those you believe you ought to have. Think of your Queen's love and gratitude, but let our love be a secret between us. Do you understand?'

Taking Elizabeth's hands in hers, a familiar gesture that was allowed, she laid her hot cheek on them, wetting them with her tears. 'Majesty,' she whispered, 'I am your humble subject. Thank you. I do understand. Perfectly.'

'And you, mistress?' Elizabeth said to Aphra.

'I am Your Majesty's faithful subject. I know nothing of this.'

'Good. Then go home and be at peace. I grew up amongst slanderers and liars as well as mealy-mouthed flatterers and fawners, so if you think I cannot tell one from the other, be assured that I learnt to discriminate at a very early age. Your husband, Henrietta, is a rare honest man, but he is a man, for all that, so you must learn to allow him a little innocent affectionate teasing now and then. It means nothing unless you allow it to. Nor does what you heard about your mother. I have nothing but good memories of her, as I do of my own.' She held out her arms to Etta and embraced her with a most unusual combination of warmth and formality that they knew would never be repeated, after which the Queen was joined by several of her Ladies-in-Waiting and escorted out of the garden. The soft whoosh of curtsying skirts broke the silence of the night, then a singing voice as a door was opened, then the metallic clash of pikes as the guards closed ranks behind her.

Lord Somerville sat on the stone bench beside Etta, taking Aphra's hand in one and his wife's in the other. 'I ask you both to forgive me,' he said, softly, 'for bringing you into this vipers' den. I should have asserted my authority from the start. This is no place for decent, innocent women.'

'My lord,' Aphra said, 'let's not apportion blame. There's no harm done that cannot be undone…that has not already been undone.'

'Aphra's right,' Etta said. 'You did what I asked you to do out of love for me and I took advantage of your good nature, my lord. I've been a selfish fool.'

Somerville placed a loving arm around her shoulders. 'Come on then, adorable little fool. Let's go home, shall we?'

Home. It was the sweetest word in a day of extraordinary happenings that had generated too many questions for sleep. Round a blazing fire and with an array of tempting supper dishes nearby, they sat in comfortable clothes to try to make sense of things which, at the time, had passed them by without rhyme or reason. By unspoken agreement, the scandalous Magdalen Osborn was excluded from their discussion, for the Queen's suggestion that it was better to remember a mother's virtues than the slander of ill wishers was sound advice they all agreed with. As was her command that Etta should now concentrate on her marriage instead of a life for which she was clearly unfitted. There was to be no arguing with that.

The presence of Sir Elion, who had been glad to see a conclusion to Etta's ambition, made it easier for them to tie up several loose ends concerning Stephen Hoby's unwanted involvement in her affairs. 'He was a failure on every level,' Sir Elion told them as he watched the fire dance through his glass of red wine. 'And failures like him tend to seek revenge. Until it turns round to bite them.'

'Revenge?' said Etta, nestling into her husband's arms.

'On those who thwarted his ambitions, love,' Uncle Elion said. 'I've been watching him since he found a position at the Royal Wardrobe with George. We knew he'd made contact with the Spanish ambassador with a view to working for them, like some others we know. Informers are paid well according to their information and he needed contacts at court so he could discover something of what the Queen's intentions are.'

'What kind of intentions?' said Aphra. 'About what she wears?'

Uncle Elion smiled. 'More than that, Aphra. Anything to do with her religious intentions, alliances with France, or policy on Scotland, or marriage plans. These all affect her relationship with the Catholic countries, and Hoby thought he'd be able to pick up something useful by keeping his ears open. Unfortunately, he picked up Sir George's precious fabrics, too.'

'And that,' Somerville said, 'was when he was seeing you, my love.'

Etta sat up straight, but was pulled back again. Being indignant in that position was less convincing. 'You mean…you knew about him…when I asked Uncle George not to tell you?'

'Give your husband some credit, Etta,' said Uncle Elion. 'Of course he knew about Hoby. George already knew that. Nic knew of your friendship when you first met, but you'd not have been too pleased to know that, would you?'

Etta was silent. She was learning not to overreact.

Somerville smiled across at his friend with a hint of triumph showing. 'He made himself appealing to you, love, because of your likeness to the Queen and because he was sure, as you were, that you'd somehow make a connection there. So when your uncle dismissed him for theft, he forged a recommendation to Lord Robert on Royal Wardrobe paper and that's where we saw him when you first met the Queen. I sent him packing, remember?'

'But you didn't say…'

'No, of course I didn't. But that's why he decided to revenge himself on me, because he could make no more headway with you.'

'Revenge himself…on you?'

'Yes, he saw at the archery contest how Dr Dee and I knew each other and I dare say he might have overheard what Dr Dee was telling Master Leon, about his books coming from Antwerp. Joseph told me how he'd pestered you. The next thing I knew was that someone had tipped off the Stationers' wardens to visit my warehouses at the Steelyard. That was the night I had to go there and move things.'

In the safety of his arms, Etta shuddered as she recalled how she had seen Hoby in the passageway only moments later, slaking his lust on a woman. That had been a nightmare of a day. 'Foul man,' she whispered. 'How could I ever have liked him?'

'Because men like that can turn on the charm whenever it suits them,' he said with his lips against her hair. 'By coincidence, the Stationers' visit came on the very day my ships unloaded, so I had to work fast. A day earlier, there'd have been nothing to find. I knew it could only be his doing.'

She had thought he was with the Queen. How much she had misunderstood him.

'But then,' Uncle Elion said, 'he lost his job with Lord Robert, too, and that was the end of the line for him. It was George who told his lordship he was harbouring an informer, so then it was serious revenge time and as foolhardy an act as ever I saw.'

'Me,' said Aphra, very softly as if to herself. 'To get back at my father.'

'I'm afraid so, love,' said Uncle Elion, 'although one would have thought that with three possible targets, he could hardly miss.'

'Thanks to Etta, he did,' said Aphra.

Somerville raised his glass, tinkling it against the other two. 'Then here's to our heroine,' he said, sipping the wine.

She allowed it to pass with a smile, for it would have been churlish not to, but there was so much to be explained about her own self-centred behaviour since her marriage to this wonderful man, so much to apologise for, so many things to put right, despite Aphra's generous words in the garden that night.

Later, as they lay at peace in each other's arms after an ecstatic lovemaking when all their words of love had been freed, Etta vowed to make it up to him for the hurts she had inflicted.

'It isn't necessary, dearest heart,' he said. 'I knew what I was taking on when I offered for you. You told me yourself. It's over now and we're better for it.'

'I think I knew for certain that I loved you when you held that transparent silk behind my head, my darling, and told me I should wear that and nothing else just for you. Do you remember?'

He chuckled. 'I remember everything. Every detail. You are priceless.'

'So tomorrow I shall ask you to tell me all about yourself and your family. I want to know all there is to know. I'm ashamed that I've not asked before.'

'All right, and tomorrow I shall give you a task to prepare while I'm away.'

Her hand stopped in mid-caress. 'What? Where... when? Why?'

'I shall be staying at the Sign of the Bridge for two weeks after Easter.'

In spite of all her efforts to make him explain, he fell asleep before she had obtained the slightest hint of what this two-week-long task might be.

She resumed her interrogation at first light. 'Don't leave me now,' she complained. 'Not so soon?'

He pushed her back on to the bed with one sweep of his forearm, hovering above her with a scowl. 'Did you or did you not promise to obey me in all things, woman? Have you forgot so soon?'

Surprised, and rather excited, too, she blinked at him. 'Yes…er…no, my lord. Do you really want me to obey you in all things? The Queen says I ought.'

'That would be expecting too much, wouldn't it? No, I'm a realist. Let's just accept each other as we are, shall we? So let's see if you can accept this request from me. I want you to prepare a wedding while I'm away in London.'

'Whose wedding? Aphra's?'

'No. Ours.' He watched her eyes open wider with the soft dawn of understanding.

'But…?' she whispered.

'No buts. I have prepared a list of two hundred guests and you can add as many as you wish from your relatives and friends. Give your list to Joseph and I will see to it that everyone receives an invitation. Two weeks after Easter will take us into the time when marriage ceremonies are allowed again and all my captains will be in harbour. That's all the time you've got. I want a banquet of *gigantic* proportions, the best musicians, entertainment, everything we didn't have before. Questions?'

The smile that had struggled to emerge now suffused her eyes, watering them with happiness. 'And I'm to do this on my own?'

'No, you'll have Aphra. She'll help. It's now up to you, my lady. Well, what now?' His face relaxed its sternness as her arms came up to hold him.

'Thank you…thank you, my love. Of all the things I robbed you of…'

'Hush, wench. I knew a simple wedding was not

your style. I told you I could tame you.' His kiss was thorough and masterly, giving her a taste of what the future would hold.

'Are you saying you told me so, my lord?'

'Mmm…' he said, nuzzling into her neck. 'That's what I'm saying.'

For the next few weeks, Etta had worked hard to make good all the omissions of that first shabby affair when the conflicts of her heart had raged out of control. Extra hands were hired from Mortlake village to scrub and polish, to fill the larders with local produce and to prepare a feast for over three hundred guests, including Lord Robert himself. Rooms were made ready for relatives, even stabling for their horses and lodgings for the multitude of servants who came with them. In the garden, lanterns were hung from trees. Bowers, pavilions, arbours and arches were covered with white blossom from the hedgerows, the pathways outlined with garlands, outdoor seats covered with white cushions and decked with primrose bouquets, bows and fluttering ribbons.

Food was brought in from all over the county, augmented by exotic delicacies brought by Somerville's own ships docked at Southampton, the best wines, spices and rare birds' eggs wrapped in gold foil. White-covered tables creaked under platters of roast meats, fish and sweet concoctions fashioned in the shape of castles with helpless maidens on the tops. Venetian glass sparkled with wines, home-brewed ales in silver tankards, ivory-handled cutlery, white linen napkins and Somerville's best silver plate brought into use at last.

All Somerville's mercer colleagues and their wives were there on the day, and so many of his friends, captains and staff, that Etta's memory for names was stretched to its limit. Levina came, too, promising to finish Etta's portrait, and Dr Ben with his best student, Master Leon, and all those from the royal court who had shown kindness to Etta and Aphra, old Lady Agnes, their grandmother, parents and siblings, aunts, uncles and cousins, friends and neighbours, estate workers and local dignitaries. Lord and Lady Raemon, who took full responsibility for 'throwing the cat among the pigeons' in the first place had a lot of diplomatic explaining to do when asked why the happy couple required another wedding so soon. 'A blessing, not a wedding,' they said.

'Oh?' Eyebrows were raised. 'Really? A blessing… as in…*blessing*?'

'Too soon to be certain,' they said, smiling mysteriously like expectant grandparents trying not to give too much away.

No hint of this was to be seen on the appointed day when Etta appeared at the church door wearing an exquisite dress of pale-green silk brocade with a creamy-white forepart of satin embroidered thickly with seed pearls. Her long red hair had been dressed with ropes of pearls and gold threads in a maze of plaits and curls and, as Somerville had seen nothing of either her or the house during the preparations, he was smitten all over again at the ravishing sight of his beloved wife walking towards him in what some of the older guests thought was a quite indecent haste. Ever unorthodox, Somerville swept her into his arms there, at the altar, in an embrace that was eventually brought to a pause by the same chaplain who had married them. 'Ahem!' he said, above the laughter of the congregation.

So there, on a sunny spring morning at Mortlake, the marriage of Lord Somerville and his lady was blessed in the hope that it would be happy and fruitful which, if he had but known, it already was. One could hardly have called it a 'solemnisation' as there was so little solemnity about it. Bells pealed out across the river, reedy choirboys sang, ladies wept openly and men gulped as the procession walked back to the manor pelted by white blossom all the way. And then the feasting began, an event that was talked about for generations to come.

In a moment of semi-privacy, Etta managed to ask Nicolaus if he thought the preparations were an improvement, knowing the answer. 'Beloved,' he said, holding her close to his cream-satin doublet, 'this is the most wonderful way I could ever have dreamed to celebrate our happiness. Thank you, sweet thing. For everything.'

'Everything?' she said, with a coy look.

'Yes, I know what you refer to, but, yes, everything. Without that to begin with, our happiness might not have been as great as this. Look at all those laughing faces. There's your family, sweetheart. You are loved, appreciated, admired and I adore you.'

'Then I have nothing more to search for, have I? You are all I need.'

Seeing them embrace for the umpteenth time that day, guests smiled indulgently, nudging elbows, raising glasses once again. Others roamed through the gardens, bathed with warm sunshine, while a servant approached Lord Somerville to say that there were wardens from the Stationers' Company in the library looking through his lordship's papers. As he was at that moment standing quite close to Dr Dee and Lord Robert Dudley, those two went with him to see what urgent reason had brought the wardens here on such a day, though two of them could hazard a guess.

Marching into the library in some indignation ready to bawl the men out for this inconsiderate behaviour, they were confronted by a weighty official with a sheaf of papers in one hand, scowling his disapproval, and another two searching through the bookshelves behind the desk. Recognising Lord Robert, however, they froze to a horrified standstill. 'Exactly what do you think you're doing in my library?' Somerville said, ominously.

Looking from one well-known man to the other, the first bullying words emerged rather lamely. 'Er… my lords…we have…er…' his eyes shifted wildly '…information regarding…er…books written by… er…you, Dr Dee, sir…which do not conform to…er…'

'What rubbish are you talking?' Lord Robert shouted, under no obligation to exercise any politeness to these men. 'Of course Dr Dee has books here. Why would he not? Her Majesty the Queen reads them and if *she* approves…'

At that precise moment, Etta appeared in all her wedding finery looking for all the world like her royal half-sister. Taking in the situation in one quick glance, she continued the drama for real in her most queenly manner. 'And if *I* approve, who are you to come in here and disapprove? By whose authority?'

The trembling sheaf of papers in the warden's hand fluttered to the floor as he knelt and bumped his head on the corner of the desk. The other two clattered away from the bookcase and sank to the ground like deflated puff-balls. 'Majesty,' they whispered, gulping. 'Your Majesty.'

Immediately, Somerville, Dudley and Dee entered into the charade, bowing low. 'Majesty,' they said in unison.

'Well?' Etta scolded. 'Get up! Now, listen to me, little man. Every book written by Dr Dee here, and any written in the future, has my personal approval. I will not have my astrologer harassed in this way, or those of my subjects who offer him hospitality. Do you understand me?'

'Indeed, Your Majesty. Indeed we do.'

'Good,' said Lord Robert. 'Now get out of here and never again meddle in Lord Somerville's affairs or those of Dr Dee. Men have been sent to the Tower for less than this.'

A whirlwind could not have blown the three Stationers' men out of the house any faster than they quit that day, leaving Etta to collapse with laughter in the arms of the three men, who could hardly find enough words to praise her quick thinking.

'Well,' she said, 'my resemblance to Her Majesty has not benefitted me so far, so it may as well do some good elsewhere. Lord Robert, I hope you won't tell Her Majesty of this. Impersonating the Queen is an offence, I know.'

'You have my word on it, my lady. But when I have need of my Queen and she's otherwise engaged, I shall come here and see you instead.'

'Not without me, you won't,' said Somerville, giv-

ing him a friendly thump. He took Etta by the hand.
'Come, wife. I'm going to sing you a love song.'
    'Yes, my lord,' she said, smiling up at him.

* * * * *

If you enjoyed this story,
don't miss Juliet Landon's
BETRAYED, BETROTHED AND BEDDED
which is linked to
TAMING THE TEMPESTUOUS TUDOR

And for more great reads by this author, try
THE RAKE'S UNCONVENTIONAL MISTRESS
SCANDALOUS INNOCENT
MISTRESS MASQUERADE

Bibliography

Books about the Elizabethan period offer a wealth of detail, some of which is contradictory, depending on the latest research.

I have relied heavily on the following:

Alison Plowden (2003). *Lady Jane Grey: Nine Days Queen.* Sutton Publishing.

Liza Picard (2003). *Elizabeth's London.* Orion.

Ian Mortimer (2013). *The Time Traveller's Guide to Elizabethan England.* Vintage.

Anna Whitelock (2013). *Elizabeth's Bedfellows: An Intimate History of the Queen's Court.* Bloomsbury Publishing.

Derek Wilson (2014). *Elizabethan Society: High and Low Life 1558-1603.* Constable & Robinson.

Philippa Jones (2009). *The Other Tudors: Henry VIII's Mistresses and Bastards.* New Holland Publishers.

Tracy Borman (2010). *Elizabeth's Women: Friends, Rivals, and Foes Who Shaped the Virgin Queen.* Bantam.

Roy C. Strong & V. J. Murrell (1983). *Artists of the Tudor Court: The Portrait Miniature Rediscovered 1520-1620.* Victoria & Albert Museum.